IT'S ALWAYS BEEN YOU

"Your braid is coming loose," he murmured, tugging softly at the leather tie. Both his hands slid through her hair, meeting at her neck to work out the tangled braid.

This was wrong. So wrong. But hot shivers of sensation moved over her scalp and down her neck and all the way to her toes. Pleasure trickled down her spine and gathered in a pool deep in her belly. She thought she would melt right through his fingers when he finally worked her hair free and ran his hands slowly through the strands, smoothing out the waves with gentle pressure.

Her head fell back under his ministrations, her mouth parted just slightly on a sigh. She wanted, feared, *knew* he was going to kiss her. The softest touch of warm breath caressed her lips and then it was him, his mouth, his lips against hers. . . .

Books by Victoria Dahl

TO TEMPT A SCOTSMAN

A RAKE'S GUIDE TO PLEASURE

ONE WEEK AS LOVERS

A LITTLE BIT WILD

IT'S ALWAYS BEEN YOU

HIGHLAND BEAST
(with Hannah Howell and Heather Grothaus)

LORDS OF DESIRE
(with Virginia Henley, Sally MacKenzie, and Kristi Astor)

Published by Kensington Publishing Corporation

It's Always Been You

VICTORIA DAHL

ZEBRA BOOKS
KENSINGTON PUBLISHING CORP.
http://www.kensingtonbooks.com

ZEBRA BOOKS are published by

Kensington Publishing Corp.
119 West 40th Street
New York, NY 10018

All Kensington titles, imprints, and distributed lines are available at special quantity discounts for bulk purchases for sales promotion, premiums, fund-raising, educational, or institutional use.

Special book excerpts or customized printings can also be created to fit specific needs. For details, write or phone the office of the Kensington Special Sales Manager: Attn. Special Sales Department. Kensington Publishing Corp., 119 West 40th Street, New York, NY 10018. Phone: 1-800-221-2647.

Zebra and the Z logo Reg. U.S. Pat. & TM Off.

ISBN-13: 978-1-4201-0484-4
ISBN-10: 1-4201-0484-5

First Printing: August 2011

10 9 8 7 6 5 4 3 2 1

Printed in the United States of America

Chapter 1

Kingston-upon-Hull, England
September 1849

"Thank you, Mr. York. It's been a pleasure, sir. A pleasure."

Aidan York smiled grimly at the florid-faced squire. The hard, hot spark in the man's eyes couldn't truly be described as pleasure. The emotion was closer to abject relief. The man had invested all his income in a ship, and rough seas had brought him to ruin soon after.

Aidan inclined his head. "The money will be delivered to your representative this afternoon."

"Thank you." The man bowed with a jerk. "Thank you, sir."

Even as Aidan nodded, he turned away, his mind already moving on to other ventures. If he departed Hull before nightfall, he'd be back in London and on the hunt for a buyer before the ship's repairs were even started. A thousand pounds profit within a fortnight, if he calculated correctly—and he always did. Not a bad morning's work.

Stepping off the walk and onto the cobblestones of the street, he barely noticed the beauty of the scene that spread before him. Kingston-upon-Hull was a bustling river port—the clean streets and quaint lanes of the old town were crowded with goodwives and servants, sailors and merchants, all industriously occupied. Several faces turned up to look at the sky just as the sun broke through the clouds. Aidan did not look. There were arrangements to be made, deals to be brokered. The weather concerned him not at all, unless, of course, it affected the shipping schedule.

Outpacing the crowd swirling around him, he turned right to head toward the docks and the small office he'd let there. But his rush was interrupted when he found himself on a narrow lane that was even more crowded than the last. Unable to bear the slower pace, he bit back a growl and searched the lane, looking for an opening, a break in the crowd.

His eyes caught for a moment, moved on, then blinked as something clicked with razor sharpness in his mind. A tightness in his chest struck him, immediately familiar regardless that it had been years since he'd last felt it. Before he could think to resist the urge, he began a quick study of the people in front of him. Women, men, children. He shifted through them like cards at a table.

There. A woman walked far ahead, her dark green skirt kicking out slightly with each step she took. The plain wool fabric of the dress revealed nothing; her hair and face were completely concealed from his gaze by a rather large, very plain hat.

Aidan frowned at the way his pulse leapt. He was

being ridiculous. Pitiful. But his eyes followed with close intent, taking in the details of this stranger. The line of her shoulder, the tilt of her head.

Sneering, he cursed himself for the terrible hope that bloomed in his chest. Even if there were something familiar in her walk, it certainly was not Katie.

He swallowed hard and forced himself to look away.

He had not done this in years. Had, in fact, thought he'd left this stupid impulse well behind him. Still, his pulse stuttered and his cheeks betrayed him with a hot flush. His gaze jumped back to search her out. As if in a trance, he slowed his pace and watched the woman stop to unlock a cheerfully blue door. She left it open to the cool day and disappeared inside.

One step out of the flow of traffic, Aidan studied the building. Just a small, tidy row of shops. The sign above the door she'd entered read HAMILTON COFFEES.

Perhaps the woman was Mrs. Hamilton. She certainly wasn't Katie. It never was and never would be. He'd known that long enough that it shouldn't hurt anymore, but somehow he still felt that ache in his throat. His lips thinned at the idea of grief. Even his sorrow had finally come under his control in the past few years. He could not let it loose again.

Inhaling slowly, he focused on the heavy smell of the shipyard that hovered over the whole town. Water and tar and wood. He closed his eyes and listened for the incessantly screaming gulls. They sounded as much like money to him as any pile of clinking gold.

When he opened his eyes, he was calmer. The blue door was just a door. The shop was just a shop. At some point, the woman would appear again. She'd step outside for a breath of fresh air or to sweep dust from the walk. And she'd be a woman, not a ghost. Then he could walk away and send the past back to hell where it belonged.

He waited. Waited as carriages and carts rumbled by, blocking his view for torturous seconds, waited as a rotund woman entered that dark doorway, then left again with a small package. He waited until the pressing urge lifted, and he knew he could move on. He didn't need to see the mysterious woman again.

She was not Katie.

Aidan turned away from the shop and walked in the other direction.

"Penrose," Aidan grunted.

Penrose appeared in the doorway that separated the two spare rooms they'd rented for the week. "Sir?"

"The post."

His secretary reappeared a moment later with a small stack of letters. "Shall I arrange passage back to London for this evening, sir?"

Aidan meant to say yes. He was done here. He should've left already.

He eyed the letter on top of the pile, recognizing his brother's handwriting. "Give me a moment," he said instead of offering a real answer. Penrose disappeared. He was good at that.

Fully aware that he was using the letter to procrastinate, Aidan sliced through the seal and unfolded the paper. As a tool, the note proved ineffectively short. A few pleasantries and news of his sister's honeymoon trip. And then a warning that their mother was planning another house party. "Cousin Harry has hinted that he may marry soon, and Mother insists he will need an audience when he announces his betrothal. She seems unconcerned that Harry has yet to reveal which lady has caught his eye. One can only pray she invites the right family."

Aidan managed a smile at that, though the idea of another trip home filled him with dread. He loved his family more than anything in the world, but they knew him too well. Whenever he was home, they watched him with wary sadness. They loved him, but they wanted the old Aidan back.

He sighed and rubbed a hand over his skull.

He wasn't a boy anymore. He was past thirty-one, his brown hair already starting the march toward gray at his temples. You'd think they would take the hint that he'd never be that boy again.

Granted, he was no longer grief-stricken and angry. But he could not seem to rid himself of the space in his chest that left his heart knocking hollowly around.

Aidan folded the letter from his brother and halfheartedly cursed the day he'd met Katie Tremont. Given the choice, he could not say with any honesty whether he'd take back the joy of having loved her just to have peace. He probably would. A few months of tortured happiness were not worth years spent grieving, not unless one had an ambition to take up poetry.

But, at the time . . . My God, at the time he would have sworn her kiss worth risking death itself. A smile tugged at his mouth at the melodramatic thought. He'd been only twenty-one, after all, and head-over-heels in love with her.

"Christ," he murmured as he made himself pick up

the second letter. This was good news. Rumors of a warehouse fire in Calais were confirmed, but his buildings had been spared. His business would profit by the wounding of others, and that bothered him not in the least. If it had been his buildings lying in ash, his competitors would snatch up his profits with clawed hands before the timbers had cooled.

Tragedy always benefited someone in the end. Hadn't he taken his share of the benefit from Kate's death?

"Penrose," he said hoarsely, ignoring the ice that crawled along his neck, "you reviewed the letter from Augustine?"

"I did. Excellent news."

"Indeed. Renegotiate the terms with Coxhill for the brandy. Supply will be limited for the quarter at least."

"Yes, sir."

"And, Penrose?"

The slim young man paused, midturn, before spinning back toward Aidan.

"Find out which trains are leaving for London tonight. But . . . don't book our passage until I return."

Penrose didn't even blink at the odd change of plans. "Of course, Mr. York."

Aidan had to return to the shop. He thought he'd successfully exorcised all his love for Katie, all his grief. It had been so long ago . . . an eternity.

But now the memories were back. Memories of her easy smile, her wide brown eyes, her soft hands tentatively touching the skin of his chest, his arms . . . everywhere. These images still shone clear in his mind though they now had a faintly stale feel—as if they were not real memories, but short vignettes he'd viewed once too often since her death.

He wanted them to fade again. If he didn't walk into that shop, didn't disprove this, she might follow him back to London and stay with him the rest of his life. Unacceptable. His life was just as he wanted it, and he intended for it to remain unchanged. He had a house, money, work to keep him occupied, and bedmates when he wanted them. He didn't need a long-dead love hanging about and complicating things.

Aidan retrieved his hat, angling it low over his eyes as he stepped out into the late sun. He kept his gaze straight ahead and pondered a trip to Italy in the spring. His strength lay in France, but his trips to Italy were becoming more profitable. Though lately, he'd had a good run buying disabled ships like the one he'd purchased this morning. He had money to sink into these projects, after all. Too much money, as he didn't seem to know what to do with it.

He could buy property, and had done. But what was he to do with more land or houses? It was only him, after all. Horses were tempting, but he felt like the worst sort of owner when he found himself with horses he'd never ridden and couldn't even recall purchasing. He cared little for fashion and less for gold and jewels.

No, he didn't need more money, but the triumph of making a profit lured him on. Each dollar made into ten felt like a victory over . . . something.

He turned a corner, and there it was, two blocks ahead. His feet wanted to slow, but he kept his pace steady. He wouldn't hesitate before a damned coffee shop as if it were a threat. He'd march straight in and put an end to this farce.

But before he could close the distance, a man in a wine red coat stepped over the threshold of the shop and shut the door behind him.

Aidan stopped, leaned his shoulder against the brick wall of an apothecary, and waited for the chance to put a stop to this.

Chapter 2

Gulliver Wilson's gaze slid over her shop, over the long oak counter, the smooth, dark wood of the floor. "You should be more careful," he intoned in his stuffy drawl.

Kate looked down and studied the green wool of her sleeve, willing herself not to lose her temper. "As you say, Mr. Wilson."

"This town is not so quaint as it seems."

"So you've told me." Her wry tone must have bounced off the man's thick head. He only nodded soberly and stroked his chin, eyes still crawling with that assessing squint she'd come to recognize.

"There's no reason to go about town by yourself, Mrs. Hamilton. I'm happy to escort you anywhere you have need to go."

Kate didn't reply to that, she only stared flatly at his pursed lips and wondered when he would leave. These visits were usually mercifully short.

"You may simply send a note 'round."

She continued to ignore him.

"Well . . ." He twitched down the hem of his red coat. "I'll check on you tomorrow."

"I assure you that won't be necessary. I am quite capable of looking after myself."

"A woman alone can never be too careful, Mrs. Hamilton."

"My husband would not have sent me ahead if he wasn't sure of my safety. Good day."

"Good day," he snapped before stomping away.

She watched with narrowed eyes until he stepped into the street and closed the door behind him. Irritating little bug. He owned the tobacco shop across the street and kept an eye on her from his desk in the window. Worse, he'd dropped in almost every day for the past two months, looking over her property and her person with an arrogant air. Her nose crinkled with distaste at the thought of his shiny eyes resting on her bosom.

What did he want from her? Perhaps he suspected that there was no Mr. Hamilton and hoped to marry her himself one day. Or he believed that she and her husband were permanently separated and he could become her lover. Whatever he imagined, in his eyes Kate was a woman without a man, and he meant to step in and fill the breach.

"I think not," she muttered with a humorless smile. Gulliver Wilson didn't stand a chance of even taking her for a stroll on the street, much less a run to her bed. The mere thought made her shudder as she went to the counter and pulled her ledgers from their perch beneath it. Freedom was finally hers and she intended to keep it.

She was no longer helpless. She'd opened this store with help from no one—and had turned a profit in less than three months. A soft feeling bloomed inside her at the thought.

She'd never dreamed, not once in the past ten years, that she could be this content. This . . . happy. *Happy.*

Was that possible? She hadn't even bothered dreaming of happiness for so long. But she now had a home. She had peace. Self-sufficiency. And *anonymity*. That was a sort of peace in and of itself.

Kate inhaled deeply, savoring the aroma of roasted beans before letting her breath out in a rush. She loved this place, loved the sharp scent of the room and the rays of the sun creeping over the hard-worn floor. The silence of late-day also gave her time to check her figures and make plans for new shipments.

A few more weeks and winter would arrive. She hoped it would be cold. A bad winter would be good for sales, but that was not the sole reason she wished for cold. It had been years since she'd seen snow—ten endless years—and she'd almost forgotten it. A small flutter touched her belly at the thought she might never have seen winter again. Just the idea of a long life spent in Ceylon disturbed her enough to dry her mouth and tighten her throat.

But there was nothing to fear. She'd left the strange shores of Ceylon far behind her and returned to England as soon as was possible. She'd taken only the money that belonged to her, and a knowledge of coffee she'd managed to gather up in her decade on the island.

Now Ceylon was a world away, and she could only pray it would stay that way. Actually . . . she could pray, and she could take every precaution.

She'd lost so many pieces of herself over the years. Some in small bits, and some in great cataclysms that had rocked her to her core. It was as if the very things that made her a person had been removed. Nothing so metaphorical as her heart or her soul, but a very real foundation of stones that held her up. And now, she was carefully piecing those stones back together, with her own hands and her own hard work.

Reassured by the thought, she glanced down to the book she held.

HAMILTON COFFEES, the engraving read in gold script. The lettering had been a luxury, but she was so pleased with it. She was only Mrs. Hamilton now. She was not Katie Tremont. She was not Katherine Gallow. Just Mrs. Hamilton, an unknown woman with no Christian name. She had no family, no past, no lover, no coffee plantation burying her in heat and deceptions. And no husband who'd ever show up and reclaim her. A perfect life, as far as she was concerned.

And she would let no one take it away from her.

Aidan stopped just inside the doorway of Hamilton Coffees. The afternoon sun shone warm and high, casting the interior of the shop in shadow. Standing silent for a moment, he let his eyes adjust to the dimness of the building and inhaled. The rich scent of coffee gave him a comfortable feeling—a reminder of countless damp days as a child spent watching his father drink his coffee as he reviewed the daily papers and planned his morning.

As his eyes adjusted, Aidan looked about the place. He'd expected a typical coffeehouse, full of tables waiting for customers to stop in and enjoy company and biscuits. Instead, the small space was lined with lidded bins. Labels were attached to each, no doubt a description of the contents. Hamilton Coffees was a coffee merchant, a very profitable position if one knew the market well.

The room seemed deserted, but once he took a step inside, Aidan saw it was actually L-shaped. A small wing extended to the left of a door on the far wall. And there sat the mysterious woman, bent over a workbook and completely absorbed in her task. He took the chance to study her. She was absolutely unremarkable. Light brown hair pinned up beneath a small white cap. Green dress completely free of any adornment.

He couldn't begin to guess her age—she was angled a little away from him—but even as he thought it, she turned slightly, allowing him a good view of her profile, and his world lurched with a violent shudder.

It was not her, could not be her, but his heart began a slow, hard thump of recognition. The street sounds filtering in from the open door faded to a dull buzz in his ears.

Her nose was straight and fine. Her lips full and rose red. She was older, certainly. Thinner. But . . . Holy God.

"Katie?" The word escaped his lips before he could form the will to stop it.

She stiffened. It was a subtle movement but obvious to him, he watched her so intently. Odd, though, she did not turn toward him, did not glance up. In fact, she bent a little more closely over her ledger.

"No." He heard the low word but did not see even a small parting of her lips. Then her chest moved as she drew a deep breath. She closed her eyes. "I am Mrs. Hamilton."

He felt strangely calm, looking at this stranger, hearing Katie's voice in her words. Time slowed, allowing him to notice all the small details of the moment. The way her hand curled tightly around a pencil. A strand of nut brown hair that had fallen free of its pins to rest against her cheek. The stiffness of that lush, unforgettable mouth.

"Katie."

Her lips fell apart just a bit then as she inhaled sharply. "No," she said again, finally lifting her head. Her closed eyes opened slowly, unwillingly, and met his.

The world sped up with a terrifying ferocity when he caught her brown gaze and knew, finally, that it was her.

"Katie," he breathed again, the only word he could think past his confusion.

Her face was a terrible mix of emotion—grief, yearning, fear. Before he could speak, that glimpse of turmoil was gone, closed behind a rigid wall of polite indifference. "I'm afraid I'll have to ask you to leave, sir."

He stared at her, drank in the sight of her—her slightly square jaw, her lovely skin, the thick hair held back in a merciless knot. An hour seemed to pass before he realized what she'd said. "Pardon?"

"The shop is closing early. You'll have to leave."

"Leave? It's *me*. Aidan."

"I know who you are."

He frowned, blinked, then felt a veil of shock begin to lift from his mind, exposing a maelstrom of anger and excitement. "What the hell is going on here?"

Her expression did not budge. "I am closing the shop early."

"Closing the—?" The words evaporated in his mouth, leaving a gritty film. He could only stare at her, openmouthed, utterly stunned at her calm. Perhaps he had lost his mind. Perhaps she was only a stranger and he was imagining that she looked like his dead lover. But she did not look confused. She knew him.

"How can you be here?"

Her eyes blazed with fear, only for a moment, then she turned on her heel and walked toward the doorway in the back wall.

Aidan's mouth numbed. "You were dead."

She stopped, spun around and pinned him with a glare. "Dead? What do you mean?"

"They told me you were dead."

"Who told you that?"

"Your parents. Your parents, of course."

"My *parents*. Well, that is not surprising, I suppose, though I cannot fathom their reasoning. I am not dead," she added needlessly. "Please leave my shop."

"The hell I will."

Her eyes narrowed further, but her breath shuddered so hard in her throat that he could hear it.

"Please don't . . ." he started. His mind was spinning, spinning. This was Katie. His lover. The girl he'd meant to make his wife. The woman who'd *died* ten years before.

"Katie, damn you. You'd better start explaining."

"Damn me?" she ground out behind her teeth. "Damn you, you cold bastard."

He took a step toward her, reaching out blindly, meaning to touch her, to shake her, but she jerked away from him and bolted into the dark room behind her. He heard her ragged breath, heard the slap of her shoes on the floor, then a bright shaft of sunlight pierced the dim as she opened a door to the alley.

By the time he recovered himself and followed, she was gone, the alley deserted. He stood there in the shadowed air and wondered if he'd gone stark, raving mad.

Chapter 3

Oh God, oh God, oh God. Her feet kept time with the beat of the words in her head. *Oh God, oh God.* She rushed down the alley, trying not to run, trying to suppress the urge to fly into the road in sheer, blind panic. The alley spilled into the bright sun of the street. Kate looked back, saw that no one followed, and pushed into the flow of traffic.

What were the chances? What were the chances he would wander into her shop?

Turning left at the next lane, she found a deserted alleyway and stopped to lean against the rough stone. Sounds flew from an open doorway further along, the clinks and clanks of the printer's shop jostling her nerves.

Her face began to crumple, her eyes stung, and the loss of control set off a rhythm of panic in her veins. Terrified at the rush of feeling, Kate raised her head and forced her face to be still. He was nothing to her, nothing. He'd sent her away long ago. He'd forgotten her until it was too late.

He was nothing to her. And yet she'd run from him.

Fled from her own home as if he could harm her. It had taken her years to build up some semblance of her old courage, and now she'd dropped it and run as if her hard-won bravery was a worthless rag.

What was he doing here? What did he want? And most importantly, *how had he found her?*

Her legs weakened. She slid down the wall and crouched there, listening for pursuing footsteps.

He could ruin everything.

She took a deep breath and told herself not to be a coward. He knew nothing of her life. In fact, he seemed to think she should be dead.

Closing her eyes, she drew a deep breath and tried to still the hundred questions swirling madly about her head. None of that mattered right now. She only had to think what to say to Aidan York.

Rubbing her forehead lightly, she cursed herself. She should not have reacted to him so, should have been cool and calm and completely at ease with his presence. Should have acted as though his appearance meant nothing whatsoever to her. Because it meant nothing, surely. He'd set her aside. She'd been given to another. It was as simple as that.

But how disturbing to see him again. He did not look the same. He was older, and his body was larger or harder or simply more intimidating. She might not have recognized him if not for his voice shaping her name. *Katie*. It sounded like an old secret. Or an old betrayal.

"Faithless wretch," she whispered, pressing a handkerchief to her hot face. She had loved him so much. With every fiber of her earnest, eager heart.

"Missus?"

Kate jumped, pushing herself up along the wall at the man's graveled voice.

"Be ye all right, missus?"

"Oh, yes." She tried to smile at the hunched figure of the local rag picker, tried to remember his name. "Yes, um. I'm well, thank you."

"Ye look a mite bloodless."

"The sun. I think I shall return home. Get out of the heat."

The man glanced around at the shadows of the lane. "You do that, missus."

Kate set her teeth and pushed away from the wall. But she didn't turn back toward her shop on Guys Lane. Instead she walked. Walked for blocks until the pain had numbed. Until she'd calmed down. Then she headed back to him.

She had a masquerade to maintain, after all. She could not back down from it now. Not even for Aidan York.

Aidan stared out the small front window before resuming his pacing. He felt like a wild animal, wanting to growl, to snap at someone or something.

He could not get his mind around the situation. She had not died ten years ago and seemed not to even know she should be dead. Unless that was just part of the lie. Where the hell had she been? His confusion made the specter of madness more real.

Through the glass of the front window, Aidan watched a woman stop and peer curiously at the closed door. After the first customer had come in and asked after Mrs. Hamilton, Aidan had turned the lock. He was in no mood to act as substitute shopkeeper.

This woman put her hand to the glass to peer blindly around. Her round face and the avid curiosity in her eyes reminded Aidan of his mother. My God, his mother was going to love this story. She wasn't an unkind woman, but gossip was gossip after all, and the story of Katie had always been a delicious one.

Mrs. Hamilton. Was she married then, or had been? Had she run off with someone else, leaving her parents to concoct a story to cover her indiscretion? The possibility stunned him.

He glared out the window for the hundredth time, watching for her. He would have some answers, if, of course, she hadn't disappeared again. The thought turned his blood cold, stopped his heart completely.

Just as his hand curled into a fist, he heard a small sound from the back room and twisted to find her standing there, smiling tightly.

"I apologize for walking out." She jerked her fingers vaguely toward the alley door.

"What happened?" he snapped.

"I . . . I just . . ." She paused to swallow. "I was only surprised to see you. Of course I was."

"No, not that. I don't understand what happened. To you. What *happened?*"

"I have no idea."

"No idea? We argued, Katie, and then you disappeared."

Her smile slipped and she glared at him. "We argued, and you told me to go."

"I was angry!" he shouted, but Kate cut him off with a sharp wave of her hand.

"There's no point in discussing this. All that matters now is you've found me."

For a moment, the clouds of confusion parted, and Aidan caught a brief moment of hope.

But Katie shook her head as if to warn him away from

such foolishness. "How did you find me? How did you track me down?"

"What?"

"I need to know. I . . . I have no wish to present myself to my family. Do they know I've returned?" Her fingers twisted nervously together, and anxiety tightened her brow.

"Returned from where?" he asked before shaking his head. "I have no idea what you're talking about."

"How did you *find* me?"

Aidan threw his hands up. "I saw you on the street! I followed you here."

Every muscle in her body seemed to freeze solid. "That's it?"

"Yes! A ridiculous happenstance. Meaningless and random."

She looked thrilled by the circumstances, but Aidan felt only a growing horror. If he'd left that office a few minutes before, or a few after, Katie would've walked on, unnoticed.

"Katie," he said on a strangled breath. "You still haven't told me what happened. Did you . . . the ship . . . did it sink?"

She spared him a distracted glance. "The ship?"

"To *Ceylon*."

"Oh, that. No. But it hardly matters now."

"Don't be absurd. Of course it matters." He took a step toward her but was stopped when she raised a hand.

"It was a lifetime ago. What story could I tell that would make any difference? I can't . . . I can't think. And I wish you would just *go*."

Strange that words could cause such stunning hurt. Aidan drew his shoulders back in an attempt to hide the force of the blow. She wanted him to go. And he could only imagine staying. For hours. For days. Staying until he'd satisfied himself with every detail of every second of her life since she'd left.

"Did you mean to leave?" he asked softly.

Her mouth twisted into a grimace for a brief moment, but she stayed silent.

He tried again. "You said you would marry someone else."

"You told me I *should,*" she whispered.

Weariness seeped into his limbs and muffled his brain. It had been an argument between children. Had she really married someone else because of their foolish, angry words? She must have. Her name was Mrs. Hamilton now, after all. And of all things, she was a coffee merchant.

His shoulders felt too heavy as he glanced helplessly around the small, spare room. "You're married?" he asked.

"I am," she said quickly and without emotion. Her hands tightened their grip on each other.

"Your husband?"

Her eyes fell to the floor. "He's not in England at the moment."

Aidan ignored his unfortunate relief. He studied her, taking in her patent discomfort, her downcast eyes, and he could not identify the emotions scrambling inside him. "Do you really want me to go?"

"Yes."

"How can I?"

"I have a shop to run," she said simply.

"The door is shut. Leave it for the day."

He knew her answer when she met his gaze. When had her eyes ever been so cool? "There are deliveries to be made. I cannot ignore them."

But stubbornness was new to her, and Aidan had

worn stubbornness like a skin since the moment he was born. "Fine. But I'll come back."

"But . . . why?" she asked, though resignation was writ clear on her face. Whatever she was feeling, she could not imagine he would leave this be.

"We owe it to ourselves to figure out what happened, don't we?"

She shook her head. "I don't see what difference it could possibly make."

"Don't you?" Aidan's hand lifted the barest inch, wanting to reach out to her, to pull her against him and feel the realness of her body. Her eyes flew to that small movement and widened in alarm.

"Tomorrow then," she blurted, taking a small step back. "There is a strolling park—"

"I'll come for you."

Her eyes flew to his before skittering away. "Good afternoon, Mr. York."

Chapter 4

Kate locked the shop door behind him. Despite her words, she would not reopen today; her shaky knees could barely hold her.

Oh, this was not good. This was not safe and peaceful. This was dangerous.

She pressed a hand hard to the ache in her stomach and wondered whether she would be sick, but a few long minutes later the nausea passed and she made her way up to her rooms, to her bed, crawling beneath the thick blanket to hide under the covers.

Aidan York. My God.

The last time she'd seen him she'd threatened to marry someone else. He'd told her she damn well should. She'd hated him for weeks afterward. But in the end, she'd still thought he would save her. She'd waited for him for so long, wondering every morning if this would be the day he would come for her. . . . But all that time, he'd thought she was dead.

It shouldn't have hurt more than his abandonment, but it did. It broke her heart to think of that terrified girl, holding on to her soul so that she could save something, anything, of herself for him. Knowing that if she just hoped hard enough, he would appear in Ceylon and take her away. In truth, there had never been any hope of rescue at all.

A ragged cry escaped her lips as she tried to stifle her sobs. It was no use. A deep well of emotion was uncapped and she could not close it. The tears overflowed her eyes and streamed down her temples as she finally gave in—just for a moment, she promised herself—and allowed her throat to open. The keening that emerged was a shock and a relief. Sobs wracked her body as she thought of the life she'd lived on the other side of the world.

The rage that rushed over her did not dry her tears but turned them vengeful, and she cried into her pillow until sleep fell over her, a sleep disturbed only by vague dreams of heat and black soil and the incessant sounds of insects.

When she woke, greeted by a headache and gritty, swollen eyes, she squinted at her small clock to find that two hours had passed. Six-thirty, and she felt like she'd lain abed for days. Rain pattered the window in a soothing ruckus. Her legs wanted to refuse service, but she forced herself to rise. The shop needed sweeping, the counters wiping. And she should eat.

Life moved on. She'd learned that lesson, at least. Life moved on and she must keep the lie going. It would not go well for her if she dragged around her shop like a grieving widow.

She washed her face and took her hair down to brush it before twisting it up again. Her hair had once been her vanity. In Ceylon it had become a heavy veil that seemed to capture all the moisture from the air and press it to her skin. She'd yearned to shave it off, as many of the men had done. Who would have cared, after all?

But now it was neither vanity nor curse, it was only a chore to be completed.

Turning her mind from the past, she pinned up her hair and hurried down the stairs to set a pot of water on to heat. The present was problem enough. And after that crying fit, she felt almost calm. She'd meant what she'd said to Aidan. What could any explanations matter? She was alive and finally well. And Aidan certainly looked no worse for wear. Older, yes, but strong and healthy. His gloves had looked cut from the finest kid. His hat had been of the latest style.

And nothing, after all, could be changed or taken back. So the present was her only concern. And there were small problems, in addition to the large ones. Her ongoing war with the old stove, which either refused to hold heat or charred anything she tried to cook. The nearly empty bin of beans from Sumatra and the wholesaler's promise that he would surely have more by Friday. And of course there was Aidan, who meant to return.

She felt sick at the idea, but even his return was a small problem. He would come and he would go, and that would be that. He would have no reason to tell her family. He'd certainly have no reason to try to track down her husband.

She opened the back door and swept the floor, then poured herself a cup of her new coffee blend before putting a sausage on to cook. She couldn't afford a daily maid, and she was determined to master the simple act of cooking a meal. So far the results had been less than perfect. In fact, she'd given up earlier in the week, but she could not bear another dinner of cheese and bread. She was forced to dare the stove.

Kate sipped her coffee and glared at the pan. The

sausage was barely sizzling. She added more coal, then jumped back with a hiss.

"Evil thing," Kate muttered to the stove, bringing a burnt fingertip to her mouth to soothe the sting. The flames looked too high now, but the sausage was finally cooking. Poking at it with a long fork, she prayed for the best.

What an exhausting day. What an *awful* day. And she still had to prepare her first delivery for the Stag's Horn, one of the best inns in town and her first big client. She'd almost forgotten, and that was only proof that nothing good could come of Aidan's return.

She gave the sausage an angry poke, and in revenge, it rolled away to reveal an underside burnt to black. Kate screeched in wordless frustration, reached for the handle of the pan . . . and remembered at the last possible moment that she didn't have a rag to protect her from the heat.

"Ha." She reached in triumph for the cloth, absurdly proud that the sausage hadn't goaded her into burning her entire palm. "I'm far more clever than you," she insisted with a smug smile—at the sausage, at the stove, at the whole kitchen.

The rumble of a man clearing his throat chased her triumph away and sent her twisting around, rag clutched like a shield against her chest.

"The door was open. . . ." Aidan gestured toward the alley.

Kate closed her mouth with a snap and glared at him. What was he doing here, taking up far too much space in her tiny box of a kitchen? "You're not supposed to return until tomorrow."

He looked as tired as she felt. A small frown caught between his brows, his wide mouth tightened with tension.

And those strong shoulders looked hard as stone. "I . . ." He shifted, clasping his hands behind him as he glanced toward the door. "I can't wait until tomorrow, Katie. Can you?"

She tried to ignore the bright pain in his eyes. "I can't have a man in my shop after hours. It's unseemly."

"Perhaps dinner at the inn then?"

"As you can see, I've already started my dinner."

He raised an eyebrow. His nostrils flared. "I think you may be in need of a new plan."

She opened her mouth to refuse him again, but her nose caught the acrid odor of burning fat and she groaned instead. "Oh, no."

Spinning back to the stove, Kate jerked the pan from the fire—using the cloth—and banged it down onto the cool side of the stove. The sausage was black and crispy, and tendrils of smoke curled tauntingly up from the pan. Her eyes narrowed, her hands clenched into tight fists.

"The inn?" he murmured.

She would have ordered him out with no hesitation if there'd been any hint of amusement in his voice, but she heard none. Willing herself to calm, she let out a long, slow breath before turning to face him.

"No." Her tone was rude but she wasn't screaming and stomping her feet as she wished to do. That was something.

His jaw clenched, but he held tight to his frustration as well. He dropped his head and frowned at the floor instead of her. "All right. But you said there was a strolling park. It won't be dark for a half hour yet. Perhaps we could walk."

She found herself staring at the top of his head. His brown hair was shorter now, but it still looked soft as sable to her. Out of the blue, a memory assaulted her. Of her hand sliding into his hair. Of her fingers gripping the soft strands as he lowered himself over her . . .

"Just a walk," he whispered. "Please."

"I'll need my cloak." She'd meant to snap the words in irritation, but they emerged as more of a rasp. "Excuse me." She dropped the rag on the small table and covered the fire before she walked serenely up her stairs. But once she closed the door at the top, she had to lean against it to try to draw a breath past her blocked throat.

She'd *forgotten*. She'd forgotten everything, and that had been good. To *not* remember. To not know him. She could not bear much more of this. Aidan was a ghost to her, and she needed him to be unreal.

So she removed her apron and folded it before walking slowly across the room to retrieve her gloves and her cloak. She would walk with him, and then it would be done.

She couldn't get her dry throat to work, so she descended the stairs and said nothing. He offered his arm, and there was no choice but to take it, though the contact brought a shiver of uneasiness to her belly and made her glad she at least had her gloves. Aidan had not worn his, she saw with a glance at his tanned hands.

She refused to remember his hands.

They strolled in silence, halfway to the park before he cleared his throat to break the tension hovering between them.

"You've been living in Ceylon?"

She shook her head and lied. "India." Ceylon was a small island, after all, and she might be known as a notorious murderess. She couldn't let him know a thing.

Silence returned, descending with surprising weight. Kate made a conscious effort to relax the fingers that gripped his forearm.

"So . . . that is where you learned the coffee trade?"

"Yes, my hus—" Swallowing the word, Kate cleared her throat again. "I lived on a coffee plantation."

"Did you return to England recently?"

"A few months ago. As soon as I was able, actually."

"You did not enjoy India?"

That surprised a laugh from her. The strained sound drew a look from Aidan, but she rushed on before he could probe. "I did not enjoy the heat."

"And that's why you returned?"

Here it was. She didn't hesitate over the story. "My husband wished to start a new venture. Coffee distribution. Due to our own plantation and his contacts in the community, we can guarantee the highest quality of product at the lowest price."

"But where is your husband?"

"The . . . the heat made me ill, so he sent me ahead to start the shop. He is in India for the moment, arranging new contacts."

"I see," he said in a way that made his confusion clear. "Are coffee shops really so profitable?"

"It is only the first step." Hands clenched tight together, she waited for him to kick at the cracks in her story. Why was she running the shop herself? Why did she have no workers? Why would her husband not travel with her?

Just as he seemed about to speak, the strolling park appeared before them and distracted him from his study of her face. His eyes swept the grassy square before he led her to sit on a small bench sheltered beneath a willow tree. Kate perched there and stared at the dying leaves of the tree, waiting for him to speak again.

She felt him shift toward her. "What happened? How did this . . . happen?"

Her breath swelled in her tight chest. "I don't know. After we quarreled, I returned home. I was so angry. You told me we couldn't marry—"

"We *couldn't*."

Kate closed her eyes, remembering the awful things they'd said to each other. She'd called him a coward, and he'd called her a naïve, stupid child. "You're right," she murmured. "We couldn't marry. So I married someone else."

"In Ceylon," he said flatly.

"India," she said again, feeling the lie on her tongue. "And that is what happened." Oh, but that so simplified it that she couldn't honestly say it was the truth. She didn't care.

Aidan pushed to his feet, shoving one hand through his hair. Kate felt stupidly jealous of that hand.

"That is *all?*" he bit out. "That is all you have to say? You could not marry me, so you married another?"

She shook her head, knowing he could not see, and said nothing.

"But they told me you'd died. *Why?*"

Why, indeed? Because she'd resisted the marriage? Because she'd refused to agree? Because they'd intercepted letter after letter begging him to come for her? Perhaps he had come for her, and her parents had been forced to fabricate her death. But she said none of this. Instead, she shrugged. "My father meant to make an advantageous match."

"I remember," he said dryly.

"My husband . . . he had money. Lots of it, and a desire to see the governor of Ceylon replaced. My father had influence over government appointments but never enough money. It was exactly the match he wanted."

"Exactly what I could not offer," Aidan grumbled.

"Yes."

"And you simply agreed?"

"I had no choice."

His head snapped up, and he looked at her. Really looked. Grief etched his handsome face, she realized suddenly. Lines of pain and weariness beyond his years. She'd been cruel not to see it before. She could not imagine what she'd have felt if she'd thought him dead. "I'm sorry they told you I was dead. I'm sorry."

He seemed not to hear her. "They forced you to marry him? They forced you to go to India?"

Her spine stiffened. Her skin burned. That wasn't grief on his face. It was pity. *Pity*. In his quiet words. In the softening of his eyes. Grief was there, yes, but pity rode close on its coattails, waiting to take over.

She set her shoulders back and decided to put an end to this. "Yes, well . . . I was privileged to travel to exotic lands and meet interesting people. Not many young girls are offered that opportunity."

His face went rather blank at that, she saw with satisfaction. "Oh. Of course. It was not altogether horrible for you then?"

"Certainly not." An impossible smile stretched her mouth. She'd be damned if she'd have him leave here feeling sorry for her. She was not the stupid, stupid girl she had been. She would not have anyone thinking of her that way.

Kate stood, forcing him to join her as she stepped onto the path. Aidan frowned at the grass as they walked, frowned at his feet, at everything but her. "Your time in India has been a benefit to you, it seems."

She made a sound of agreement.

"What was it like there?"

"Hot. The plantation was isolated and somewhat

primitive, I suppose. The animals were strange. . . ." Her voice faded away at the thought of the strange animal who'd been her husband. It had taken her so many years to understand him.

She felt Aidan's arm tighten like a wary cat beneath her fingers as he prepared to ask something he didn't wish to.

"Were you comfortable with your life there then?"

"Comfortable? Yes. It was a very comfortable life. We must have had twenty servants inside the house alone." Not one of whom had ever spoken to her of anything but their duties. Kate had come to think there was nothing more disorienting than living for years in a house full of people who refused to see you. Only her stepson, a boy her same age, had watched her, and Kate had eventually wished him blind.

Setting the disturbing memory aside, she studied Aidan for a moment from the corner of her eye. He looked confused and a little angry, his jaw ridged with tension.

She fought the impulse to appease him. She was done being that woman. She'd eventually found a small purpose in Ceylon. If Aidan wanted to wish her miserable with her husband, then he deserved his own misery. Could he not wish her happiness? After all, he didn't look as though he'd spent the last decade locked in an asylum, mad with grief.

"It was a long time ago," she said. "We were young. And naïve."

Aidan winced as if he remembered with perfect clarity the words he'd shouted at her that day.

Kate made her mouth smile. "You were right, you know. We couldn't have married, so how else could it have turned out?"

He did not answer her, but seemed lost in thought as they circled the park before heading back toward her lane. The sun was setting, the air cooling around them. The coldness soothed her nerves. She inhaled deeply, filling her lungs with iciness. When she exhaled, she felt at peace, and she leapt into that peace with a final lie. "Perhaps it was better this way. If I'd married a man in England, it would've served neither of us well."

He looked dumbstruck at the idea.

"I'm glad you came tonight," she said. "But we should return now, I think. And say our farewells."

"I thought I would return tomorrow evening. Perhaps dinner—"

"I'm already obliged for tomorrow evening," she interrupted. "A reception."

"Can you not bow out?"

"The dockmaster is hosting it. It would not do to insult him when our family business depends on timely shipments."

"I see." Green anger flashed in his eyes and silence fell again. He said not another word until they stopped before the door of her shop. "I'll bid you good night then," he said flatly.

"Aidan." She could not keep the weariness from her voice. "We must say farewell. There is no point to this."

She expected an argument, but what she got was worse. His eyelids dropped slightly. His jaw hardened to steel and edged forward. His eyes glinted cool fury.

When she'd known Aidan, he had not often lost his temper, but when he had, he'd become intractable. And he'd looked exactly like this.

Kate sighed. "Good evening then," she murmured. "And . . . please do not mention me to anyone. I am not

Katie Tremont anymore. I no longer know my family and I do not wish to. Please."

He nodded and she turned to unlock the door. Her fingers were clumsy. It took her a moment to even find the keyhole. Just as her hand slipped off the key, she felt Aidan's large presence draw close to her back, felt his warm fingers slide over her gloved hand.

"Here." His voice rumbled just inches from her ear as he guided the key into the lock. Kate twisted it, quick with panic, and pushed the door open. She moved to escape him, but before she'd shifted more than a few inches, before she could get free of his heat, that voice touched her ear again, impossibly soft. "I am so glad I found you."

A shiver slid up her spine, icy, feather-light. She closed the door behind her, not daring to even glance in his direction.

Chapter 5

The third glass of whisky went down more quickly than the second. Aidan didn't notice the subtle taste of peat and oak. All his subtler senses had deserted him hours before.

Katie was not only alive, but she was here. Here, in his reach. He didn't know what to feel about it. The strong veil of anger that overshadowed his other raging emotions surprised him. He actually felt angry that she was alive, ridiculous as it was. Angry that he'd been tortured by grief when she had been alive and well in India.

Perhaps the *well* rankled most. It seemed as though she'd settled in nicely to her life on a coffee plantation, married to some faceless man. Surely, if she'd wanted to, she could've avoided the marriage. She could've turned to Aidan. She'd claimed to love him. She'd given herself to him.

He chastised himself for the anger even as he gave in to it and raised his hand for another drink. She'd only been a child. Well, not quite a child perhaps, but at most a very, very young woman. She hadn't reached her majority, and her father had refused Aidan's offer. They could not have married, not for three years, at least.

A curse escaped his lips. These thoughts were meaningless, futile, and yet they seemed unstoppable.

He pictured Katie as she had been—confident, mischievous, daring. She had dazzled him, had even been slightly overwhelming in her exuberance. The very first time he'd seen her he'd been enchanted, captured by the contrast of her demure white dress and the sharp glint of humor sparkling through her eyelashes. She hadn't even been out yet, had only been allowed to attend dinner at her family's ball before being forced to bed before the dancing. But she'd been confident enough to smile in his direction and exchange a few pleasantries over dessert. And when her mother had ushered her quickly out at the end of dinner, his fate had been sealed. What young man could resist forbidden fruit?

But how different she was now. She seemed to have grown into stillness. She was beautiful though; still lovely in a quiet way.

Beautiful and *married*. Did she love the man?

The question stuck in his mind, a barbed thorn, irritating and painful. Did she take her husband to her with the same breathless excitement she had Aidan? It was maddening to think so, despite the dozens of lovers he himself had entertained in the past years.

Aidan snorted at the comparison. His nights with women had little enough to do with love. Nothing, actually, to do with it. That was the point—to keep as far away from love as possible.

The fourth glass of whisky succeeded where the others had failed and actually quenched his thirst. Aidan stared at the last drops of amber liquid, at the dim light wavering through the thick glass. What did he really feel, underneath the anger and jealousy? The emotion was familiar in a vague, distant way, and he thought that perhaps it was relief.

Setting the glass against the tabletop with a distinct thump, he pressed his fingers hard against his eyelids and watched lights dance against the black with exhausted fascination. His tired mind drifted for a long moment, floating with the blurry peace liquor provided. The anger softened, the pain lost its edge. Ten minutes of time not revolving 'round Katie.

Unfortunately, he'd used drink to dull his mind once too often in the past, and his brain ground slowly back to life, eager to remind him of the damage being inflicted to his eyes. Reluctantly lifting his face from his hands, Aidan stared blindly at the stained oak of the table.

It was only eight, according to the distant chime of the inn's clock. He'd planned to see her tomorrow but now had to fight the urge to rush back to Guys Lane and toss rocks at her window. She wouldn't appreciate it; the woman obviously wanted him gone. Why the reluctance to see him? Given a choice, he would have clung to her side and stared at her for days.

"Idiot," he muttered darkly. She had a husband. Little wonder she didn't know how to react to the unexpected appearance of an old lover.

Restlessness twitched his limbs with sudden urgency, pressed at his head. Aidan surged up from his seat, wincing when the chair tipped and hit the floor with a loud clap.

"Sorry." Ignoring the curious stares of the few other patrons, he righted the chair and stalked out the door, moving with determination, as if he actually had some destination in mind. The need to take action clawed at him, but there was absolutely nothing to be done except stalk and glare at people. There was no changing what had happened. The past could not be corrected.

By the time the fresh air settled the churning of his stomach and cleared his head, Aidan saw that he'd made his way to a less-than-respectable area of town. Good. One of the lounging drunks might make a move toward him; a sailor could stumble out of a tavern looking for a fight. But he walked on unmolested, unnoticed, until he finally arrived at the docks and made his way to the *Valiant*. She was small and sleek, and Aidan could well afford to repair her storm damage and get her sold quickly. A few repairs to make her seaworthy and she could be run up to London for a full rerigging.

There was nothing to keep him here, nothing but Katie, and he couldn't hang about much longer with no more reason than a need to be near her. Still, he could stay to supervise the repair job—it would take at least a week, perhaps two.

A week or two. That would allow him time to make some peace with this situation. To say his farewells to Katie and send the past back to hell where it belonged. He kicked a cigar butt into the debris-strewn waters below, and as he watched the moon glint off the ripples it created, he wondered why his blood felt warmer beneath his skin than it had in years.

Chapter 6

"Mrs. Hamilton!"

Despite her weariness, Kate felt a genuine smile tug at her lips as she finished tying up a sample of ground coffee.

Lucy Cain had come to call. The woman was lively and bright and Kate actually liked her. Miss Cain was smart enough that she had decided not to marry. Despite her father's grumblings, she told everyone who asked that she was happy without a husband.

"The day is finally here!" Miss Cain trilled. "This little dinner is my favorite of the year."

Kate smiled. "A little dinner, is it? I understand half the town is invited."

She tossed her red curls over her shoulder. "Pah. My father's business associates and every married couple in town, if I'm not mistaken. And not a soul to gossip about gentlemen with."

"I'm sure to be a disappointment as well then, I'm afraid."

Miss Cain's eyes narrowed with mischief. "Really? And yet I hear that you've been strolling with a handsome gentleman, Mrs. Hamilton."

"You . . . I . . . Pardon?"

"Oh, indeed," she giggled. "The baker's wife saw you and has been joyfully spreading the news."

Kate rushed to her tall counter and took a seat behind it so that she could shuffle ledgers about and look busy while she panicked.

"My word," Miss Cain said. "You've turned red as a cherry, Mrs. Hamilton."

"I'm sure I don't know why."

"Perhaps you've only taken too much time in the sun." She aimed a pointed look at the gray light in the window. When Kate didn't answer, the girl clapped her hands. "Well, I'm relieved to see you are not so awfully serious as you have seemed. From the moment we met, I knew there was something about you I liked."

Kate had been confused by that from the start. Lucy Cain had brought a basket of cakes and breads before Kate had even finished arranging the shop, then she'd sat and talked with—or at—Kate for the next hour. She'd concluded that visit with the argument that there were so few young, lively women in Hull that they must band together.

So confusing. Kate was not young and lively and felt disturbed that Miss Cain could make such a strange assumption. Kate was nearly thirty, first of all. And she was so *tired*. Much as she loved her shop, she sometimes wished she could stay abed all day.

Miss Cain, on the other hand, fairly vibrated with energy. In truth, she made Kate feel very old. And she made her smile when no other could.

"Do you have a gown?" the girl asked.

"I do."

Miss Cain cast a doubtful glance around the shop. "And a girl to help you dress?"

"I'm sure I shall manage."

"Nonsense! I'll send my maid along! And the carriage too!"

"Miss Cain, that's unnecessary."

"Yes, but it shall be *fun*. Don't you wish to have fun, Mrs. Hamilton?"

Fun? It was a temptation. . . .

Miss Cain drew close to the other side of the counter and reached out to take Kate's hands in hers. Her gloves were dainty and white, and Kate imagined her bare hands must be too. She was so very young.

"Mrs. Hamilton, you remind me of my sister. Have I ever told you that?"

She wanted to draw her hands away, but the girl's fingers curled tighter.

"She is close to your age, but she is not free like you. You understand? She lives beneath her husband's thumb. And you . . ."

Kate felt a moment of pure, horrifying fear. A surety that somehow this girl had found her out. But then she met Lucy Cain's sweet brown eyes and saw in them a wisdom she had never noticed.

"You remind me of her," Miss Cain repeated. "So please let me send my maid and a driver. And let us enjoy ourselves tonight, because there is no husband about to tell us we must not."

Inexplicably, tears clogged Kate's throat with the suddenness of a clenching fist. What could she do but nod?

Miss Cain gave her hands another squeeze before she stepped back. "I shall see you tonight then, Mrs. Hamilton."

"Please," she managed to say. "Call me Kate."

Her smile stretched to a blinding grin. "Yes, I think I shall. And you must call me Lucy."

Warmth prickled through her so quickly she pressed a hand to her chest. "All right," she said. "I will."

"Mrs. Hamilton!" a gruff voice called, startling her from this new place where people called her Kate. She stood and rushed toward the alley door to find a great oxlike man standing in the doorway. She recognized him by his white curls. He was the new driver who brought supplies from Mr. Fost's warehouse.

"Good day, sir. Have you brought the Sumatran?"

"I'm not right sure, ma'am. I've got four crates here for you. Hope one of 'em has what you like."

"Bring them in, please."

He set them in the short corridor, stacking them against the wall. "Did I hear your husband was in India, Mrs. Hamilton?"

She glanced up from her examination of the label on the first crate. "You did."

"I've a brother there. With the John Company, 'course. Where abouts is your plantation? Perhaps you might know him. Can't be too many Englishmen there. I reckon you all know each other."

Neither of the first two crates was Sumatran. "The plantation is quite isolated. In Mysore. I'm sure your brother has never been there. There were no Company stations nearby."

"Oh, I'm sure, ma'am."

She stood and put her hands on her hips. "There is no Sumatran here. Will you please tell Mr. Fost that I cannot go another week without?"

"I'll pass that on, and hopefully I'll be along with it shortly. Afternoon, ma'am."

Kate dusted off her hands, then remembered Lucy and hurried back to the counter. "I'm so sorry!"

"Oh, please don't apologize. I swear my father gets up

from every meal at least four times to tend to some emergency. I wouldn't know what to do with undivided attention. But I must go now. So many things to do before the party. Are you excited?"

Kate smiled. "I suppose I am."

"Of course you are. It will be impossibly wonderful." Lucy reached for Kate and clasped her tight in an unexpected hug. "I am so pleased you are coming. Good day, Kate."

After Lucy swept out, Kate found herself humming a waltz as she went about her work.

Lucy had entered like a spring storm, and just as after a storm, the air of the shop felt cleaner and brighter now. She'd swept all the staleness away, and even Kate's worries about Aidan York could not keep her from watching the clock in anticipation.

Lucy Cain was a force of nature and Kate had finally let herself be overtaken. And it felt . . . fun. She could almost hear the slide of another stone back into place. The tragedy she'd left behind did not matter. This was a new life, and already she was stronger.

Chapter 7

There was no point in staring into the wardrobe. She owned only one dress that could possibly be worn to the Cains' reception. Though it was modest and staid like the rest of her gowns, the material set it apart—a dark aquamarine silk that seemed to cast shadows upon itself when she moved. She ran a hand over the lovely fabric and felt a thrill course along her spine.

Silly, she supposed. She'd once worn gowns of silk and lace and fabrics shot through with silver. But this was a new time, a new place, and this dress made her happy.

She refastened her hair into a roll at the base of her neck and studied her own face in the mirror. What did Aidan see when he looked at her? She traced one finger over her cheekbone and the tiny scar that still lingered. Her face was thinner, certainly. She thought she looked tired, but perhaps the slight hollows in her cheeks sculpted her into a mysterious beauty.

She smiled at that, and though her smile was slightly marred by the small pucker of the scar, it was a real smile. The sight of it set her eyes sparkling. She was no beauty now, if she ever had been, but she was free. And despite all her brave thoughts of living a solitary existence, she was excited about the party. And she was trying very hard not to be excited about her suspicion that *he* might be there. She'd been on pins and needles all day, waiting for him to step into her shop. He hadn't, and her suspicion was growing into a knot in her stomach.

"Mrs. Hamilton?" a tentative voice echoed from downstairs.

"I'm here!" she called back. Lucy's maid hurried up the stairs.

Before Kate could finish thanking her for her troubles, the short, round maid was tugging Kate's corset strings with brutal strength.

"I'd say we can get another two inches off that waist, missus."

Kate put an alarmed hand to her stomach. "I don't think that's—" But she watched in amazement as the tightening stays pushed her breasts higher. Her fingers slid up to hover over the pale skin of her bosom. When she dared a breath in, the mounds of her breasts swelled. "Oh," she breathed.

Did she still have this body? Was she still a woman beneath all her ghosts and memories? How very strange.

"There we are," the maid muttered. "Lovely."

The maid swept the dress over Kate's head, briefly turning her world into hills and folds of twilight seas. Wanting to hold on to the moment, Kate closed her eyes and did not open them until every tie had been tied and every hook fastened. When she opened them, she saw a stranger in the mirror. A slim and regal woman whose face showed false depths of peace and confidence.

She realized then that she needn't have worried she'd be recognized and connected to her parents or her departed husband. There was nothing of the rosy-cheeked optimist she'd been as a girl. And she was no longer the dull-eyed wraith she'd become in Ceylon. Not quite.

"Are ye ready then?" the maid asked.

Kate nodded. "I'll be down in a moment."

The bodice didn't dip low, but with the corset tightened so expertly, the barest hint of rounded bosom was visible above the neckline. Kate traced the pads of her fingers over her skin, amazed that she could look so feminine.

She had sold all her jewelry, so she didn't even have a brooch to pin to her dress, much less a pendant to draw the eye to her skin. But for the first time in years, she touched the barest hint of rouge to her cheeks and lips before retrieving her slippers and cloak.

By the time the coach stopped in front of the Cain house, Kate was shaking with nervous excitement. After she handed her cloak to a footman, she clutched her reticule tightly between her hands and looked around. A thrill spiraled through her at the sight of dozens of elegantly dressed people.

In Ceylon there had been parties, but David had never taken her. A few women had stopped by the plantation upon her arrival, wanting to know who she was and what news she had from England, like vultures picking at the carcass of her lost life. But David had sent them away.

Eventually, they'd left her alone.

The sound of bright laughter distracted her from her memories, and she looked up to see Lucy Cain hurrying over. Her red curls were piled high atop her head, and an emerald green dress showed off skin as pale as untouched snow.

Kate closed her eyes as the girl hugged her. "You look so beautiful, Lucy."

"And you are lovely, Kate. So pretty. If your handsome

gentleman is here, he will prostrate himself at your feet in worship! What is his name?"

"Have we begun to gossip so soon?"

"It is always time for gossip, silly."

"Well," Kate murmured, "he is not my gentleman, as you know. I have no idea whether he'll be here or not."

"If he is, may I borrow him for a turn about the gardens? As he seems to belong to no one."

Kate kept her smile bright as she answered. "Of course you may. Though I cannot say whether he belongs to someone or not. He's merely a business associate. Now tell me all the other gossip. I am a blank page, you know. Fill me up."

Lucy's eyes blazed with joy as she took Kate's arm and swung her around. "Splendid. Let's see who is here."

Half an hour later, Lucy was in the middle of the scandal of Mrs. Mortimer—who married her husband's apprentice before Mr. Mortimer was even cold in his grave—when Kate found her eyes drifting. When she spotted Aidan York watching her from the doorway of the parlor, she didn't feel even a twitch of surprise.

In that moment, she knew she had dressed for him. When she'd smoothed her hair and touched pink to her lips, she had known he would come.

Lucy's words snapped to a stop when he drew near.

"Mrs. Hamilton," he murmured. "You look amazingly lovely." His deep voice stroked over her as he offered a bow.

"Mr. York," she said in answer, her chest so tight she had to look away from him. "Miss Cain, may I present Mr. Aidan York of . . ."

"London," he filled in.

"Oh, sir!" Lucy trilled. "What an honest pleasure."

He bowed over her hand. "I have cause to do business with your father on occasion, Miss Cain."

"Are you a sailor, sir?"

"I am in shipping," he answered, bringing a frown to Kate's brow. She had been so eager to avoid examination that she hadn't asked a single thing about him. Shipping. What could that mean? When she'd known him, he'd been the second son of a modest baron, with nothing to recommend him as a husband. Nothing except his wit and smile and gentle hands. Nothing except his love.

Aidan's warm laugh filled the space around her, and Kate blinked herself back to the present.

"Coffee," he was saying. "I've provided Mrs. Hamilton a shipment once or twice."

"Oh?" Lucy chirped. "I had no idea importers provided such immaculate service, sir. I am thoroughly impressed."

Aidan's answering smile was all charm and affection. "May I offer my service to you now by delivering punch? Or perhaps champagne?"

"Oh, champagne!" Lucy insisted. "Thank you, Mr. York."

His smile touched on Kate for a bare moment, and she felt it like a charged arc between them.

"Kate," Lucy hissed as he walked toward a servant. "My goodness. That is *him,* isn't it? The man the baker's wife saw you walking with?"

"He . . . he's an importer, as he said," she stammered, her lie making her words skip like stones on a river.

Lucy wisely ignored her. "He is so very handsome! And the way he looks at you . . ."

"He hardly looked at me at all."

"Exactly. He could not bear it, Kate!"

"Don't be ridiculous," she whispered as Aidan walked back with two glasses. "I am a married woman!"

"Ladies." His voice was all rumbly good humor. She actually shivered at the sound of it.

"Thank you, Mr. York," Lucy said. "Now if you'll excuse me, I must greet some of our other guests. A buffet is being served in the ballroom. Perhaps you might escort Mrs. Hamilton to a table?"

Kate knocked her elbow hard against Lucy's but the girl didn't even wince before she walked away with an innocent smile.

Aidan offered his arm. "I have worried about the state of your stomach."

She pressed a hand to her waist. "Pardon?"

"The war with your stove. I assume it is a drawn-out affair? The beast is clearly a hated and vicious adversary."

"Oh." She tried in vain to tighten her mouth against a smile. "You were not supposed to see that, and you're horrid to bring it up."

"On the contrary! I'm offering my support. A warrior needs her strength. Shall we approach the buffet?"

"You're not clever," she murmured. But he was. He always had been. So she took his arm and dipped her head so he would not see her smile.

"I saw that," he whispered, and the softness of his words slipped along her skin. Disturbed, she concentrated on the quick glimpse of her slippers afforded by each step.

"She reminds me of you," he said softly.

"Who?"

"Miss Cain."

Her eyes flew wide in disbelief. "You're mad."

"She's mischievous and bright. Happy."

His words bored a hole through her breastbone,

then sunk deep to settle in her belly and burn. She was relieved that they'd reached the buffet. She did not have to speak as he served her bits of the delicacies laid out on impossibly long tables. "Duck is a favorite, if I remember correctly?" he asked as he offered a large serving. Yes, he remembered correctly. She wouldn't let that thrill her.

When they reached their seats, there were introductions to be exchanged among the other guests. Pleasantries and idle chatter, nothing she had to turn her mind to. So she could think on his ridiculous assertion that Lucy reminded him of Kate.

Did he really still see her that way? How could he? Was it because *he* was unchanged? In his severe black suit and white cravat, Aidan looked . . . My God, he looked beautiful. Not so much like an angel as he'd once looked though. Now he looked dangerous as Lucifer.

Had he always had that knife's edge to his gaze? She wouldn't have known. In the past, when he'd looked at her, his eyes had been too full of love to leave room for anything else.

And just like that, she saw him. Really saw him. His short, slightly wavy hair and his shockingly green eyes. His wide mouth and straight nose and hard-hewn jaw. She saw the changes in him too. The touch of gray in his hair and the faint lines that creased his forehead and the corners of his eyes.

He had aged, matured in the years she'd been gone. Grown into his tall frame and wide shoulders. He was extremely attractive. Impossibly, even more attractive than he'd been as a young man. He glanced her way and caught her looking, and he smiled. He smiled, and it was as if there were a lamp inside her and someone had just struck the flame.

Panic welled in her chest and threatened to strangle her. That had been the feeling curling inside her since yesterday. *Attraction.*

"Katie."

She jumped nervously at the rich sound of his voice.

"Are you all right?" The last of the other guests at the table had departed. When she only stared mutely, Aidan waved a servant over and took a glass of red wine from the tray.

He held it out toward her, his mouth a line of concern.

"Thank you," she stuttered, and reached for the glass. The crystal chimed a pretty note when her fingers struck the rim, and a tiny wave of wine sloshed over the edge. The red stain spread in a slow circle over Aidan's white shirt cuff. Kate stared in horror.

What was she doing? What would people think?

"It's fine," Aidan said in a rush as he reached for her hand. "It's nothing." His fingers curled over her own and she thought she would dissolve into tears right there at the table. His touch felt wonderful. The heat of his skin seeping into hers. The soft rasp of his fingertips sliding across her knuckles. Wonderful.

Jerking her hand away, she stood on shaky legs. "I must go. Excuse me."

Aidan frowned up at her. "What? Why?"

"I'm sorry." She turned and fled before he could even stand, rushing past the swiveling heads of the other guests. She tried to appear calm as she hurried toward the door, tried to pretend she didn't see the startled looks of her neighbors, but her composure was completely destroyed.

First he'd brought pain back to her life, now his presence was eliciting other emotions as well. She hadn't expected this, not at all. And she could not afford it.

She reached the front door, but only managed three

steps past the frame before his alarmed voice stabbed into her.

"Katie—"

Feeling a hand close over her shoulder, she stopped, embarrassed to be running away again, humiliated that she now saw hiding as her greatest hope.

"What's wrong? What happened?"

"I just . . . I have to go." She was stammering. *Stammering.*

"Here." Aidan took her arm and led her gently down the stairs and into a hidden corner around the side of the house. "Tell me."

His warm fingers touched her chin, a startling contrast to the cool air. She closed her eyes against the beautiful pressure of him tilting her face up. She tried not to remember this same touch, long ago, this same motion just before he'd pressed his lips softly into hers for the very first time. Her eyes burned, wanting to weep.

"Katie—"

"Don't call me that!" She heard his sharp inhalation and shook her head. "I'm sorry," she whispered. "Please don't call me that. I'm Kate now."

"All right," he said carefully.

"And . . . I'm sorry but I can't see you again."

His fingers held her chin for a moment, tightened almost imperceptibly before they fell away. "Of course." She didn't dare look at him, didn't dare to see what emotion chilled his voice. "Then I will take this opportunity to say good-bye. I'll leave for London in the morning."

"Yes. I think that's just as well. I didn't mean . . ." She forced her eyes open, willed away the tears before they even formed. "I only meant that it is too strange, seeing you. It's discomfiting. And there are . . . There is my husband. I'm sorry."

His mouth had lost its gentleness; the cold shadow of his eyes fell impersonally on her face. "Of course," he repeated. "Would you like to return to the party?"

"No."

"Let me walk you home at least. Did you bring a cloak?"

He retrieved her cloak and reappeared again. This time, he did not offer his arm, and she was grateful. He was far too real now to touch.

They walked as strangers, silence between them like another companion. Clouds passed the moon and shifted darkness over them, only to be banished by the bright lights of windows they passed. In and out of shadows they walked. He did not speak until they reached her narrow lane.

"Katie . . . I mean, Mrs. Hamilton . . ."

Her feet slowed, but she didn't stop and turn to him until she'd passed into another patch of darkness.

"I'm sorry," he said. "I'm sorry for how things ended between us. If I could go back, I'd change so many things."

She could not see his face, thank God. She could pretend it wasn't him as she nodded. "I'm sorry as well."

And what else was there to say? They made their stiff farewells at the door, she avoiding his eyes, he bowing perfunctorily. Then she fled into the shop and up the stairs to lie down in her bed fully clothed, wrinkling her best dress and not caring in the least.

He was leaving.

She was relieved and somehow burning with anger also, because even his departure disturbed her, flooding her with desperate regret.

My God, how could she be attracted to him? Granted, he was handsome, he always had been. But she'd not looked at a man with anything more than a distant sort of weariness in so long. She'd assumed herself immune to men and their charms.

Staring at the ceiling, she watched pale light fade as the moon rose past her window. The darkness thickened. She stared.

Her body had betrayed her. It seemed to have some memory of Aidan and the love she'd once felt for him, the passion. The idea was foreign to her now.

She knew, intellectually, that she'd once wanted him, even that she'd enjoyed making love with him, but she could not really remember it. It was as if it had happened to someone else, someone who'd told her the story. She knew he'd touched her body but she could not recall the feeling of it. Her mind was crowded with the impersonal grip of her husband's hands, his blunt fingers digging into her flesh. Worst of all, she had ruined those memories of Aidan herself.

David Gallow had been her husband, and so she'd shared his bed. Still, for the first few months of her unwanted marriage, she'd thought Aidan would come for her, so every time her husband had taken her she'd been tortured with guilt. She betrayed Aidan, letting another man do that to her. It had seemed impossible Aidan would still want her, could still desire her, if she let another man touch her.

In defense, she'd tried to fill her mind with thoughts of him, ignoring her husband's impersonal assaults. She'd thought it would lessen the betrayal, thinking of Aidan. Instead, it had obliterated all her memories of his gentle attention to her body.

Kate couldn't remember their lovemaking, but her

body seemed willing to draw him near again. She could not do that. She was not *free* to do that.

The flat blackness of her bedroom blanketed her. He would leave tomorrow. She felt the wet tickle of a tear inching slowly down her skin and thanked God that he was going.

Chapter 8

Aidan tossed the remainder of his cigar onto the rocks beneath the train platform and strode down the steps. He headed for the crowded street where Penrose had already hailed the carriage. By the time he threw open the door of his modest Mayfair townhome, any sense of calm that the train had rocked into him had vanished.

"Shall I bring your personal letters immediately?" Penrose asked.

Aidan wanted to snap at the man, but he could not decide how he should answer. Instead of shouting, he bit his tongue and brushed past his secretary to retreat to his study. With a sneer, he took a seat behind his massive mahogany desk. The piece was a monstrosity that had come with the house, likely because it wouldn't fit out the doorway.

Penrose said not a word as he retrieved a glass of whisky for Aidan, then disappeared through the door that led to his own smaller office beyond. The fluttering sounds of paper being sorted filtered through the door. Aidan stared absentmindedly out the large window next to his desk and thought of nothing.

He finished the tumbler of whisky, and Penrose brought him the decanter and a few pieces of correspondence before retreating again.

Aidan ignored the papers before him and resumed his study of the window.

"A note from Mrs. Renier," Penrose murmured when he reappeared to add another letter to the pile. Aidan snapped that one up and looked it over. She was in London for a brief stay while her husband was on the Continent. She had instructed the butler not to place the knocker on the door, but a private dinner in her salon would not be an imposition.

At their last private dinner he'd fucked her on the table before the soup course had ended. The footman had dropped the fish course in the doorway, but they hadn't bothered to stop what they were doing. She had simply bared her teeth and growled at Aidan to pound her harder. Perhaps that kind of mercenary focus was exactly what he needed.

Aidan folded the letter and considered her offer. He'd already ended the affair, and he was usually unforgiving in that regard. The invitation should have irritated him, at the least. On a bad day, he might've been enraged by it. What the hell kind of day was he having that he was actually tempted to take Mrs. Renier up on her offer?

Aidan frowned at the window. Perhaps it wasn't a bad idea. If he resumed his normal activities, that would be proof that Katie's resurrection meant nothing. "Penrose."

His secretary materialized in the doorway. "Sir?"

"Please inform Mrs. Renier that I will join her for dinner tonight at nine."

"Yes, sir. And Mr. Scarborough's invitation to tomorrow's lecture?"

"Pardon?"

Penrose's gaze slid to the desk, and Aidan saw that there was now a tall stack of correspondence there. He'd only made it through one piece in—he glanced at the clock—an hour.

He cleared his throat. "I'll look over the other business later."

"Later, sir? All of it?"

"Yes, all of it. Leave me be."

Penrose nodded and shut the door to his little room with a wary look. Normally Aidan let nothing come between him and work. Today he simply swung back to the window.

Katie had turned away from him . . . and he'd let her. Her claim of being disconcerted had wounded his pride and pushed him on his way—exactly the outcome she'd been looking for, he realized now. The lie that he'd only wanted to say good-bye had come easily to his lips. He'd been trying to wound her as she had wounded him. Instead, he'd seen relief in her eyes.

But why was she so disturbed by him? When he'd boarded the train, he'd told himself that she was married now and cared nothing for him, but that made no sense now that he'd shed his anger. If she were indifferent to him, completely absorbed in feelings for another man, his presence would be less than disturbing; it would be inconsequential. But he'd affected her, and that meant she still felt something.

"Hmm." The progress of a slowly strolling couple occupied his eyes as they passed on the walk in front of his window, but his mind was still far north of London.

Perhaps he had exited the field prematurely. That story about her husband was poppycock. No man would let his wife live halfway around the world if he loved her.

And no decent husband would let his wife toil in a shop when he had funds enough to run a plantation.

She'd left her husband. She must have.

Still, it had nothing to do with Aidan. He'd pass an evening with Mrs. Renier just to prove it.

He told himself to leave off staring out the window and be productive. An hour of work and he could bathe and dress and set off for Mrs. Renier's house and a few hours of oblivion. But he was so damn tired.

Weariness pulled at him as if weights hung from his wrists and ankles. The feeling should've been familiar. He never slept well. But usually his tiredness was a restless ache. This felt more like a shroud of lead.

He glanced at the clock. Seven P.M.

Perhaps the sleepless nights in Hull had finally caught him up.

"Penrose," he said sharply.

The poor man looked downright worried as he rushed into the room.

"You may depart for the evening."

"But, sir—"

"On your way out, tell Whitestone to ready a bath."

"Of course, but if I may . . ." Penrose held up a sheaf of papers.

Aidan caught sight of the seal at the top of the first page. An important contact in France. Someone he'd been waiting to hear from. But his head felt ready to explode and his bones seemed to want to fall from his skin.

He reached for the decanter and poured himself another glass. "No," he finally answered. "Not tonight."

"Oh. Of course." Penrose hesitated a moment, as if waiting for Aidan to admit he was only joking.

Just as he turned away, Aidan gave in to one last impulse. "Have you sent the note to Mrs. Renier yet?"

"I have it here, sir." He raised a small square of paper.

"I've changed my mind. Let her know I'll come to dinner tomorrow."

"Of course," Penrose said as he retreated.

Relief spread through Aidan's muscles. Tonight he would simply have dinner and a bath and find his bed. He didn't need a woman's body tonight. He didn't need to exhaust himself, he was already there.

He took his bath, then drank too much, forgetting dinner altogether as he fell into bed. Amazingly, he got through the night with no dreams, but he woke with a memory, and a certain mission. A sense of purpose that had nothing to do with his work, for once.

He had to return to his family home, not to visit his mother or his brother or any of the dozen people sure to be hanging about. He had to return and find the box he'd hidden in the attic so many years ago. Because the contents of that box would give him a reason to see Kate again.

Chapter 9

"Aidan, my darling boy!" His mother enveloped him in an energetic embrace as he bent down to kiss her cheek.

"Mother. How are you?"

Her arms squeezed harder. "Thank God you've come! It's madness!"

The words didn't cause any alarm. His mother's world was always in crisis. "What's happened now?"

"Your cousin Harry," she wailed. "He means to propose to . . . to *someone,* and I'm sure he's chosen Miss Samuel, but he refuses to confirm."

"Confirm what?"

"That he means to ask for her hand!"

Aidan shook his head. "But he hasn't asked yet, correct? Perhaps he'd like to wait until the woman has accepted his suit."

"Oh, but there is planning to be done! We must have a party to announce it, and it must be before my birthday, and there is only so much I can do without knowing who the bride will be. It is all so frustrating."

He frowned. "There are two Miss Samuels, aren't there? Which one do you mean?"

"I don't know! If your sister were here, she could surely find out more. I've asked her to return."

That caught even Aidan off-guard. He'd been reaching toward the sideboard for a drink, but he stopped to frown at her. "You asked Marissa to return early from her honeymoon?"

"Well, she is the Miss Samuels' best friend."

His brother, Edward, stepped into the drawing room, and Aidan met his bemused gaze with his own. "Ah. Completely logical then. What did Marissa say?"

"Pooh. She didn't even mention my request in her next letter. Just went on and on about the sights of the Ottoman."

Edward snorted loudly enough to convey his exasperation to their mother. "Good for her. It's almost as if she's a sane person."

"Baron," their mother snapped. "Don't be snide. If you would only order Harry to tell us the truth, I daresay he would."

"Ah," Edward said, reaching past Aidan to snag the whisky he'd poured. "But I am almost a sane person myself, you see, so I won't order him to do any such thing."

She snatched up her skirts and marched for the door, seemingly forgetting how thrilled she was to see her sweet younger son. "You are all so very difficult." She'd only just disappeared through the door when her head popped back past the doorway, bearing a happy smile. "Aidan, how long shall you be here? I'd like to have a welcome home dinner in your honor."

"Only a day, I'm afraid. And I was here a scant three weeks ago, so it hardly bears celebrating."

"Everything bears celebrating, Aidan. You know that."

She left them with that cheerful truth, while they both

stared in silence at the empty door. As often as not, this was how she left any room.

"Well, then," Edward said a full ten seconds after her footsteps finally faded. "What are you doing back so soon?"

Aidan poured himself another glass and collapsed into a chair. "I was told there was an emergency."

"That's never brought you home before."

He tipped his glass in acknowledgment. "Right. I need to retrieve something I left behind."

"Surely you could've just sent a note."

"Mm." He left it at that as they both sipped their whisky.

"Did your business in Hull go well, then?"

Aidan was aware, as he always was, that his relationship with his family had dwindled to polite and guarded conversation. It wasn't the way he wanted it. Somehow it had just happened. He'd been so angry that first year. At himself and his family and the whole damn world. And instead of dissipating, the anger had merely buried itself more deeply over time, like a badger digging in. He'd used it as a barricade to keep everyone at a distance, but what of times like this, when he needed someone near?

He missed Edward, he realized. He missed the unspoken friendship of a brother.

"You can't tell Mother," he said quietly.

"Tell her what?" Edward asked, his head tipped back to rest against the chair.

"What I'm about to tell you."

Edward's eyes opened slowly and he raised his head to meet Aidan's gaze. "What is it?"

The moment he had his brother's attention, Aidan wished it gone. It was too much. He dropped his eyes and looked into his glass as if it were the one with the secret. "She's not dead," he murmured.

"Who's not dead?"

"Katie."

A dull thud punctuated the word. Edward's glass had slipped from his hand and landed on the carpet. "Pardon?"

"Katie's alive."

"But . . . I don't understand."

"Ha." Aidan's smile was drawn. "Neither do I, but there it is."

"She survived the shipwreck?"

Aidan finally found the courage to meet Edward's gaze. Not the courage, actually, but the ever-present anger. "There was no shipwreck. She was packed off to India to marry a rich farmer, and she arrived quite safely. The shipwreck was a ruse."

Edward looked as stricken as Aidan felt. "But why?"

"I've no idea. She claims she knew nothing of the tale. Perhaps it was only that I kept returning to her home, demanding to see her, and had to be swatted away like a pesky fly. Perhaps it was meant to hide the shame of her family selling her to a farmer with no name and hoards of money."

His brother leaned forward, eyes growing wider. "Wait a minute. You've seen her?"

"In the flesh. She's running a coffee shop in Kingston-upon-Hull."

"Katie Tremont? Running a coffee shop? That makes no sense."

"No," Aidan said. "No, it doesn't. And she's not Katie Tremont anymore. She's Mrs. Kate Hamilton."

"Oh. Yes. Of course."

Of course. As if any of it made any sense. "I must ask

you to keep this in your confidence. Her family has no idea she's returned to England."

"Aidan . . ." Edward's voice had gone ragged at the edges, as if his throat was too tight. "If it weren't you telling me this, I wouldn't believe a word. Why has she not told her family?"

Aidan shrugged. "Her father died last year." He felt no emotion as he spoke the words. He'd hated the man for a long time, but now he didn't even feel triumphant.

"Yes, but her mother! And her brother is the earl now."

"I have no idea why, Edward. She asked me not to resurrect her, and I agreed."

"Jesus Christ," Edward breathed. "Katie Tremont. Will you . . . ? What will you . . . ?"

"She's married. Her husband is still in India, but she's married."

"I see."

But of course, Edward could not see any more than Aidan could see. It was a ridiculous farce. Or a tragedy. A poorly written play, whichever it was.

Edward retrieved his fallen glass and took Aidan's as well. He refilled them both before collapsing back into his chair. "Thank you for telling me."

"I had to tell someone. And you . . ." He tipped back the whisky and swallowed it all in two long gulps. His throat burned, but so did his eyes. "I wanted to tell you."

"I'm glad."

Aidan cleared his throat, dislodging any trace of emotion that might linger there. "Are my old trunks still in the attic?"

"I believe so."

"Good. I need to go through them." He pushed up from the chair, aware that his brain wobbled a bit with the movement.

"You're retrieving something for Katie?"

"I am."

"Aidan."

Aidan set the glass down carefully on the table, not happy with the warning in his brother's voice. "Yes?"

"She's married. You said so yourself."

"And?"

Edward set his own glass down hard. "Only you would treat that so casually."

"What the hell is that supposed to mean?"

"You know damn well what it means. But Katie Tremont is not just some jaded, bored wife. She is the woman you used to love. And she's the woman who never *once* contacted you in the past decade."

"I'm well aware of that. You needn't fear for my heart, brother. It's no longer tender. I've spent years banging it against other women's backs, as you kindly point out."

"Aidan—" Edward started, but Aidan shook his head.

"It is only the truth." He was out the door and headed for the stairway before his brother could stop him.

He cursed as he bounded up the stairs, briefly sorry he'd said one word about Katie. He wasn't stupid. He knew they were both changed. But that was why he wasn't afraid. She was married. There was no chance at a tender, innocent reunion. There was no chance he'd tumble into love again and beg her to marry him. She was someone's wife. And if she was an unhappy wife, well what woman wasn't? He had some experience in unhappy wives, after all.

After Katie's supposed death, the women of the ton had taken an uncomfortably avid interest in his return to the social scene, and that was before he'd even made his fortune. Young women, especially, suddenly began treating him like a rare treasure that had been plunked down in their midst. He'd finally solved the mystery of his appeal weeks later when one of his lovers had made a confession—all her friends were half in love with him, taken with a rumor that he was grieving the death of a secret lover. *That* was why they wanted him: because he'd lost Katie.

He'd been coldly furious at the time, sick that Katie's death had become titillation for the ton, and yet he hadn't stopped. He'd used the bodies of those women to forget for a few moments, and so he'd used her death as well. As that realization had sunk into his bones, he'd only become more dissolute.

The guilt and the drink had nearly killed him. And then a cousin in France had proposed a partnership. He'd needed an English contact, and Aidan had needed . . . what? To prove himself? Certainly the idea of making a fortune had appealed to his sense of revenge. Kate's father had rejected Aidan's suit because he'd had no means to support a wife. Or her family, in retrospect.

So he'd gone to France, drawn by a desire to show Kate's father up and, if truth be told, by the idea of drowning his sorrows in Frenchwomen for a time. Eventually, he'd found that he could drown his sorrows in business, as well. That deal had saved him. But not his soul. Not his conscience.

After a time, it hadn't been Katie he'd grieved for, but the man he'd meant to be. He'd betrayed himself with his actions.

When he reached the fourth floor, Aidan was happy for the dimness. It helped alleviate the sudden stark fear that Kate would find out what kind of man he'd become. But no. No, her own desire for privacy would protect his secrets. And who would ever tell her?

He lit the lantern that hung on a nail on the wall, then opened the door to the attic stairs. Once he reached the warm, dusty black of the attic itself, he turned up the wick on the lamp. Narrow trails snaked through the boxes and crates, leaving little room to maneuver. Thankfully, he found his chests stacked near the door, as if they had awaited him all this time.

The top chest contained nothing but old clothes as far as he could tell. When he lifted the lid of the bottom one though, he found what he'd been looking for. Nestled among the books and papers lay a large wooden box, carved with his initials. He hesitated a moment, watching the box with a wary look, as if it might lash out and injure him. He'd purposefully packed it away to remove the temptation of revisiting his memories of her. Blowing out a long breath that sent dust motes dancing wildly, he took the box from its coffin, set it on a crate, and opened the lid.

It was all there, the pitiful leavings of his secret time with Kate. Twelve letters—lavender paper covered with her looping script. A tiny white lace handkerchief that had once smelled tormentingly of her perfume. A pressed flower she had included with a note. And there, underneath it all, the thing he'd come here for.

The heavy gold pocket watch had been her grandfather's, she'd told him as she pressed it into his hand. She'd given it to Aidan as a pledge of love, bidding him hold it for her until their marriage. He still remembered the way his fingers had shaken as they closed around it. They'd just made love for the first time, both of them nervous and overwhelmed with emotion as they gave their innocence to each other.

Jesus, they'd been fools. Certain, as only young people can be, that the world would genuflect before their love. Only a month later they'd been shouting at each other in frustration, helpless in the face of her father's refusal.

And then she'd been gone.

Every day for a year Aidan had carried this damned watch over his heart until he'd finally grown so disgusted with his own grief that he'd packed everything away in this box and never looked at it again. Until now.

Slipping the watch into his breast pocket, feeling the familiar weight settle against his chest, Aidan made his way out of the attic with a grim smile. He now had the perfect excuse to see Kate again, whether she wanted him to return or not.

Chapter 10

"My husband will be arriving soon enough," Kate said past clenched teeth, turning her back on Gulliver Wilson to resume dusting the coffee bins.

"It's inappropriate for you to remain alone so long," he grumbled.

Kate let her mouth fall open with shock at his impudence, though in truth she wasn't shocked at all. "Really, Mr. Wilson, you are being utterly inappropriate. It is hardly your place to question the actions of my husband, sir."

He cleared his throat. "Perhaps Englishmen raised in the Orient don't understand the correct care of a lady, madam."

"Perhaps you don't understand that you're behaving outrageously! I'll bid you good evening, sir."

The blasted man actually stayed where he was. She glanced past her shoulder to find him frowning down at her. He was a bully, and he wanted her to be cowed by him, but she refused to comply. A whole minute ticked past before he nodded and made his way to the door.

The moment the door closed behind him, Kate stood

straight and twisted her hands into her apron. Mr. Wilson was too suspicious. What if he decided to "helpfully" track her husband down and ask when he planned to join Kate in England? It was too soon for this. If it was discovered that Mr. Hamilton didn't exist, her business would be ruined. But that sort of information would take months to ferret out. Years even. And no one would connect her to David Gallow. More importantly, no one would connect her to David's death or the horrible threats of his son.

Her stomach ached at the thought. Not for the first time, she almost wished she'd stayed in Ceylon long enough to know the outcome of that night. But she'd had no choice. She'd promised David she'd never reveal the truth, and so she'd had to run.

The letter hidden beneath the countertop was another worry buzzing around her head like a hornet, but she wouldn't rush over to it and hold it in trembling hands like some helpless young girl. Instead, she finished her dusting like the responsible business owner she was, then she stowed away her rags and duster and sat calmly down at her stool.

The letter had arrived from London two weeks before. She'd taken it out every day to stare it down as if it were a snake. A Mr. Dalworth claimed to be writing as a representative of a very important planter in Ceylon. He'd heard of Hamilton Coffees and wanted to discuss a deal with the shop owner personally, perhaps saving all interested parties a good deal of money in the process.

Mr. Dalworth did not name the planter. Kate felt suspicious of that, yet she could understand the reasoning. The planter would not wish to anger his current broker. Still, it made her nervous. What made her even more nervous was that Mr. Dalworth would be personally traveling to Hull this week.

Why?

Kate glared down at the letter for the hundredth time. Mr. Dalworth's client wished to know Mr. Hamilton's background and reputation. If only Mr. Hamilton actually existed, it would be simple information to provide.

This was exactly the type of deal that could help her business flourish. Exactly the purpose behind all her scheming. She knew the product, after all. She knew it from the moment the woody sprouts pushed from black soil. She knew when the beans must be picked to hold the greatest flavor. And most importantly, she knew which plantations took more care than others. Which owner demanded his workers pick the most beans, and which owners taught workers to pick the best.

But no one would believe a woman could know so much, which was exactly why she'd invented a husband upon her return to England. Just for a little while, then she'd lay him to rest. It wasn't such an awful lie, surely. Her real husband was dead, and she deserved to make something good of her years on Ceylon.

But an inquiry from an anonymous planter in Ceylon? A coincidence or a trap?

Kate took a deep breath and looked around her shop. This life she had built. This good and right thing she'd carved for herself out of darkness. A year ago, she would have lowered her head and curled her arms around herself, afraid to take a chance. But now she thought . . . now she thought she would rather go down kicking and screaming, mad with fury. If it was a trap, she would fall into it and wait for the chance to attack the man who'd laid it.

She carefully folded the letter, zipping her finger over

the creases to seal them tight. Then she slipped the letter back under the counter and dusted her hands. And now her workday was over, and a sizzle of anticipation traced through her body.

She slipped the latch and rushed to the back room, her boots raising a happy riot against the wood floor. Purposefully ignoring the kitchen and the two burnt dinner pots that awaited her attention, she grabbed her hooded cloak from a nail on the wall and pushed open the alley door. The air that greeted her when she stepped outside was startlingly crisp.

Kate paused for just a moment to inhale the delicious coldness, ignoring the various alley odors that lingered about. The warm spell had finally broken, and the weather she'd been waiting for had arrived.

Rushing down the alley, she eyed the sky above hopefully. Flat gray clouds hung still over her head like great, floating promises. She wound her way through the lanes until she reached the strolling park, then veered away from the ancient willow, choosing a bench on the opposite side of the lawn. There was no sense in reminding herself of Aidan.

The wind sent brown leaves skittering over the grass as she sat down and gazed across the park. It all thrilled her—the dry sound of the dead leaves, the hard bite of the air, the wind's cruel caress as it snuck into the folds of her cloak.

The grocer, Mr. Johansen, had predicted it would snow before sunset. She was ready.

Sitting as still as the stones that made up the bench beneath her, Kate waited and thought of nothing, refusing to allow even a hint of an idea or memory to form in her mind. She simply closed her eyes and breathed.

She'd discovered over the course of her time abroad

that heat was a fortress, a prison. It oppressed the body and the mind, suffocated the soul. The cold was liberating. She suspected that, if she wished, she could rise up and fly away on a stir of the wind.

A tiny pinprick struck her cheek. Then another.

A fan of bittersweet euphoria swept through her body. Eyes still closed, she turned her face up to the sky and felt a dozen more snowflakes land on her skin. Her mouth stretched into a wide, unfettered grin and a sobbing laugh escaped her.

Seconds later, her face now wet with melted snow, she opened her eyes to see flakes floating, dancing, blowing through the air. A weight lifted from her heart at the sight. It was silly, she knew. She'd been back in England for months now, but for the first time, she felt she'd returned.

She'd wondered sometimes, particularly since Aidan's departure, whether she really belonged in England. She felt so changed, so foreign. It had even occurred to her that she'd died on that island and this was some sort of death dream. But sitting here in the cold, watching the dim light of the hidden sun grow dimmer, she knew she was home. A few hot tears mixed with the dampness on her cold cheeks as darkness finally fell over the park.

She should go. She was looking forward to lighting a fire in the stove and working on her mending, just enjoying her small parlor with its yellowing walls and ragged furniture. She'd received some excellent Madeira in trade and planned to have a glass to help warm her before she retired to her bed, a bed the perfect size for her and her alone. But for now, she was content to sit here, to shiver and breathe.

Time stretched by, her nose began to numb. Taking a deep breath, she drew in the cold and looked slowly around, memorizing the sight of the light silver veil of falling snow, setting it carefully in her mind before rising to start her stroll home.

She'd reached a peaceful place again. A week ago she'd been frantic. All the control she'd exerted over her life had threatened to crumble and leave her soul naked to the elements. Over and over again, she'd imagined how different life would've been if she hadn't been sent to Ceylon. Or even if she'd only known Aidan hadn't abandoned her. She could've escaped if there had been someone to run to. If she'd had hope, she would've found a way to make her way back to him. But she had stayed. Stayed and faded.

Oh, it had eaten at her heart for long hours—the thought of what could have been. But after that first endless night of trembling hands and raw emotions, she'd forced herself to calm. She was fine now. Just fine.

Avoiding the front door—and Mr. Wilson's prying eyes—Kate passed through the mouth of the alley, counting on the brightness of the snow for visibility. A few feet in, a prickle of unease swept over her skin, but she ignored it. These days found her curiously unafraid of physical danger. She'd sailed alone all the way from Ceylon with little thought for her safety. The leering looks of the sailors had been easily quelled by cold stares of her own. The men seemed able to sense her impervious contempt of them, and they'd left her alone. It was almost like magic, this fearlessness. A strange magic though, since it had failed her in the face of Aidan York.

"Kate."

She jumped, and for a moment she fell into a well of fear. It was him, her stepson, come to confess his awful love for her again. Come to threaten her with his awful lies. She slid a foot back, preparing to race away.

"Kate, it's me."

Finally, she registered the familiar voice. Aidan. Not Gerard. A chill shivered through her body, setting her hair on end as she searched the shadows for Aidan. He finally took a step forward, revealing himself.

"What are you doing here?" she asked through clenched teeth.

"I have something for you."

She took three shallow breaths, then shook her head in exasperation. "Aidan, you can't be here. You have to go."

His forehead furrowed into a frown as he glanced around with concern. "Is something wrong?"

"Ha! Yes, there's something wrong."

Obviously worried, he stepped toward her as if to take her arm, but she pulled quickly back and turned to the door. Her mind turned frantically, trying to find a way to make him go and stay gone, but her brain refused to offer a solution. With no idea what to do, she found herself moving through the door with him close on her heels. Clutching the folds of her cloak around her as protection, she turned and met his gaze. His eyes were expectant, his mouth grim and beautiful.

Trying to ignore the sudden silence between them, Kate busied herself with lighting a lamp. She didn't know what she was hoping for—the floor to open up and swallow him whole? It seemed unlikely that he would show a sudden desire to depart after waiting in the snow for her. His eyelids dropped almost imperceptibly.

"Oh, very well," she muttered in resignation, and removed her cloak, holding out her hand for his coat. She was rewarded with a wide smile as well as his wet garments.

A glance at the stove showed her kettle still steaming on the warm top. "Tea? It's a bit late for coffee."

"Tea would be wonderful."

She took her time preparing the tea tray, aware, all the while, of his eyes on her. What did he see? Who did he think she was?

Without a word, she picked up the tray and headed up the stairs; he followed with the lamp.

"Let me get the fire." He was already kneeling at the small stove, striking a flame. It was completely inappropriate that he be here, in her private rooms, but that horse was already miles from the barn. Still, his presence disturbed her.

"I thought you'd gone to London." Turning away from tending the tea, she made no attempt to pretend happiness at his arrival.

"I did. I returned to check the repairs on my ship."

His ship? She would not ask him about himself. Instead, Kate perched tensely on one of the small chairs and poured tea as he took the seat opposite. The width of the table between them was a relief.

"I have something of yours. I thought I would bring it to you as I was returning to town anyway."

"I'm sure that wasn't necessary."

Instead of replying, he gently placed a package on the table. It was small: a square of carefully folded blue cloth wrapped in a silver ribbon. Hesitant, afraid what she might find, she reached out and lifted it, feeling the weight of his gaze on her as she untied the ribbon and unfolded the package.

"Oh!" The sight of the burnished gold, engraved elaborately with a delicate forest of leaves, tightened her throat. With slow reverence, she turned the watch over and brushed her fingers along the smooth-worn metal where her grandfather's thumb had rubbed away the design. She breathed in the scent of old metal. A memory surfaced, of her grandfather in his library, staring into the flames of the fireplace, thoughtfully stroking the watch as he puzzled something out. A hundred other memories assailed her, all of them of her grandfather, all of them good. He'd been a constant in her life. A man who was always kind and warm and funny, at least with her. Even as a small child she'd been aware that others were intimidated by him, even afraid of him, but Kate had worshipped him—and been adored in return.

A click of the clasp and it opened to reveal hands frozen at the six and the ten. The watch had kept this same time for years, even before her grandfather's death. The familiar sight drew another picture from that hollow in her heart.

Aidan's face, flushed with the hour they'd spent in each other's arms. His eyes, shining with fierce emotion as he cradled the watch in his palm. *A promise,* she'd said, *a pledge of my love until we can be together*. He'd embraced her then and rained tiny kisses over her eyes, her jaw, her neck. *I love you,* he'd whispered again and again. *I love you.*

Kate placed a hand protectively over her throat, guarding the tightness that settled there.

"I know how much it meant to you. I wanted . . ." He shrugged. "Well," he added quietly, "it's returned to its rightful owner now."

Closing the watch with a loud click, Kate tried to end the memories of Aidan with the same efficiency. "Thank you. I hadn't thought of him in years." The thickness in her throat muted the words.

His hand lifted, and she watched warily as he reached slowly toward her face. His thumb brushed her cheek, catching a tear she hadn't known had fallen. Eyes closing of their own accord, she helplessly savored the tenderness of that small touch. How many years had passed since anyone had touched her without demanding or punishing or directing? The thought was jarring. She'd grown up with the gentle hand of her mother, the affectionate arms of her nurse and her governess, the steady touch of her maid. Then there'd been Aidan. . . .

Odd that a person could go almost a decade without a kind touch and not even realize it.

The feather touch of his thumb became the warm press of his whole hand. She allowed herself just this moment of pleasure and turned her cheek into his palm, pressed her skin against his heat. Just a second of contact, then she stood swiftly and walked away from him to look out at the night through her tiny window. The floorboards creaked as he rose. She waited anxiously for the sound of his footsteps coming close, but he didn't move, didn't even seem to breathe.

Silence stretched taut between them, plucking at her nerves. When he finally spoke, he left the past behind. "You seem to have the beginnings of a successful business here."

"Yes," she answered breathlessly, some of the tension leaching from her body. "It's very exciting." Her eyes focused on his reflection in the window and caught his quick grin.

"Exciting?"

"Yes. Well, I think so. You probably think running a shop would make for a tedious life."

He moved a few steps toward her. In defense, she turned to face him and his smile. "On the contrary," he said. "I find business invigorating. I think one must find it exciting in order to be successful."

"What is your business then?"

"I started importing years ago. Now I invest, generally. Ships, textiles, industry. Anything I think will make money."

"Oh, that does sound fascinating."

"It is. When you're good, it is. If you're not, then it's just terrifying."

"That good, are you?"

He laughed, the sound a delicious vibration in her belly. "I can afford to be confident."

Smiling, Kate tried to ignore how comfortable it was to simply be with him. There had been an easiness between them from the very first moment they'd met.

"And what about you?" he asked. "How did you come to this?"

The easiness vanished like a dream. Clearing her throat, she straightened and edged past him to retrieve her cup. "I already told you. I missed England, and my husband had an idea for new income."

"Yes, but how did you come to run the shop? How did you even know you would like it?"

"I . . . I . . ." She didn't know what to say. In truth, she hadn't known any more than that she'd needed to leave Ceylon and she'd needed an income as well.

Aidan cleared his throat. "I suppose you help with your husband's estate."

"Yes! Yes, exactly. He has a son from his first wife, so he helps with the planting side of it, but there is so much more than that."

"And you have no children of your own?"

She'd been expecting the question, but it still squeezed her chest. He sounded so casual as he asked. So polite. "No. No children. And how is your family? Is your mother still well?"

A moment passed, but when he answered his voice was light. "She is as she ever was."

Despite her nervousness, Kate couldn't help but smile at the thought. "She has not mellowed with age?"

"Oh, God no. In fact, I'd say her imagination improves weekly."

"And your brother? Has he made you an uncle, at least?"

"Not yet, much to my mother's loud lament. But my sister just married. You remember Marissa?"

"Of course!" she said, though she hadn't thought of her in years. "I was amazed by her. So beautiful and cool even as a child. If I had to guess, I'd say she married a dashing prince from a foreign land."

"On the contrary, an untitled Englishman."

"I don't believe it."

He winked. "Believe me, neither did we. But she loves him. Even I can see that now."

Even I? What did he mean? "And you, Aidan? You've never married?"

"No."

Alarmed by the thrill that sparked inside her, she made herself smile lightly. "Surely you're sought after?"

"Yes."

She waited for him to continue, but he said nothing more. Her throat strained. She wanted desperately to ask why he'd never married but wouldn't let the words pass her lips. It was none of her business.

"As for your family—" he started.

Kate drew in a sharp breath and stepped back. "What do you mean? You promised not to tell them—"

"No. I said nothing. But I believe your mother is well. And I see your brother on rare occasion in London. You do not wish to see them at all?"

She didn't close her eyes, though her lids fluttered down for a moment. Her injuries were old and long since healed. "No," she whispered. "My brother and I were never close." Even if she had a desire to see her family, she couldn't. Her masquerade would be finished, of course. But more than that, if Gerard had spread his lies about her, they'd surely have heard.

Aidan drew near and put a hand to her elbow. "Are you all right?"

"Yes. Thank you for bringing my grandfather's watch."

"I wanted to return it to you. And I wanted to see you again," he said. His soft words seemed to echo in the room, but the tender stroke of his voice must be her imagination.

"I'm truly grateful." She turned from him as she carefully voiced the dismissal. It was not subtle. He could not mistake it. She cringed when he made no reply. "It was kind of you to bring it to me."

"Kind."

Kate nodded and listened to the censorious silence that fell once more. From the corner of her eye, she could see his intent gaze.

An endless moment passed before he sighed and shifted. "I'd hoped we could be friends."

Staring desperately at the wall, she pressed her lips tight together.

"You were my best friend once, Kate."

Her lungs strained to draw breath through her rigid throat, her muscles shivered with suppressed emotion. She'd told herself she wanted only solitude, but his words exposed the lie. If he'd asked to be her lover, she could've sent him away with conviction. To be friends, though, as they'd once been . . . The idea set off a fierce yearning inside her.

Tears overflowed her burning eyes. She raised a trembling hand to her mouth just as his arms came around her. She smelled snow and salt water in the wool of his coat. Aidan York was *holding* her.

"There's too much between us," she whispered through her tears.

"Nonsense. There's no reason in the world we can't be friends."

"There's too much between us," she repeated frantically.

"The past is the past, Kate. We're both different people now." His hand smoothed over her hair, soothing her frenzied nerves. "I'm not willing to lose you again. I've not had a true friend since the day you left England."

He couldn't know what that meant to her, to hear that no person had ever replaced her in his life, just as no one had ever taken his place in hers. He needed her, and, oh God, it seemed she needed him too. But could she believe him? She'd once believed every word he'd said, but her father and time and distance had ruined that for her.

But those old doubts could not expand when his arms were around her.

"I'm married," she breathed in one last attempt to push him away.

"I know."

This was a terrible idea. Sending him away had been the right thing to do, but she didn't think she had the strength to do it again. Kate breathed in the scent of him, of his clothes and his soap and his skin, and felt the blank terror of jumping from an unknown height. She deserved this small thing, didn't she?

Taking a deep breath, she braved the leap. "I was planning a long walk along the Humber tomorrow. The shop is closed on Sundays."

He was still, stiff, then his muscles shifted and moved slowly into relaxation. "I was thinking of a walk myself. Would you like company?"

Sniffing self-consciously, Kate nodded into his shirt, unable to speak past the emotion that pressed against her throat. *Friendship,* she told herself as her heart danced in her chest. *And nothing more.*

Chapter 11

It was as dreary a day as he'd ever seen. Gray light, gray sand, gray rocks, gray water. And Aidan was sure his frozen toes were an alarming shade of that same color. Watching Kate as she stepped lightly beside him, he wondered if she were walking on the same icy beach as he. A happy pink glow suffused her cheeks, and her eyes seemed to throw off gold sparks.

"It's cold," he groaned.

"So you've said." She gazed serenely out over the rippling water, a small smile playing about her mouth.

"You seemed to need reminding."

Her smile widened when she turned toward him. "You should go home and warm up. We can walk together another time . . . when it's not too cold for you."

"It's not too cold for me," he protested in as reasonable a tone as he could muster. "I'm only concerned about you."

"I'm perfectly well. You, on the other hand, look positively frozen."

She seemed so cheerful about it he couldn't help but laugh. "Why are you enjoying this so much?"

"You'd enjoy it too if you'd baked in the tropical sun for years!"

"I suppose I would," Aidan conceded, happy with her enthusiasm, if not the weather. "And if you can bear the cold, I'm afraid my pride wouldn't survive the embarrassment of retreat."

"Such a gracious escort." Her grin was saucy, relaxed.

Aidan grunted obligingly, but he was secretly thrilled. She was a different woman today. Her smile came easily and she took his arm with a natural grace instead of wariness.

His offer of a platonic friendship had relieved her, it seemed, removing the tension that hovered about her like a storm. It was no idle offer on his part. She *had* been his last true friend, and he'd missed the ease and comfort of being near her.

"How long will you be staying this time?" Her voice broke through his thoughts.

"Well, I'd only thought to check on the progress of repairs on the ship, but the workmanship is impressive. I'm considering leaving her here for the complete overhaul. It'd be to my advantage to have a good shipyard outside the confines of London." The advantages began to form and clarify in his mind even as he spoke. Cheaper port fees, a faster turnaround. The work itself definitely came cheaper, and the craftsmen seemed reliable.

And Kate was here.

"It's colder here, though," he added with a sidelong look at her. "The river tends to ice."

"Oh, so subtle! Fine. I give in. Let's get you back inside to warm your delicate toes."

Aidan smiled at her with unabashed pleasure, whirling

her around to walk back toward town. "My delicate fingers are quite frozen too."

Kate surprised him by giggling. She really was so different. Perhaps he was too. He couldn't remember the last time he'd walked for the simple enjoyment of it. Actually, he could. Of course he could. It had been with Kate, along a rocky river shore quite like this one, her hand held tightly in his. And then they'd spied that old boathouse. . . .

A strange shimmer of warmth swept from his chest down to his fingers at the memory. It was a feeling much like the wonderful, painful anticipation she'd inspired in him years ago. A need to touch her, sweetened by the knowledge that she'd welcome his touch. The sensation rocked him. This was what he'd never felt with other women. Only Kate had ever made his fingertips tingle, made his breath catch in his lungs with anxious want.

And she still did, apparently, though he tried to rein in the feeling. It could be only nostalgia or some desire to recapture what they'd lost. But there was no recapturing that.

Still, it was hard not to give in. Hard to stop himself from touching her face when she turned to smile at him, hard to keep from sliding an arm around her waist as they walked. It was even harder to think that in a few minutes or an hour or two hours, he would have to say a casual good-bye and retreat to the inn until the next day. A need to be near her pulsed in him, and he wanted to indulge it, to quench it.

"Have you tired of my company or may I impose on you for dinner this evening?"

"Oh, certainly," she answered quickly, her smile turning to a frown. "Although . . . dinner . . ."

"Never fear." Aidan tipped his head toward town. "I already asked the innkeeper to prepare a basket. I did not wish to strain your hospitality."

"Oh," she replied archly, "is that what you were thinking?"

"What else?"

She narrowed her eyes at him suspiciously, but he kept his expression angelic.

"What if I were to tell you that I put dinner in the oven before we left?"

"I'm sure I don't know what you're implying," he said.

"No?"

He shook his head.

"Oh, fine. You win. I'll pretend you don't think me an absolute disaster in the kitchen."

"Lovely."

Kate laughed, and God, but it was a gorgeous sound. Aidan tried not to imagine the idiotic grin on his face as he stepped back into town.

She wasn't sending him away. He'd see her again in an hour. Less than that. And he didn't plan to bring only dinner. He'd purchased a chess set that morning from a shop near the dock. It was winter, after all, and far too cold to spend every day touring the town. But chess . . . a single game could take hours. Hours spent inside, together, in front of a warm fire.

The gray sky suddenly seemed bright as summertime.

It was dark in the alley when she opened the door to his knock. A tingle of danger spread down her belly as she stepped aside to let Aidan in. If anyone saw him entering . . .

But Aidan smiled the smile of a pleased child and held up the basket.

"Is that roast chicken I smell?"

"Perhaps." He shifted the basket away from her reaching hands and inclined his head toward the stairway. Kate led the way eagerly, her mouth watering at the smell. She had no doubt it'd be the best meal she'd had in weeks.

Aidan was immediately busy with laying out the meal. He'd brought everything, as far as she could tell—food, plates, silverware, napkins, even wine and glasses. The bounty quickly overwhelmed her small table. As she craned her neck to see past him to the feast, his broad shoulders shifted toward her and he handed her a glass of wine.

"Is this a celebration?"

His eyebrows rose in surprise before he smiled warmly at her. "No, but I suppose it should be." He touched his glass lightly to hers. "To you. To our renewed friendship. To our continued success in business endeavors. To the simple fact that we are both alive."

"Yes," she replied softly, unable to tear her eyes from his gaze. He still smiled, but his eyes turned serious—intense and unwavering. He raised a glass to his mouth and she did the same, mirroring his movements. The sweet, sensual taste of the wine filled her mouth like summer fruit.

"Do you like it?"

"It's gorgeous."

"Yes," he murmured, green eyes suddenly hot as they moved over her face.

Blinking hard, she stepped past him to take a seat at the table, intent on ignoring the knot that formed low in her belly. The moment passed unacknowledged, and they settled into the meal, finishing the bottle of wine long before starting dessert. Tired and full, they both subsided into silent contemplation of their wineglasses.

"What are you thinking?"

Kate blinked and shook her head to clear the cobwebs—the wine, actually—from her head. "Nothing. Why?"

"I just want to know. You must be someone different now. We were so young. You must have scars and memories."

A sudden constriction tightened her chest. Was it possible he really did see her? Her hand drifted to her cheek, to that small scar high on the bone. The playful light in his eyes faded to puzzlement as they followed the movement. His own hand rose to hover over hers for a moment before he brushed her fingers aside and set the lightest of touches against her skin.

"What is this?"

She shivered at his soft touch, at the low rumble of his voice. "Nothing."

His fingers feathered under her chin to tilt her face toward the lamplight as his thumb smoothed along her cheek. "A scar."

She tried to offer a coy smile. "You're not supposed to mention such things."

She felt the pressure of his fingers tightening on her chin even before his face stiffened with anger. "What is this?"

"Nothing. A riding accident. There was a mud slide. I was lucky," she added cheerily. "I escaped with only cuts and bruises." Meeting his gaze unflinchingly, she watched his worried anger turn to sympathy.

"I hear India can be dangerous."

"Yes."

His fingers fell away from her skin. "Well, I'm glad you're back in safe, staid England then."

"Not so glad as I am." She reached distractedly for her glass only to find it empty.

"Shall I open another bottle?"

"No. No, I've had enough."

Nodding, Aidan stood and stretched, drawing her eyes up the long line of his body. She suppressed a sigh and looked away from the beautiful sight of him.

"I've brought you something."

He opened the basket he'd brought from the inn and withdrew a flat, square package.

"What is it? Some other remnant I left behind in England?"

"Open it."

Surprised and wary, Kate untied the string and folded back the paper to find a plain wooden box beneath the wrappings. When she flipped the small latch of the walnut box and lifted the lid, she found only more wood. Truly puzzled now, she worked the piece of wood up and out of the box, finally spying the chess pieces cradled in a nest of cloth.

"A chess set! Thank you."

"The piece you're holding folds out into a board."

She opened the board, marveling at the hidden hinges that held the four squares of wood together. It was a simple set otherwise, the pieces basic and painted.

"You told me once that you played with your grandfather."

"I did. And thank you, but you shouldn't have bought me anything." Her hands belied the words, stroking the smooth edge of the white queen.

"It was purely selfish. I'm hoping you'll consent to play with me. We never had a chance before."

She looked around the small, worn room. He shouldn't be here. She shouldn't have invited him in. Widow or married woman, it wasn't right. But her old nature was returning. The rebellious soul that had gotten her into trouble so many times.

Aidan only wanted to be friends, after all. There was no chance of more, not with the lie of her marriage sitting between them. Not with the bloody mess she'd left behind.

"Of course," she finally said.

He smiled as she began to clear the table. "I don't play well," he warned as he unpacked the pieces.

"I do." Warming at the smooth stroke of his laugh, she surprised herself by smiling at the pleasant feeling. *Just friends,* she reminded herself sternly, if with little enthusiasm.

After he'd set the last piece on the board, Aidan opened another bottle and refilled the wineglasses. At her raised eyebrow, he shrugged and took his seat. "It's thirsty work getting trounced."

The game was over in thirty minutes.

"I warned you." Aidan sighed at the sight of his king, solidly cornered.

"How can you be so dismal at strategy and yet so good at your work?"

He shrugged unapologetically. "I suppose if there were some motivation for me to learn . . ."

"Like money?"

"Something like that, yes."

"I'm afraid I've nothing to offer to sweeten the pot." Kate regretted the flip words as soon as they left her mouth, but her wine-drugged blood sang sweetly at the sudden heat in his eyes.

"No? Nothing?"

Her lips dried. She licked them, inadvertently drawing his eyes to her mouth as she shook her head.

"And if I said you did?"

Unable to control the compulsion, she wet her lips again, fascinated by the way his jaw hardened at the sight. The wine was definitely affecting her judgment. She wished there were no table between them, wished he could simply lean toward her, lower his head and touch his mouth to hers. A small sigh escaped her at the thought, a heavy tension invaded her belly. She focused on his lips then, on the handsome shape of them and the firm line of his mouth. She wanted to remember how his lips felt on her skin, wanted to create new memories to replace the ones lost.

There were so many little things about him her mind had left behind. The thin white line of a scar trailed into his hairline at the right temple, the result of a childhood fall. A cowlick at the crown of his head that interfered with the careful, elegant cut of his dark hair and made her want to twirl a finger through the little swirl it created.

Her heart contracted at the thought of how he'd once belonged to her, how she'd once been able to reach out and touch him with perfect aplomb. Now she had no right to him, no reason to put a hand to the nape of his neck, no excuse to stroke her fingers over the short cut of his hair.

But perhaps he meant to give her that right. Aidan rose, but instead of walking away, he went to his knees in front of her. His hand brushed over her temple. "You never pierced your ears," he said, his fingers brushing the sensitive lobe of her ear.

"Pardon?"

"You were so eager to."

"How can you remember that?"

"I remember." His hands edged farther back, sliding into her hair. The touch was slow, dreamy, and Kate's eyes closed of their own accord.

"Your braid is coming loose," he murmured, tugging softly at the leather tie. Both his hands slid through her hair, meeting at her neck to work out the tangled braid.

This was wrong. So wrong. But hot shivers of sensation moved over her scalp and down her neck and all the way to her toes. Pleasure trickled down her spine and gathered in a pool deep in her belly. She thought she would melt right through his fingers when he finally worked her hair free and ran his hands slowly through the strands, smoothing out the waves with gentle pressure.

Her head fell back under his ministrations, her mouth parted just slightly on a sigh. She wanted, feared, *knew* he was going to kiss her. The softest touch of warm breath caressed her lips and then it was him, his mouth, his lips against hers. The spicy warmth of wine invaded her senses until it was all she knew. It was comfort and unbearable excitement. It was fear and need and desperation.

Kate heard a soft sound of want, knew that it was her own quiet moan, and opened her mouth to him. His tongue glided inside. She felt the shock of it as if she'd never been kissed, as if all those kisses they'd once shared had been an invention of her lovesick brain. Still, she wasn't tentative—sliding her tongue over his, she arched her neck into his hands, offered her mouth up for his pleasure.

It was his groan she heard this time as he deepened the kiss, his hands a wild tangle in her hair. Her heart swirled up and out of her chest with joy. She felt light as air and just as insubstantial, as if she would dissolve into puffs of clouds at the slightest touch.

Her fingertips tingled, wanting to float away, so she placed them purposefully against his chest to tether them to something solid. He was definitely solid. At that touch of his body, her spirit rushed back into her flesh. She was no longer feather light. She was hot and languid, heavy with the desire that pulsed through her veins. Terrible need blossomed in her when Aidan slid a firm hand down her side, following the line of her corset to her waist and then to the curve of her hip.

A strangled sob rose up in her throat, escaped against his lips. His hand tightened briefly on her hip and then he pulled back from her, abandoning her to her need. She curled her fingers into his coat, thinking she could simply hold on to him and stop this moment from ever ending, but his lips lifted from hers and he was whispering her name.

"Katie."

She didn't open her eyes, didn't want to let the world back in.

"Are you all right?" His hand smoothed her hair again, hushing her vibrating nerves.

"No," she answered with a small, hiccupping laugh.

"No?" His voice was a beautiful murmur as he pulled her a little closer and pressed a long, sweet kiss to her forehead. "No, I'm not all right either."

What was she going to do now? Horror flooded through her.

He must have sensed her torment. When she opened her eyes, she found him shaking his head. "Please don't regret that, Kate."

"Aidan. I can't—"

"No. We don't need to talk about it now. Just promise you won't regret it."

She looked into the beauty of his green eyes, stared hard into the depths. There was hunger there, and tenderness, and the icy glint of deep pain as well. Pain she had caused.

Fine. She didn't wish to talk about it anyway, to push her lies deeper. "Yes," she said. "All right."

Nodding, he stood and paced several feet beyond the table to stare at the flickering light of the stove. She stared with him, savoring this lull before the coming storm. They would have to talk sometime, after all.

Anxiety took hold of Kate's shoulders, tightening the muscles like drying rope. They would have to talk about it, it was inevitable. They could only be friends. He must know that. She should say it aloud, but not now. Not when she still tasted him on her tongue.

He cleared his throat and turned back to her, his hands clasped tight behind him. "Mr. Penrose insists I must return to London soon."

"Oh?" She tried not to sound relieved.

"No weeping? No gnashing of teeth?"

She tried to think of something tactful to say.

He smiled briefly, as if to reassure her, but it did not hold. Within seconds, his mouth went straight and grim. "Kate . . . Is your husband really coming to England?" Despite the question, there was no curiosity in his eyes. No doubt. He knew. Knew there was no true marriage, even if he didn't know the reason. "He's not, is he?"

"Does it matter?" she asked. Another statement poised as a question.

"Of course it does."

"No," she countered. "We can't . . . I can't . . ."

He didn't say a word, but his gaze never wavered from hers.

In the end, she said, "I'm sorry," and he looked away.

"It's very late. Thank you for a lovely evening."

Her mind was muddled, slow, and she only stared up at him for a long moment, marveling at his tall grace. They had fit together perfectly once—his lips just reaching the bridge of her nose, her own mouth always searching out the line of his jaw.

Dazed, she watched him frown and open his mouth to speak, but he hesitated before he finally said, "I'll return again before I leave for London."

A few minutes after the door closed behind him, she rose unsteadily from the table and put herself to bed, thoughts of his mouth swirling madly through her dreams.

Chapter 12

Aidan eyed the *Valiant*'s new mast as it was hoisted into place. The smooth wood reached toward the gray clouds that hung above them, threatening snow. He stuffed his hands into his pockets and rocked back on his heels.

"Are you married, Penrose?" Aidan's words floated toward the sky on white wisps.

"Pardon, sir?" Penrose asked.

"Do you have a wife? I assume not."

Penrose looked shocked to have been asked a personal question. "No, sir."

Ropes creaked as men heaved the lines taut. They were watching from the dock for safety's sake, but if the mast fell, it would fall much farther than this. Aidan observed with a narrowed eye. "And have you ever been in love?" Silence greeted his words and he turned to his secretary. "It's a simple question, Penrose."

Penrose's face was slack with shock. "Sir, I don't . . . that is to say . . ."

"Well?"

"I don't know. I suppose I was once. As a young man."

Aidan glared down at Penrose's smooth cheeks and

slim frame. "Hm." His blond hair glinted in the pale light. The boy was likely twenty-four or twenty-five now, but he seemed so young. "So you were in love once, but then it dissipated, correct?"

"Dissipated?"

"Yes. You ceased to love her."

"I—I shouldn't like to be so callous. We did not suit."

"I see."

He turned his eyes back to the mast and the ropes that stretched from it. A dozen workers held tight to those lines, holding the mast steady. Aidan felt as if he needed the same ropes lashed to him.

"Perhaps," Penrose started before coughing lightly. "Perhaps I didn't love her at all. It was likely an infatuation that simply faded."

"An infatuation," Aidan murmured, trying to convince himself that this was just the word that applied. Even if it had been love with Kate so many years before, those feelings had long since died. This was something new and . . . temporary.

By God, he'd had trouble turning his mind to business today. Last night her wine-flushed lips and welcoming eyes had been a glorious torment. Then her gaze had touched his mouth, and he'd been lost in the desire to feel her. Her skin, her lips, the wild disarray of her hair . . .

He'd kissed her. He'd kissed her and known immediately that it was right.

No, not right. It couldn't be right, because she was a married woman. Granted, he'd taken a shameful number of married women to his bed, but this was *Katie*.

Snow began to fall, and Aidan absentmindedly donned his hat, still eyeing the workers.

Kate was not just a thoughtless means of distracting himself for a few hours. She was not just a body. And she was clearly not experienced at this type of affair. She'd been thinking of repercussions before the kiss had ended.

Still, there'd been no denial at his guess about her marriage. If she'd loved the man once, she did not love him now. She likely didn't love Aidan either, but she felt something. Nostalgia, or infatuation, or pure and simple lust. Need tightened his groin at the thought.

What the hell was he going to do? She'd snuck inside him, and now he could see the danger he'd overlooked. He'd been hollow for so long, and the space inside him had been cut out in her shape. How could she not fit perfectly?

"Mr. York!" The bright feminine voice pierced his brooding thoughts. For one painful heartbeat, Aidan thought it was Katie. And it wasn't anything like lust that made his pulse tumble.

But as he turned, his heart tripping with anticipation, he saw Lucy Cain hurrying toward them, her cheeks pink with the cold. Her smile was wide and welcoming and he felt churlish for his disappointment.

"Miss Cain," he said, sweeping his hat off to bow. "What a pleasure."

"Look at you, Mr. York. Why, I think you're even more handsome in the snow."

He winked as he rose, then tilted his hat toward Penrose.

"May I introduce my secretary, Mr. Penrose?"

Penrose blushed as Miss Cain offered her hand and a saucy smile. "An honor, miss."

"So polite. You must bring him to luncheon today, Mr. York."

"Luncheon?"

"You see, my father wondered if you could join us. I think he's discovered how rich you are."

Aidan laughed. Yes, this girl reminded him of Katie in so many ways. "I would love to join you for luncheon. Mr. Penrose?"

"Yes," Penrose stammered. "Of course. Without a doubt."

"Then, Miss Cain, shall we?" He offered his arm, feeling a lightness in his chest as she placed her gloved hand on his sleeve. He had a brief, searing hope that Kate would be at the Cain's when he arrived but pushed it away. She was a married woman. It would do neither of them good to be seen so much together.

But he could think of her as often as he liked. No one could keep him from that.

Hard pellets of snow tinked against the windows as Kate drew swirls and circles on a torn piece of paper, idly considering when to kill her husband. The planning felt cruel, despite that Mr. Hamilton had never existed. As for David . . . he'd been dead nearly nine months now. It could not matter to him.

She'd wanted to wait a year after arriving in England before declaring herself widowed, but things felt so different now. And her business was doing tolerably well. She'd chosen the location so carefully. A town small enough to have escaped the notice of another dedicated coffee merchant, but prosperous enough that certain households would demand the finest roasts and blends. Four local estates had already paid her a generous amount to secure their own private roast, available to no one else. It was exactly what she'd hoped for.

But now she was beginning to tire of the masquerade of

marriage. She could put out word any time that her husband had died of a sudden fever. Everyone in England seemed to think the Orient was rife with deadly dangers, after all. No one would doubt that a man might fall over twitching and gasping with no warning at all.

So she could get rid of Mr. Hamilton, but there was the larger problem to be faced. What about Gerard Gallow? She didn't think she'd hurt him badly that night. She hoped that the sickening crack she'd heard had been only the bottle and not his skull. But he'd fallen so hard to the floor. Still, despite the blood that had trickled from his head, his eyes had fluttered when she'd nudged him.

So she'd run. She'd run for her freedom and her life and her sanity. She hadn't dared search out news from Ceylon once she'd reached India. If she looked toward Ceylon, she'd reasoned, it might look toward her.

But now she wished she'd paused for just a moment. If she'd stopped to look back, she would at least know if Gerard was all right. She hadn't meant to hit him so hard. And even if he were fine, had he tried to convince the world that she had killed David? She hadn't hurt her husband, but who would believe her over Gerard?

It was time to find out the truth. She could not bear the uncertainty anymore. It had seemed a small sacrifice a few weeks ago—living alone, needing no one. But now she faced a new possibility. Maybe she could need more than that. Maybe she could still be a whole woman with wants and dreams and desires.

She'd kissed Aidan York, after all.

My God, she'd *kissed* him. Opened her mouth to him. Rubbed her tongue against his as if she'd never spent a day apart from his body. She was supposed to be a married woman, yet she'd licked at his mouth as if she were starving for it.

What must he think of her today? What did she think of *herself?*

With a great sigh, Kate rubbed her hands roughly over her face, wondering how she would look at him again. Would it be worse if he came today or if he didn't? She felt stupid now. Stupid that she'd got caught up in the intimacy of the moment. My God, there was a time when she'd convinced herself that he'd never even loved her, thanks to her father's cruel words. And now she found herself wondering if he might love her still. It was absurd. And exciting.

Kate picked up her grandfather's watch and rubbed her thumb over the cool metal. As soon as she'd touched the watch, she'd remembered giving it to Aidan and all that had come before that.

The secret, stolen moments that had eventually led to that day. The frightening excitement of hurrying along the river bank, toward the old boathouse. They hadn't planned to let things go so far, but the kissing had led to touching and it had been so good. And Aidan's hands had been gentle and sweet. Just as his mouth had been. Just as it still was.

He hadn't hurt her at all that day in the boathouse, though he'd asked over and over again to be sure. If there'd been any pain, it had been swallowed up by her trembling excitement.

Curling her fingers over the watch, Kate squeezed her eyes shut and felt warmth seep out of her body and into the metal. This was ridiculous. This was not why she'd returned to England. Not by far.

She pushed aside her lethargy and retrieved paper and pen from under the counter. She wrote a simple, short letter for Lucy's father. As she sealed the letter, anxiety plucked at her nerves. It hurt every fiber of her being to ask about Ceylon, but after all, it had already asked about her. That Mr. Dalworth would arrive soon. Today or tomorrow, if he kept to his word. And any good coffee merchant would want news from Ceylon. Certainly it damaged her masquerade not at all to inquire after old newspapers from the East.

The alley door opened with a bang, and her heart jumped to her throat. She rushed to the back, thinking it must be Aidan, but instead she found Fost's white-haired driver.

"Oh, thank heavens!"

The man tipped his hat. "Good morning, Mrs. Hamilton. 'Tis nice to be so warmly welcomed."

"Hush, you. It's the coffee I'm thrilled to see. Please tell me you've brought the Sumatran?"

He chuckled throatily. "I asked specifically this time. Told Mr. Fost I wouldn't dare cross your threshold without it." He reached down and hauled up the crate that lay at his feet. "Where would you like it?"

"In the front room, please. I'll need to put it out immediately. Oh, this is wonderful." At his nod, she hurried back into the shop with a relieved sigh. She wasn't confident with her supplier. He always came through with the deliveries, but often at the last possible moment. The Sumatran was supposed to have arrived on Friday, and here it was on Monday.

Still, she'd struck a profitable bargain with him and hated to start from scratch with someone else.

The driver came in with one last crate, and Kate sighed. "I apologize if I've been prickly. And I thank you for being so kind."

"It's no bother, ma'am."

"How is your brother?"

"Well, I think. He don't write often and I don't read often, so news is far between. And your husband, ma'am?"

"Very well, thank you."

He opened his mouth to ask another question, but Kate heard the front door open and raised a hand to stop him. "I'm sorry, I must see to the shop."

"Of course, ma'am."

"Close the door when you're through," she said as she rushed back to the front.

As if she'd been sent to counter every ounce of Kate's anxiety, Lucy Cain rushed in on a cloud of snow. "Good afternoon!"

Kate grinned at Lucy's dramatic entrance. "That's a happy response to such weather," Kate said, though she felt the same joy at the storm.

"Oh, it's not the snow that has me grinning. It's the company."

"Me?"

"No, not you! I just dined with two handsome bachelors."

"Is your stance on marriage evolving then?"

Lucy gave a look of horror as she swept off her cloak. "Heavens no. If I marry, my days of flirting with bachelors will be over."

"I suppose you're right." Kate rose to prepare two cups of coffee in her sampling pot, no longer nervous about Lucy's presence. She'd stopped by nearly every day since her father's party to gossip and laugh and even to discuss coffee.

"Aren't you going to ask *which* handsome bachelors I dined with?"

Kate wracked her brain, trying to snatch up a few of the names Lucy had mentioned, but the girl talked so quickly that names always seemed to fly right past Kate's ears. She pressed down on the coffee. "Was one of them the gentleman with the pink waistcoat?"

"No. One of them was Aidan York!"

The handle slipped out of her hand and her knuckles rang the pot like a bell. "Oh! Mr. York, you said?"

"Yes, indeed. And his secretary, Mr. Penrose. He's quite serious, isn't he?"

Kate set her hands back to the pot, hoping to buy herself a moment of thought. Lucy had dined with Aidan this afternoon? Anxious curiosity filled Kate's chest, urging her to blurt out question after question. Instead, she cleared her throat and spoke very carefully. "I'm not sure. I've never met Mr. Penrose."

"Well, you must meet him. He's quite striking. Golden hair and lovely blue eyes! But I think I made him nervous."

It shamed Kate to admit it, but Lucy's interest in Mr. Penrose inspired a sharp stab of relief. But her heart still hammered as she carried the cups to the counter. "So? How did you find yourself dining with them?"

"My father finally found out more about your Mr. York's investments. Impressive, I gather. Father was quite eager to invite him to luncheon. If I'd had any warning at all, I would've invited you as well."

"Oh, I'm sure that's—"

"You know . . ." Lucy put her chin in her hands and leaned over the counter. Her eyes glowed with innocence, and that was never a good sign.

"What?" Kate asked warily.

"When I mentioned your name, I could've sworn I saw Mr. York's eyes light up."

"Lucy . . ."

"Oh, fine."

"I'm a married woman—"

"I know. I know. It's just that . . . There's something about him, isn't there?"

Yes. My God, yes, there was something about him. There always had been. Something that drew people to his side. Something that made people smile. Kate had felt honored to be a part of that once, but she couldn't be part of it now.

She tapped the countertop. "Tell me more about this Mr. Penrose."

Her words prompted a flood of description from Lucy. Kate was so distracted that she only caught the occasional bit of coherence. Mr. Penrose was apparently both dignified and nervous. Solemn and soulful. Though he didn't speak much, she could read volumes in his eyes. And despite his reserved nature, he seemed to be much younger than Aidan York.

Kate's brain spun around the words *Aidan York*, and seemed to get caught there. This situation was fast becoming intolerable.

Lucy's voice broke through her thoughts. "But it's just as it should be. I'm far too young to catch his eye at any rate."

"What?" Kate asked. "Who?"

"Mr. York, silly. You're closer to his age, I should think."

Funny that Aidan had seemed old enough to be unobtainable when she'd first met him. She'd thought him so mature and manly. Now she felt old enough to be his governess. She smiled at the strangeness of it all. "Men always like young women, Lucy. It doesn't matter how old the gentleman is. They're attracted to girls who are bright and lovely and untouched."

"Untouched?" Lucy raised a saucy eyebrow, but even

as Kate laughed, Lucy's smile faded. "And that's the reason I shall never marry."

"Oh, I don't mean a man won't love you once you've aged. There are plenty of husbands who don't stray."

"That's not what worries me, Kate. It's the brightness. It seems an awful trade to make. I don't want to fade away for the sake of a man. And I think that might be the unavoidable cost. My friends, my sister, and . . ."

She didn't finish the sentence, but Kate knew how faded she'd become. "And me," Kate finished. Lucy didn't know the half of it. Sometimes in Ceylon she'd looked down at her own hands and marveled that she couldn't see right through them.

"I didn't mean . . ."

"I know. But it's true. My husband wasn't cruel though. He rarely required anything of me, and yet, in that place, I was nothing more than his wife. I filled a role that didn't truly exist. So sometimes it seemed that *I* didn't exist."

Tracing the edge of her cup, Kate realized that whole months had passed like that in those early years. Months when she'd felt nothing. But that seemed another life now. These days she felt so much. Too much.

She looked up to find Lucy watching her with a frown, her teeth worrying her bottom lip.

"What is it?"

"You said 'wasn't.' He 'wasn't' cruel."

Panic wrapped her chest and seemed to crush her ribs in its grip. She'd grown too relaxed and tripped herself up. "I—I . . ."

"I suspected you'd left him for good."

"I . . . What?"

"Your husband. You've left him, right? That's why you returned to England."

Miraculously, Lucy assumed the same thing that Aidan had. Perhaps that only made sense. Who would ever suspect that a woman would pretend her husband was alive when he wasn't?

Lucy seemed to take her silence as an admission. "I wish my sister would leave her husband. She comes home sometimes, but she always goes back."

"Perhaps he's not so bad."

"No, he's bad. But they have two children now. If she'd left the first time he hit her . . . But she didn't. And even if he weren't so bad, I have to wonder if marriage isn't all the same. Have you ever known a woman who wasn't diminished by it?"

Kate thought about it. She sipped her cooling coffee and riffled through her memories. Her own mother had been cowed by her husband. She'd never stood up to him over anything, not even her daughter being shipped to the other side of the world.

Only a very few of Kate's friends had married before she'd left England, and she'd had no friends in Ceylon. Still, she could not say she knew any woman whose marriage had made her more lively or more vibrant. So was every woman diminished? It seemed so.

She opened her mouth to answer, but then she thought of Aidan's mother. There was a woman who seemed in no way diminished. She was filled with wild emotion, and by all accounts had only grown more vivacious with every passing year. Though her husband had died when Kate was still in England, he'd been alive when Kate had first known the family. They'd been a fairly happy couple.

"Yes," she finally said with a smile. "Yes, I have

known women who were undiminished by marriage. Perhaps we should only be more careful in our choice of husband. Or perhaps we should be stronger ourselves."

"Or . . ." Lucy drawled, "perhaps we should avoid the problem entirely and treat marriage like the plague."

"Even if it involves Mr. Penrose?"

Lucy giggled and the darkness of the moment was gone, just like that.

Kate had spoken of her marriage, and her unhappiness, and it felt like nothing more painful than . . . memory. Just memory, fading as it was exposed to the light.

"Kate," Lucy said, leaning even closer so that she could speak in a whisper.

Kate narrowed her eyes in suspicion. "What?"

"I've heard that in London all married women take lovers."

She jerked back. "That's not true!"

"I don't know. I think it might be."

"Well," Kate sputtered, "it hardly matters. We're not in London."

"Still . . . Mr. York is from London. Perhaps that is all that matters. He provides the excuse of worldliness."

"Nonsense! Lucy Cain, you should be ashamed of yourself."

Lucy shrugged and one side of her mouth tipped up in a sneaky smile. "I'll see if I can summon up the will."

"Oh, I doubt you will bother."

"Probably not."

Kate rolled her eyes. "Regardless, will you deliver this letter to your father?"

As if her work was done, Lucy stood and clapped her hands together. "I will. Good afternoon then, Kate.

Forget I ever said a thing about it." She retrieved her letter and set off with a jaunty wave.

But of course, Kate couldn't forget. Not for a moment. Perhaps she did not need to kill off her manufactured husband. Perhaps she could simply think like a man and have everything she wanted at once.

Chapter 13

Aidan smiled into the snowflakes as he walked, thinking how Kate must be enjoying the weather. Perhaps he should buy her Sir William Perry's account of his expedition to the Arctic. She'd likely adore the descriptions of unbearable cold. He made a mental note to have Penrose order the book as soon as they returned to London.

He didn't want to think about leaving though. He felt content here, and not only when he was with Kate. But at the moment, all his good feeling had to do with the sight of Guys Lane ahead. His heart pressed against his throat in anticipation.

When he turned the corner, there was Kate, as if she'd been waiting for him.

She locked the front door of her shop and turned toward him, and when her eyes widened in surprise, he saw joy in them. Joy for him like embers glowing in the snowy dusk.

"You can't keep coming here," she said when she reached him.

Aidan blinked in shock. Whatever fantasies he'd had

about how she'd respond after that intimate evening, this wasn't it. "What do you mean?"

"I can't have people talking."

She was concerned about appearances, not his actual presence. Suppressing a smile, Aidan took another step back and clasped his hands behind him.

"I'm a married woman. People on the lane will gossip."

"Are you asking me to come in through the back?"

One side of her mouth curved up as she brushed past him to walk up the lane.

He followed her around the corner and watched her tug her hood lower before she started walking again.

"There's no one out in this storm, Kate."

"That's why I'm allowing you to accompany me."

"And may I ask where we're going?"

"*I* am going to speak to an importer. You may walk with me, but I can't have you there when I negotiate."

"Why?"

She stopped abruptly and tilted her head up to meet his eyes. "That's a ridiculous question."

"I don't know what you're talking about."

"Oh, for God's sake, Aidan. Don't be dense. If you're there he'll speak to you because you're a man."

She started walking again, leaving Aidan to follow, slightly dizzy with confusion. Here was another new Kate. This was obviously a woman who had started a shop, despite that ten years before she'd been a pampered girl of the ton and had never worked a day in her life. He would've admired this new side of her if she looked at all open to kisses and flirtation, but she looked as if she'd box his ears if he got close. Still, he dared to reach for her hand and place it on his arm to slow her pace.

Though she shot him an annoyed look, she left her hand where it was. He felt her side press against his forearm as she took a deep breath. "I cannot afford the appearance of impropriety. Surely you can understand."

"Of course. The appearance."

She turned enough that he could see her eyes slide over his chest. "Yes."

Aidan's heart jumped into a crazed rhythm at that one simple word. This was real, this possibility that she could be his again. It wasn't his mind weaving phantoms into feelings. She felt it too. And even if they were both imagining this pull . . . didn't that make it real?

He felt light-headed, so dizzy he wanted to laugh. Yet they walked on, as if the world weren't swaying beneath his feet. As if his heart wasn't thundering in overjoyed panic.

He tried to remind himself that she was married, but what did that matter to him? He knew well what little hold those bonds placed on women's bodies.

Kate's hand left his arm and she said, "Wait here," before disappearing around a corner. By the time he caught up, the only sign of her was a weathered door swinging closed. The rough, splintered wood of the building rose up at least two stories. A warehouse.

Aidan was left waiting like a lost child. The snow pelted his hat, then dripped off the brim in watery clumps. But the cold no longer cut through him, because all he could feel was the premonition of Kate's touch.

Kate carried her happy anxiety into the warehouse and turned it into boldness. She glared down at the open bag of roasted beans and snarled at the man who offered it. "You are a fool."

He snorted in arrogant contempt. "I assure you, Mrs.

Hamilton, that this is the finest quality of Coorg coffee on the market."

"And I assure you, Mr. Fost, that it is not."

"Madam, if your husband were here to offer you guidance, he would—"

"If my husband were here, you would not try to pass off this rubbish as Coorg."

He seemed uncowed. "If you will only note the beautiful darkness of—"

"Exactly how many years did you spend living in the East?"

"Pardon?"

"I spent the last ten years of my life on a coffee plantation, Mr. Fost."

"I'm aware of that, but I doubt Mr. Hamilton allowed you to stroll the fields."

Frustration flashed to rage, and Kate's muscles ached with the need to hurt this man. She pointed her finger in his face and bared her teeth. "You listen, sir, and listen very closely. A quarter of these beans were picked green and another half are not much better than that. If you have a functioning brain in that head of yours, you will not send me another crate of less-than-questionable quality and try to pass it off as something better. Do you think my husband would've sent me here on my own if he did not trust me with his livelihood? You insult us both."

He held up both hands, his eyes finally brightening with alarm. "Mrs. Hamilton, please. I swear to you, my London roaster promised me this was an excellent lot." The man's placating tone had finally risen to desperation.

"There is really no point in my continuing a business relationship with a man who's either dishonest or too ignorant to realize his supplier is cheating him."

She could see him struggle with his pride for a moment

before he finally gave in with an inclination of his head. "I apologize, madam. This won't happen again."

"It had better not. I'm aware of your tenuous situation, Mr. Fost." His eyes widened dramatically. "You would do very well to keep me happy."

"Of course."

"Other distributors may not even know the difference between stable muck and arabica, but I expect to be treated as a professional."

"Yes, yes. I can assure you, I will send only the best, the most valuable of my supply in the future. I'm grateful for your understanding."

A stream of apologies followed her out the door.

Kate sighed as the door banged shut, leaving her in the snowy dusk. Mr. Fost was having a rough spell. One of his major buyers in Leeds had retired. It truly wasn't her concern, not when her profit was at stake, and she refused to feel sorry for him. But he had done her a service of sorts, reminding her of why she'd started this masquerade in the first place. Without the ghost of a husband behind her, she would not be able to establish a solid footing among the men in this business. And they were all men.

It had only been wishful thinking on her part, to hope to give up her lies so soon. Kate was so wrapped up in her temper that she didn't see Aidan until he moved away from the wall he'd leaned against. In all honesty, she'd forgotten he was there, and she felt twin jolts of alarm and joy at the sight of him.

"You didn't have to wait," she said quietly.

"I'll assume that was a poor attempt at a joke."

The snow had picked up. The world was silent around them as she took his arm. The muffled crunch of their footsteps was the only sound in the world as they walked. And her breathing. And her pounding heart.

"I feel . . ." she started, but the words stuck in her mouth, as if they didn't wish to emerge.

"Yes?" Aidan prompted.

"I feel I should send you away."

"But why?"

"You know why."

She dared a glance at him and found him scowling at the snowy street. "Don't let the past years come between us," he said softly.

"It's not so simple," she whispered. "I've had a whole life since then. And you don't appear to have been living as an ascetic monk."

She felt the jump of startled muscles in his arm. "I haven't claimed to."

"Lucy tells me you have your finger in everything."

"I—I don't— Pardon?"

"You're no simple investor. You haven't been quietly toiling away for the past decade. You're a rich and powerful London gentleman now."

She felt his fingers curve over her hand, and Kate slowed to stop. Aidan circled around until he stood in front of her. "Do you know why I'm rich, Kate?"

She shook her head. Snowflakes landed on his lips and melted there.

"Because I was determined to never be supplicant again."

"Supplicant to whom?"

"To your father. To anyone like him."

Kate felt the strange pain of a ghost sliding through her. "My father? You really asked him?"

The frown on his face didn't budge. "What do you mean?"

"You asked for my hand? You truly tried to persuade him?"

Aidan shook his head, and water slid off his hat like teardrops. "What are you talking about? You know I asked him. It was the entire reason we argued."

"I know." She nodded, only a faint movement, but she couldn't seem to stop it. "Yes, of course."

"Kate." He lost some of his tension, and he reached for her. His gloved fingers curved under her chin to still her movement. "What do you mean?"

"It's silly, but . . . He told me you didn't."

He tilted his head in puzzlement.

Kate tried to smile. "I never believed him. Not at first. But then . . . you didn't come for me."

"Who told you what? You're not making any sense."

"My father. He denied that you asked for my hand."

"My God, Kate! That's ridiculous. Why would he say that?"

"Because," she whispered, tilting her chin out of the grasp of his fingers. "Because I told him I couldn't marry anyone else. I told him I'd already given myself to you."

"Oh, Kate," he sighed.

"He said I was a fool. That you'd used me like a . . . like a rag and then tossed me away."

"No . . ." His face went white. "That's not true. I asked for permission to marry you. I begged for it on my knees. I swear to you, I did everything but kiss his boots."

She nodded again, but stopped herself before she got lost in the motion. She couldn't speak, and the pressure in her throat was one big mass of relief. Despite her initial, violent rejection of her father's words, at some point they'd rooted in her mind. He'd kicked at one of those stones that held her up, and eventually the seed he'd planted had worked into the cracks like a weed, splitting her certainty wide open. And when that stone had tumbled out, she'd known that Aidan had taken her virginity without any intention of marriage. She'd thought herself in love with a falsehood.

But Kate slid a new stone back into place. Aidan had loved her, and she hadn't been a fool.

"I did come for you," he said.

For a moment, she picture him in Ceylon, searching the harbor towns for any sign of her. Her heart clenched in pained hope. "You did?"

"I came to Bannington Hall. Over and over. They said you wouldn't receive me."

Her heart fell. "I was with my mother's family," she whispered.

He'd never known. He'd said it before, but somehow it hit her now. She'd waited and waited for him to come to Ceylon to rescue her. She'd been so patient. So true.

But slowly, as the weeks had crawled painfully by, she'd realized that he was never coming for her. He didn't want her. Why else would she still have been on that godforsaken island? Why else would she still have been that strange man's wife?

Her heart had shriveled up, condensing to a hard, tight knot in her chest, and she'd realized with a quiet kind of horror that Ceylon was her life from then on. Her *life*. That isolated, foreign place her home; that cold man her husband. No one was ever coming to take her away. And so much of her had crumbled then. There might never be enough stones to fix that.

Remembering that first year in Ceylon, Kate clenched her hands tight. Snow bit at her face and she tried to breathe. "I sent letters," she whispered. "But of course you never got them. Even then, I didn't think you did."

His hand touched her again, smoothing over her cheek. "Don't cry, Kate. Please."

Was she crying?

"I came for you," he whispered urgently. His arms curved around her. He pulled her into his arms and moved them toward the shadows of an alley. "I came for you. I swear I did."

She nodded again, her cheek scraping over his wool greatcoat, but she was crying hard now, gasping for air. He couldn't truly understand because she'd never tell him.

"How could you believe that about me?" His breath rushed over her forehead, turning to ice where her skin was wet.

I don't know, she meant to say, but the words wouldn't come. *I didn't, truly.* A few minutes later, her sobs finally subsided.

"Come," Aidan said. "Let's get you home."

For once, she felt no outrage at being ordered about. She walked through the evening with snow swirling through her vision and felt she was drifting through clouds. They moved toward the alley, avoiding the front door.

Once they were in her kitchen, he locked the alley door and took her cloak.

She looked blankly toward the stove. "I should heat some water. . . ."

"No." And when he turned her toward the stairs, she

went blindly, numbly. The same numbness cradled her as he unlaced her dress and loosened her corset.

"I did it," she whispered, her voice reed thin.

"Did what?"

"I told my father the truth about us. That's why he sent me away. And that's why he told you I was dead."

"No." His fingers worked along her spine, freeing her from the awful constraint. "He would never have lied to all of England just to keep the second son of a baron away from his daughter. I've been thinking about it. Hell, I can't stop thinking about it."

When the corset finally let loose its grip, Kate drew a glorious breath that steadied and soothed her all at once.

"Your father has always been arrogant and proud. He loves nothing better than expounding on his bloodline and complaining that England has lost its respect for tradition. How could he then admit that he'd sent his daughter to the East to marry a stranger with no bloodline to speak of? Can you imagine him explaining that to his friends at the club? He welcomes a foreign stranger into his family, all for the sake of filthy lucre?"

She supposed he was right, but she was too bone-weary to take it in.

When she was down to her shift, Aidan lifted her and took her to her bed. She went with no objection, holding on to his neck when he bent to throw back the bedcover, curling into a tight ball when he laid her down.

He left her and returned within moments to wash her tear-streaked face with a handkerchief dipped in cold water.

When he was done, she closed her eyes and turned away from him.

"I'll leave," he said, and suddenly Kate's mind cleared. She didn't want him to leave. Not at all.

"Stay," she whispered to the wall. Miraculously, he heard her.

The scrape of his boots halted. She felt his eyes on her, but she felt no nervousness.

"I'll sleep in the parlor," he offered.

"No. Stay here. In my bed."

Silence again. And then she heard the sounds of cloth against cloth. The same noises of the forest in Ceylon, oddly. The shushing sound of leaf brushing leaf in a steady breeze. The room went dark. When Aidan lay down with her, his trousers touched her legs, but his arm was bare when he curled it over her.

He leaned close and pressed a kiss to the skin just below her ear. She felt as free as one of the birds in the jungle forest, flying high above the grasping green leaves.

Whispering against her neck, he urged her not to worry.

And so she wouldn't. Not tonight.

Chapter 14

Kate stuck her head back into the bedroom and just as quickly withdrew. He was still asleep, sheets tangled around his trouser legs.

She'd already dressed in a panicked rush in the parlor and gone downstairs to brew coffee. Now she didn't know what to do. Her hands shook, her muscles ached with a trembling need to flee. She paced to the window and stared out at the mist. And then she laughed.

Aidan was in her room. Aidan was in her *bed*. The knowledge filled her up with a raw heat that felt like sunshine. Like the merciless sunshine in Ceylon, except this was a heat she welcomed. She hadn't felt anything like it since . . . since she'd been a girl. Since she'd loved Aidan.

But she wasn't a foolish young girl now, and this wasn't love. It was desire. Hope. It was living instead of existing. Ceylon had changed her, but it hadn't pulled her soul clean from her body as she'd feared.

No, her soul had definitely been intact when she'd lain in bed and stared at Aidan's bare chest this morning. Her heart had thundered with nervousness, but that hard pulse had pushed her body to arousal. They'd lain together before, but only in stolen, rushed embraces of rumpled clothing and hushed moans. She'd never seen his bare chest or the strong lines of his arms. She'd never awoken to find his cheekbones brushed with pink warmth and his hair a wild mess.

My God, he was beautiful. Even more handsome than he'd been as a boy.

Today, his beauty didn't scare her. Instead, it filled her with giddy joy. She gathered up that joy, retrieved the coffee tray, and made herself walk into the room.

He didn't wake when she set the tray on the table next to the bed, so Kate took that as permission to look at him. He was in her bed, after all. Surely that conveyed some small degree of possession to her. And how could she not look? His shoulders were so wide and stroked with mysterious hollows. The secrets of his body called to her fingertips, begging for exploration. But when she looked to his face, she found his eyes open and watching her with sharp intensity.

"Good morning," she said before she could give in to the impulse to jump up and run away.

He rose up on his elbows. "I'm sorry. I meant to wake before dawn. Your neighbors . . ."

"We'll need to take care when you leave. A few titillating rumors are one thing, but the scandal of a man stealing away in the morning . . ."

"I'm sorry," he said again.

"I am the one who asked you to stay, Aidan."

He paused in the act of sitting up. "Yes," he said softly. "You did. And nothing could have made me leave."

She tried to stop a smile and failed. "Nothing but the morning?"

Aidan frowned as she handed him a cup of coffee. "Nothing but a meeting with the shipbuilder at nine A.M., but perhaps I can send a note to Penrose and have it postponed." When she sat down on the edge of the bed, Aidan propped himself against the wall and watched her.

"It's enough that you stayed the night."

His gaze caught between heat and wariness. "Enough for whom, exactly?"

Kate ducked her head and smiled at her hands. Yes, that was heat she saw in his eyes. And it had definitely been life she'd felt in her veins. Her pulse beat a tattoo that urged her to move faster along this path. "It was enough," she finally whispered. "For now."

When she looked up, his gaze was sharp as a blade. A blade that wanted to cut the seams of her clothing and remove it from her body.

"You're right," Aidan said, the words so soft they floated toward her. "It was enough. I've never done that."

"Done what?"

"Slept in a woman's bed."

No, that couldn't be right. She shook her head.

"Slept," he said, his voice dropping even further, "in *your* bed."

He'd been with other women. He must have been. But she understood what he was telling her. He had not cared enough to spend the night in their beds. But he'd stayed in hers.

He could be mine. The fierce knowledge took hold of her like a ruthless hand. *He could belong to me. Again.*

Power flooded her veins. She wanted him. And she need make no other decision besides that. She had just told him that sleeping was enough, but in that moment it became a terrible lie. And if she wanted him, now was the time. He'd said himself that he was leaving for London soon. Perhaps even today. But right now he was in her bed.

"You're right, though," she whispered. "It wasn't enough, was it?" All the power in the world could not convince her to meet his gaze at that moment. Instead, she watched his chest expand with a deep breath. She wanted to touch it. She wanted to know the taste of his skin.

She forced her eyes up, made herself meet the green heat in his gaze. And then she said the words. "It's only seven. Would you lie down again?"

His brow fell, his eyes clouding with confusion, but he didn't ask what she meant. Instead he handed her the half-empty cup, and slipped back down to the mattress.

Kate couldn't pause to think, or fear would stop her. So she put her hands to his chest and spread her fingers wide.

His ribs eased down as he sighed. The long slow exhalation seemed to go on forever. His lips were parted, his eyes dark with question. He didn't know what she wanted from him, and she could understand that. She didn't know what she wanted either, aside from the feel of his skin under her hands.

She slid her fingers down, feeling the warmth, the contrast of smooth skin and crisp hair. Down farther, over the muscles of his belly. She watched as they jumped beneath her touch.

Her taut shoulders relaxed by slow degrees as she fell into fascination. He was so hot. So alive. Her hands wandered all over his torso, from his stomach to his shoulders, over the dip of his breastbone and the swell of his muscles and the steely curve of his ribs.

She became lost in her exploration, nearly forgetting,

oddly enough, that he was there. Not even noticing his deepening breaths and clenching hands.

"Katie," he finally said, her name a low rasp.

Blinking from her trance, she saw the tortured pain on his face, and she smiled. "Will you touch me, Aidan?"

"Ah, God," he moaned, and framed her face in his hands. He pulled her down, covering his body with hers, and guided her mouth to his.

Kate groaned when his tongue entered her. She scrambled higher on his body so that she could slant her mouth over his and kiss him with all the yearning that coursed through her veins. Aidan drank her up with just as much urgency.

His hands roamed down her shoulders, over her back, to her hips. She settled her knees on either side of his hips, and her body went heavy and hot. Every muscle, every inch of skin burned as his tongue thrust into her, a rhythm she knew. A rhythm she *wanted.*

Kate reached for her skirts to ruck them up. When she was settled more soundly against him, she broke from the kiss and sat up.

The sight of him beneath her hit her like a brutal hand. His face was flushed, his eyes glittered. His expression struck some beautiful line between tenderness and cruelty. And above the edge of her skirts, he was naked and so very lovely.

Determined not to lose her courage, Kate inched down and reached for the fastening of his trousers.

"No," he said, startling her. "No. It won't be like this. Not this time."

"What—" she started, but Aidan was easing her up, off the bed. "No," she said as he rose as well.

But then he eased her around and he reached for the

buttons of her morning gown. "Oh," she sighed. "I can do it."

"No."

That simple word stilled her hands. She watched as he slowly unfastened each button, then spread the dress down her shoulders and off her arms. She stared at the pale skin above her white chemise. Her dress fell, pooling around her feet.

Her corset was laced loosely so that Kate could hook the clasps herself. Aidan popped the first hook free.

"Wait," she whispered. She hadn't looked at her own body in so long, and now she realized what a dreadful idea this was.

His hands froze. "What's wrong?"

"It's so . . . It's so bright."

"Oh, Katie," he murmured. "Close your eyes." So she did, only because she didn't want this to stop.

She kept her eyes closed as her corset loosened. She squeezed them tightly shut when his hands drew the shoulders of her chemise down. When he untied the delicate string of her drawers, his knuckles pressed the naked skin of her belly, and she began to tremble. Linen caressed her thighs as it slid to the floor.

And then the room pressed into her whole body. The cool air. The wisps of wind when Aidan moved. She could even feel the light on her, naming her a woman nearly thirty, a whole world away from the young girl she'd once been.

"I've waited a lifetime for this," he said. His hands gripped her hips, and she opened her eyes to find him kneeling on the floor before her. Wetness rushed to the place between her legs as Aidan pressed his open mouth to her ribs. His tongue stroked up, up, until it brushed the curve of her breast.

Kate felt her throat open on a sigh. This was . . . It was beautiful. Even in the light, it was perfect. Yes, her breasts were heavier now, but Aidan's mouth worshipped the flesh. Yes, her hips were wider, but they served the needful purpose of giving his hands the perfect curve to grasp.

His mouth closed over the deep rose flush of her nipple, and Kate cried out. He sucked at her, and a shimmering, vibrating tension began to pulse deep inside her, spreading through her body like rings of water until her fingers trembled and her skin buzzed.

By the time he lifted his head and his green eyes rose, Kate was caught in a storm of her beating heart and straining lungs. She could do nothing but stare down at his flushed lips in wonder. How could such a simple touch of his mouth draw her sex so desperately tight? Now she remembered why she'd been so foolish all those years ago. Because being foolish with Aidan had been worth any price, any risk. Because she'd been *alive* with him.

"You're so beautiful," he said. "I could never have imagined how lovely."

His hands turned her hips, and urged her down to the bed. The linens were cool and crisp against her backside, while Aidan's hands were hot as they slipped down her thighs. In that moment, she decided there was no more vulnerable place in the world than the inside of a woman's thighs. She shook as his thumbs trailed lower. He parted her legs and bent his head.

"Aidan!" she gasped, trying to scoot back.

"Let me. Please."

Kate shook her head, but he wasn't watching her, and she let her knees be eased apart. She let him slide between them, let his mouth touch her *there*.

"Ah!" she cried as his tongue touched her most secret spots. She felt each swipe of his tongue, each circle it traced. Pleasure spread over her like cracks in glass. She cried out raggedly as Aidan's mouth rubbed again between her legs, finding a little point of pleasure over and over.

He'd mentioned this once to her, in a whispered, breathless conversation. He'd told her of the things that lovers might do after they married. But this was nothing she'd imagined. It felt as though a wicked heart was beating deep inside her, separate from any other body she'd ever known.

Everything inside her clenched tighter and tighter until it burst into a thousand pieces of shimmering light. Her nails clutched the sheets as she fought to anchor herself to the world. Finally a sob was dragged from her throat, a deep-throated cry, and Aidan ceased his torment.

She was crying. She knew she was, and all she could do was let the tears slide down her temples and try not to make a sound. Aidan pressed delicate kisses along her thigh, and she tried to calm herself.

She felt the slide of his body against her legs as he rose. Then the shift of fine wool on her skin. When she opened her eyes, he stood naked and beautiful above her. His eyes met hers directly, meaningfully, and she took what he offered and looked at his body, still and proud, yet somehow vulnerable in the morning light. Her eyes lingered on his wide shoulders, the hard plane of his chest, the long stretch of muscle in his legs. She even let herself stare at his jutting manhood for a brief, thrilling moment.

He went to his knees beside the bed again. He pulled her hips closer; her knees edged farther apart. When the head of his shaft touched her open sex, her body jerked, the slightest touch of him against her jarring and painfully intense. Aidan went still. He was holding his breath, waiting, wanting. Finally, she breathed again, and he pressed forward.

There was none of that pushing, that forcing that was all she could remember of the joining of bodies. His body slid into hers as if it were coming home, as if it remembered her and the way to her soul. It was sweet and slow and like nothing she'd ever felt.

She took him inside in a smooth slide until he was so deep, filling her up, filling a void she'd forgotten existed.

"Oh," was all she could say. Aidan held motionless against her, and now he was the one whose panting filled the room. "Oh," she sighed again, "Aidan."

He slid his hands up to curve around her ribcage and then up to cup her breasts. Her moan turned into a sharp cry when he lightly pinched her nipples, sending a bolt down through to the core of her. She felt her passage tighten around him, felt his pleasure at this when he pushed even deeper.

She squeezed her thighs as he pulled back, gliding out and out until her body held only the tip of him. His hands fell to grip her hips and he pushed in again in one strong motion, sending waves of satisfaction through her belly.

"God, Kate," he ground out as he found a long, slow rhythm.

Her body registered so many things at once: the heat of his skin against her thighs, the pale play of light over their bodies, the musky scent of their sex.

She moaned and threw her head back, lost in the way he filled her up and set her free at the same time. It felt good. Better than anything she'd felt ten years before. It felt perfect, and she knew then that she'd never regret this.

His strokes quickened. His fingers tightened on her

hips. Yes, she thought. Yes, she wanted to make him shake and shatter just as she had. Kate drew her knees higher and felt him settle into that last tiny space between them.

"Ah, Christ," he moaned. He took her faster, harder, and Kate found herself crying out when he shouted his release. He slid from her body as his muscles jerked, and his seed splashed hot against her belly as he climaxed.

She covered his hands with her own, weaving her fingers between his and holding tight.

"Katie," he rasped, bowing his head as he tried to catch his breath.

She found herself smiling stupidly up at him, unable to control her joy.

When Aidan opened his eyes, his expression slid from fierceness to surprise, then he met her smile with one of his own. "Well, then."

A giddy laugh rose up and danced from her throat. "I had no idea, Aidan. I don't remember it being so . . ." She shook her head in wonder.

"I daresay it was nothing like that before. I was very young and very nervous."

"Um," she sighed happily. Her limbs were weighted, heavy with weary satisfaction.

"I'd lie down with you and cover you with kisses, but I don't think there's room in this bed."

"I don't need more kisses," she sighed.

He raised an incredulous eyebrow.

She could only laugh. "I've had everything I need, and we can't afford to lie abed regardless. The day is starting."

His smile turned tender. His eyes warmed. "Yes, it's just begun." Aidan rose, and rinsed out the cloth he'd used to dry her tears the night before. While he dressed, Kate washed herself, conscious of the strangeness of their shared space. And all she could think was one word: *mine*. He's mine again.

Foolish. And ridiculous. And not even true. But still, she told it to herself like a secret no one else could know. *He is mine again. For this day at least. He's mine.*

She drew her chemise over her head and then simply sat there. She didn't move. She couldn't. She listened to the thump from her parlor as he tugged his boots on, then the rustle of fabric as he donned his coat. A short while later, he stepped back into the bedroom and even the black silk of his cravat was respectably arranged.

He smiled at her, running a hand through his mussed hair.

"You look no different," she said, marveling at that. She felt like a different person altogether.

"Then you've the eyes of a fool, Kate," he said quietly.

Her heart stopped. And when she looked again, he was right. She saw sorrow and joy in his eyes, mixed together and turning into the depths of him. She saw his soul unshuttered, and she wondered if he could see the same in her.

"Will you come again tonight?"

"More foolishness," he said, tempering the words with a smile. "I planned to wander the alley like a ghost if you didn't invite me in."

"Ah," she said, "wailing and gnashing your teeth?"

"Yes, and rending my garments just in case you unbarred the door." He kissed the laughter from her lips and offered a gallant bow. "I'll show myself out the back door, shall I?"

"You make it sound so sordid."

His smile slipped away. "No," he said quietly. "Never that. Not with you."

She listened closely to the slow clomp of his boots

on the steps and caught the strain of a cheerfully whistled tune as the door opened and closed. She should be worried that he'd be seen. She should feel guilty for what they'd done.

But she couldn't summon up even a glimmer of regret.

Chapter 15

What had seemed so simple in the morning grew into a mass of tangled anxieties in the afternoon.

First, Gulliver Wilson had arrived on a gust of cold, damp air. She'd unlocked the door three hours before and this was only the second time it had opened. The first visitor had been a kitchen boy sent out into the icy streets to pick up an order. A slow day, indeed.

Kate tried her best to smile. Would this day never end? "Mr. Wilson."

"Mrs. Hamilton," he intoned arrogantly. "I wish to speak to you on a serious matter."

To speak *to* me, she noted derisively, not *with* me. She kept her mouth closed to avoid saying something she'd regret.

"It has come to my attention that you've been entertaining a certain strange gentleman without any sort of chaperone and with no care for your reputation."

Kate's face flushed with anger and worry. Had he seen Aidan sneaking from her home? "What do you mean?" she made herself ask calmly.

His whiskers quivered when he cleared his throat. "I

saw a strange gentleman return you from a walk yesterday evening, madam."

Thank God. Her worry burned away and set her anger free. "I can assure you, sir, that who I speak with on the street is absolutely none of your business."

"Of course it is my business!"

An outraged laugh slipped from her throat. "How so?"

"I am a respected member of this community and I cannot countenance this type of behavior. I'll not be able to offer you the prestige of my friendship if you continue to behave like a . . . a . . ."

"A what, sir?"

"A harlot!"

"Mr. Wilson." Her clenched teeth muffled the words. "I believe you know where the door is. Please see yourself through it. And don't bother returning."

His square, fleshy face turned a rather gorgeous shade of purple as he struggled to speak, his mouth opening and closing several times before he found his tongue. "If your husband knew—"

"If my husband knew you'd called his wife a harlot, I assure you he'd teach you a lesson in manners. And that strange gentleman you mentioned is a friend of Mr. Hamilton's, so I'd suggest you leave before he happens along and finds you insulting me."

Gulliver Wilson's eyes flicked briefly to the door, giving her a thrill of satisfaction. Those eyes were decidedly narrower when they returned to her. "You will not find the people of Hull quite as *exotic* as the residents of India. We expect our women to comport themselves with dignity."

Fists clenched into tight balls, Kate tried to subdue her rage. She'd lived far too long with people telling her how to behave. She'd not do so again. "You are not in a position to 'expect' anything at all from me." One more breath and she was slightly calmer. "And your tobacco is inferior and overpriced."

His eyes nearly popped out of his head at that. "Regardless, as a respected member of this community it is my duty to warn you that your indiscretions will not be taken lightly."

"Mr. Wilson, I grow weary of your insults."

"Doxy," he spat.

"Leave my shop now! And never return."

Instead of leaving, he stepped closer. "James Fost is a friend of mine, madam, and you have treated him abominably."

That took her aback. This was about Mr. Fost? Gulliver Wilson was trying to leverage his threats into a favor for a friend? She could understand that motivation, and she made herself relax.

"Mr. Fost and I have reached a peaceable agreement. Your threats are unnecessary."

"You insulted him!" he countered.

"As you have insulted me, Mr. Wilson?"

His piglike eyes glowed with arrogant dislike, but he had stupidly revealed his hand to her. Kate retrieved her pen and bent back to her ledger as if her next words meant nothing to her. "If I hear one hint of one word that you have spread about my marriage or my friendships, I shall cut all ties to your Mr. Fost. And I shall explain to him why I've done so."

Silence met her words. She scratched a few figures onto the paper.

"You wouldn't dare," he finally sputtered.

"I certainly would. And . . ." Kate remembered a tiny snippet of gossip she'd heard from Lucy. "I shall also make sure to pass on the rumors that your brother is in debtor's prison because you were heartless enough to call in his debts."

She looked up with the sweetest smile she could muster. Mr. Wilson had turned purple again.

"*And* that you have offered his wife a way to earn the money to release him. Isn't that the tale, Mr. Wilson?"

"You . . . you . . ."

"Good day to you, sir," she said. Miraculously, he turned on his heel and he went.

She looked back at her numbers and smiled. She had reason to. One of the most prominent households in town had begun to use her after bringing their coffee straight from London for the past ten years. And she'd recently begun receiving orders from country estates up the river Hull. Word was spreading.

She should have been elated. She was only mildly pleased. A few weeks ago, this measure of progress would have sustained her, comforted her. Not anymore. Now she had Aidan and tonight to think of. Tonight, which was so much of a risk, but she would take it.

Emotion surged through her, hot and icy. "I want him," she murmured, just to feel the words on her tongue. "Again." They felt awkward and foreign but left behind a tingling touch on her mouth.

She was surprised at how easy it had been. Granted, she'd had no experience as a girl, but youth and love had given her the advantage of unselfconsciousness. She'd simply thrown her body into him and assumed he could only find pleasure in that. He had. They both had.

But this time had been so very different. It had been a wonder of pleasures. Had it been different for him as well? She spent the next hour waiting on customers, sweeping the floors, and reliving their lovemaking a hundred times.

Every time the door swung open, her breath froze in her throat. And she laughed at herself each time it wasn't Aidan.

But she didn't laugh when the door opened to admit a stranger. Kate looked up from her table to see a tall, wiry man, dressed in a thick wool coat and a fur cap, as if he were traveling to Greenland instead of Hull. His face looked painfully thin in comparison to the width of the thick brown fur, and his nose was a knife blade of sharp bone.

He stomped his snowy boots on her floor. In that instant, she knew she did not like him.

"Can I help you, sir?"

"Yes. I'm looking for Mr. Hamilton."

Kate tried not to feel fear as she stood. "Mr. Hamilton is not here right now. I am Mrs. Hamilton."

"Ah." His eyes narrowed, creasing into little slits as he looked her over. "I am Mr. Dalworth. I sent your husband a letter—"

"Mr. Hamilton is in India at the moment, sir. I received your letter, though I wasn't sure what you meant by it." As she spoke, he took a little book from his pocket and began writing in it.

My God, she was doomed to be surrounded by rude, despicable men today.

When he looked up and found her frowning, he grudgingly removed his hat. "I believe my letter was clear, madam. My client wishes to know more about your business."

"And who is your client?"

"He does not mean to reveal himself until he's assured that a partnership with your husband would be profitable."

"And I'm sure I do not wish to reveal more about

our business until I know to whom I'm addressing the information."

He sneered at her words. "When will your husband return, madam?"

"He will not be here until spring, so I suggest you find a way to deal with me."

He regarded her for a long moment before inclining his head. "I'm afraid I am prohibited from revealing my client's name. He does not wish to upset his relationship with his current broker until and unless he is prepared to cease his dealings with him."

Kate arched a haughty eyebrow. "I can understand that. As long as he understands that we will reach no agreement until I've received several samples of his crop."

"Agreed," he said, and they sat down to talk money.

But when he departed, he left Kate with an uneasy tension in her stomach. She'd witnessed many negotiations at David Gallow's side. None of them had been quite so superficial or brief. Still, this was only the opening salvo, and the details would be hammered out later. She had no reason to feel such creeping dread.

She had everything she wanted right now, after all. Her work, her independence, and Aidan. The fear was just left over from her old life, and she'd banish it the moment she knew that Ceylon was behind her forever.

Chapter 16

He hadn't expected that the next time he saw Kate it would be across a crowded reception room. In fact, Aidan would've sworn it was the last place he'd wish to see her, with all these people standing between them, all these eyes who might see the need in his gaze. But now that he was here, he felt fascinated by the sight of her interacting with others.

She wore a dark amber dress that did nothing to add color to her cheeks, but the color was there. It flared brighter when she looked up to see him watching, and Aidan caught the curve of a secret smile as she turned away from him. She seemed to glow, and he realized with a sudden jolt of sorrow just how dim she had been, how little of her old shine she'd had.

She was shining now.

He dared to approach, knowing Penrose would follow. "Mrs. Hamilton," he breathed as he bowed over her hand. He introduced Penrose, then stared as the two made polite chitchat. He wouldn't normally bring his secretary to a dinner, but Penrose had been specifically invited. A dockmaster's house was an odd mix of industry and society, it seemed.

When he'd found himself unexpectedly agreeing to a dinner in the Cain home, he'd sent a panicked letter to Kate. Lucy had asked him how he meant to fill his evening, and he'd been so beset by erotic images of Kate that he'd panicked and said he planned to do nothing at all. Luckily Kate had just been invited as well, and had sent him a note to that effect. So here they were, pretending the distance between them was natural, when all he wanted to do was put his hands to her skin.

But Kate seemed at ease. In fact, she was transformed. She flashed him another teasing smile, biting her bottom lip just before she turned away for an introduction to an older couple.

She was *flirting* with him, by God.

Yes, she was transformed. She was not young Katie, though. She'd become another creature altogether. Her flirtatiousness, her humor, was now buffered by the sharp edge of resiliency in her jaw. It was an enticing combination of hard and soft and he couldn't stop thinking about exploring the contrasts.

"You watch her too closely," a woman whispered at his shoulder. Aidan's gut clenched with fear as he turned sharply to face Miss Cain.

"I'm sorry, Miss Cain. I didn't catch that."

She smiled gently. "Don't yearn for her so. I've sat her next to you at the table. You'll speak soon enough."

"Miss Cain—"

"Come. It's time for dinner. You may walk me in."

He should say something, think of the perfect sentence that would persuade Lucy Cain that he had no interest in Kate beyond business. But the idea was so ridiculous that he could think of nothing. He walked her to her seat, his mind churning. But when he took his seat next to Kate, it hardly seemed to matter anymore.

She looked at him past her lashes, and his body immediately hardened, aroused by the glow of desire on her skin.

Aidan greeted the gentleman next to him, a man who spoke French and only a few words of English. At first, he assumed that Lucy had sat Aidan next to him out of courtesy. Then he noticed that the man seated next to Kate spoke Spanish, and Kate had not a word. Polite or not, Lucy had surrounded them in a bubble of privacy.

He spoke under his breath. "You're stunning. I'm overcome."

"Overcome? How so?"

Aidan watched the life shimmer off her skin and fought the need to press his lips to her mouth, her chest, the little hollow in her throat. "You humble me," he said softly.

She looked up then, looked hard into his eyes, but any response was cut off by the server's appearance with a bottle of wine. Kate lifted her glass to her mouth.

"Try not to get sauced again," he murmured.

"Oh, that was your fault and you know it. Such a typical male ploy."

He raised his eyebrows high in mock surprise. "You're on to me, Mrs. Hamilton. Drink up."

Her laughter sounded like a purr, and he spared a glance for the rest of the table, certain they must all be caught up in this seduction. But no one seemed to notice her beauty, her spark. It was just for him.

Kate turned to attempt a few words with the gentleman to her left, and Aidan's eyes roamed to the far end of the table. Penrose was there, at Lucy Cain's left hand, an unexpected honor for a gentleman's secretary.

But Penrose looked surprisingly at ease. Indeed, he sported a smile that made him look younger than Aidan had ever seen. And Miss Cain . . . Miss Cain was now very obviously flirting with Penrose. Penrose!

A remarkable evening indeed.

Penrose's transformation distracted him for a moment, and Aidan sat back in his chair to observe Kate's friend. Miss Cain was attractive, red-haired and glowing with good health like a milkmaid fresh from the country. He could see why Penrose was fascinated—she laughed easily and often and her eyes sparked with intelligence. Her large bosom probably contributed something too.

Still, when Penrose began to laugh with a deep chortle, Aidan frowned in shock.

"What's wrong?" Kate asked.

"Penrose . . . He's laughing. I've never seen anything like it."

"He's probably intimidated by you. But Lucy seems quite taken with him."

"I suppose."

"Well, you're too young to look so disapproving."

"Me?" he asked, laughing. "I haven't been young in years."

"Don't be silly," she scolded. "You're still a pup."

Perhaps he was, now that Kate was back.

The entire dinner passed in laughter and ease. Later, he remembered little of the meal, only that Kate had enjoyed the fish course but hadn't eaten much of the heavier meat dish. He did, however, clearly remember dessert. A sweet vanilla custard that she'd licked from her spoon like a pleased kitten finishing her last drops of milk. The sight had been a teasing reminder of the many, many delights they'd never gotten around to sharing. He intended to address the omissions.

When the meal was done, he helped Kate out of her seat and saw desire in her glance. Her pupils were dilated, her eyes black instead of brown.

His own lust held in tight check, he purposefully moved away as soon as she rose. Patience would reward him. He was sure of it. But his arrogance was cut down with such suddenness that the brutality of the blow stole his breath away.

"Mr. York," a soft voice said from the corridor behind him. "What a surprise to see you here."

For a moment, when he looked at the petite blond woman, he did not place her. Her face did not prompt even a quiver of recognition in his brain.

"I tried to catch your attention at dinner, but I never could," she said with a smile that was patently false.

The smile did it. Now he knew her. He drew in a breath with such slow care that his head spun as he stepped into the corridor. "Lady Sarah. This is a surprise. What could possibly bring you to Hull?"

"My husband wished to stop and see an old friend before we move on to Bath. You remember my husband, Lord Quentin Meeks?" She gestured toward the man beside her, but he was already moving away, busily discussing railroad development with another gentleman. A good thing, as the only thing Aidan could recall about Lord Quentin was that his wife had laughed about him while Aidan took her. She'd crowed that her husband's cock was half the size of Aidan's and only a third as hard.

That was why Aidan had found it difficult to place her face. She'd only wanted it from behind that night, and he'd never contacted her again. Cuckolding another gentleman was one kind of cruelty. Joining in laughter about it was another.

"And you, Mr. York? What brings you here?"

He glanced past her toward the other guests. The men filed into the billiards room; the women strolled to the drawing room farther on. Kate was among them, but he thanked God he couldn't see her. Or did that mean she still lingered in the dining room and would stumble upon them at any moment? He felt the blood leeching from his face, felt his head grow lighter.

"Shipping, of course," he murmured, his lips numb as he spoke. "I have several investments here."

He barely knew this woman whose eyes swept down him, but he had a terrible fear that their connection was visible to others. That a reminder of that night still clung to them, the foul threads visible now that they stood so close.

Aidan cleared his throat. "What a happy accident, to see you here so far from London."

"Yes." She watched him past her lashes just as Kate had done before. His panic turned to nausea and shame. What if Kate saw them? What if his past was revealed to her in all its ugliness?

Ridiculous, of course. Lady Sarah would say nothing to Kate. She would say nothing to anybody. How could she? He forced an easy smile and gave a bow. "I apologize for rushing away after such a fortuitous meeting, but I must catch Monsieur Blanc before he leaves or he will conveniently forget the deal we struck over wine earlier."

"Oh," she said, her smile slipping a bit. "Of course."

"Please have a safe journey to Bath. And convey my well wishes to your husband."

"I will."

Aidan walked down the corridor as if he were determined but unconcerned. He pretended that a bead of sweat wasn't snaking down his temple when he passed the drawing room and continued around the corner to the washroom at the end of the hall. But once there, he closed the door and leaned against it, hanging his head and letting his breath shudder out.

All these women he'd had . . . Kate wouldn't understand that. How could she?

Heat washed over him with such force that his ears felt afire. In Kate's bed, he'd forgotten his life for a moment. He'd forgotten how little he cared for himself and others. He was not the boy she'd loved, and he wasn't a man she would love either, if she ever found out.

"She won't," he said aloud, trying to calm himself. These were not things one spoke of in polite company. This was not something a woman would tell another. *Aidan York has had me on my knees a dozen times over. What did you do with him?*

"She won't find out," he said again, finding the strength to push away from the door. Leaning over the sink, he turned on the tap and let cold water fill his hands. That felt such a relief that he lowered his face into the pool he'd created and let the icy water numb his skin.

By the time he dried his face on a towel, he felt nearly normal, though he wished for a full bath, wished to wash away the last threads of shame that clung to him. But he was recovered enough to step into the hallway with an easy air. He did not even break into a sweat when he turned the corner and found Kate there, speaking with Lucy and adjusting her cloak around her shoulders.

"Ladies," he said easily as he passed them. Kate gave only a polite smile. She was going home in the Cain carriage, so Aidan knew she would be safe. He would leave later so as not to arouse suspicion.

Earlier, he'd dreaded having to count down the minutes in the billiards room, but now he was simply relieved to have a sure escape from Lady Sarah. He proceeded straight to the corner of the room farthest from her husband and closest to the clock. Twenty minutes should suffice, and then he could lose himself with Kate again, and forget the tragedy he'd made of his life. He could be a young man again, instead of a hollowed out shell.

Chapter 17

"There's snow in your hair, poor thing," Kate said as he slipped from the icy damp of the alley into the warm box of her kitchen. She reached for him to brush the snow away, and Aidan closed his eyes at the pleasure of being touched.

"I made some tea. I know how the cold affects you."

Aidan growled at her coy smile. "Will you view me as weak forever? That day was ridiculously cold, and you were the only person mad enough to want to be outside."

"So sensitive, Mr. York. Have I injured your pride?"

"Perhaps. I plan to take it out of your hide at a later date."

Kate's husky laugh sang through him. "You may try your best."

"I will."

Her hair gleamed dark in the lamplight, her skin glowed pale. She looked ethereal, ghostly. The thought sent a slow curl of discomfort turning in his gut. She *was* a ghost, but she'd somehow been sent back to him, nearly whole. He would not forget that.

When he trailed a finger along the edge of her jaw,

she closed her eyes and smiled, as if she savored soft touch as much as he did. As he turned to hang his coat on a peg, Kate poured tea and added sugar. Silence grew between them, but it was nothing like the silence that always fell over him with other women. He had, after all, always chosen his lovers with the opposite of friendship in mind. Women who were as cold as they were hot. Women who cared nothing for his thoughts. But with Kate, it was as if he were a man at home. As if they'd told all their stories to each other and now needed nothing but silence.

There was no logic in that. They'd been strangers for ten years and lovers for only one night. But this ease between them was as real as it had ever been.

And yet she was another man's wife.

He sipped the tea she handed him, trying to dislodge the terrible jealousy from his throat.

Kate set her hand to his chest. "I wanted to touch you tonight," she whispered. "But I couldn't."

The heat of his jealousy was fanned by her admission, and Aidan lost any sense of ease. He set down the cup and framed her face in his hands so that he could kiss her. She opened for him as soon as his mouth touched hers, thank God. He was desperate for the taste of her, the sure knowledge that she was his. At this moment, she was his and no one else's.

He deepened the kiss and her hands fisted into his waistcoat, as if she'd pull him tighter still. He understood. It did not matter how close they got, it wasn't enough. It never had been.

"Come upstairs," she urged, the words warm against his mouth. "Come to my bed."

He need hear no more than that. Pulling away, he set his palm to her back and urged her toward the stairway, but she soon outpaced him and he found himself rushing to catch up.

He was not used to this new Kate yet, and Aidan was shocked when she simply reached for the fastenings of her dress as soon as she reached her bedroom. Fierce lust gripped him as he slipped off his jacket and loosened his cravat. She felt it too, this horrible, unending need to get closer, as if that could erase the distance of the past years.

He reached for the clasps at the back of her dress and as soon as it loosened she tugged it down. "My corset," she urged, but he'd never planned to hesitate at all. His hands were already at the knots, tugging them free. Kate gasped as it finally opened, her ribs expanding against the chemise that stayed pressed to her body.

Her movements slowed as if the corset's grip had made her panic, and now she was free to move with languid grace. She turned to him, meeting his eyes as she let down her hair. It tumbled around her shoulders, and his heart shook with the force of his pulse.

When her hands reached up to slide the straps of the shift from her shoulders, he sat down hard, thanking God that he actually hit the bed. She moved with such slow grace, inching the straps down and down till they finally caught at the crooks of her elbows, the shift barely clinging to her breasts.

Crossing her arms in a demure movement that tugged at his heart, she worked the shift farther. It dropped suddenly to catch at the curve of her hip.

Aidan sucked in a hard breath at the sight before him. Painful pleasure twisted inside his body, curling through his shaft until he was heavy and hard for her. She was a perfect picture, seductive and shy, her palms pressed to her breasts and her stomach smooth and white. He was almost thankful for her modesty. If she hadn't covered her breasts, he definitely wouldn't have noticed the curve of her waist that begged for the grip of his hands. He wouldn't have even seen the adorable dip of her navel or the way her belly curved out just under it.

She shifted under his scrutiny and the thin fabric lost its hold, slithering to the floor. Aidan closed his eyes to savor the image that floated behind his lids. He just wanted a minute, one minute, to chisel it into his mind before it was gone forever. Those generous hips, soft and all his, the alabaster thighs, and that dark, dark triangle of curls, drawing his gaze and his soul.

He eased open his eyes to find her watching him through her lashes as if she were a student of coy seduction, but it was only shyness, he knew—she was still hiding behind her hands. That morning she hadn't had time to anticipate, and neither had he.

"Beautiful," he murmured, reaching for her elbows, drawing her to stand between his thighs. Reverently, unwilling to rush her, he kissed each of her knuckles, gently seducing her until her hands began to relax and fall away from her body.

"I know you've already seen me," she whispered with a soft, nervous laugh. "And I guess I shouldn't worry how I've changed. I hardly think you got so much as a peek when I was seventeen."

"No," he answered as he kissed a small circle around one areola. "Those times were a bit too hurried for this sort of . . . exploration. But I can assure you"—she whimpered as he traced his tongue around that circle—"that there's never been another woman as beautiful as you."

"That's silly." Her words were faint, shaky.

"No, it's true."

The last words she uttered before he sucked her nipple

into his mouth were nearly inaudible, but he thought she said, "Thank you." But words were superfluous now. By the time he laid her on the bed, all she offered were sighs and gasps.

Aidan discarded the rest of his clothing and joined her on the narrow mattress. It was too small for sleeping comfortably, but in that moment he was thrilled to be forced close. He lay on his side to face her, meeting her eyes as he touched her body. Her gaze grew solemn as he shaped her waist and hips, and before he could touch more of her, Kate twined her leg around his and pressed her hips to his.

Pleasure and need radiated outward from that spot, making his eyelids flutter as she dragged herself up. "Kate . . ." he murmured, but she slid higher until his cock notched itself to her opening.

"Please, Aidan," she said. "Please just . . ."

What could he do but please her? He understood. It felt like years since he'd entered her this morning. Like the ghost of the years they'd spent apart.

So when he felt her leg tighten around his, Aidan pushed inside her. Just an inch. Just enough to feel her flesh squeeze him and her sigh whisper over his cheek.

"We don't have to go so fast, love."

"Yes, we do," she insisted, so he pushed higher.

"Ah!" she cried. "Yes."

Yes. Of course, yes. She was right. There was no point in waiting. All they wanted was this. She tilted her hips on his next thrust, and then he was deep within her.

Aidan spread his fingers over her jaw, and she turned her head to catch his thumb between her teeth.

Her body was so hot around him, against him, her tongue like fire on his skin. It was so much pleasure that it hurt, and as he took her in slow, careful thrusts, Aidan realized he'd never done this. He'd never faced a woman like this as they made love. Never watched every flutter of her lashes. Never watched her mouth form each sigh against his skin.

And so here was another first with Kate. He hadn't meant for them to lose their innocence that day. He hadn't planned it. But their kisses had turned to touching, and she'd sighed so sweetly when he stroked her thigh. And then he'd touched the core of her body, and my God . . . The hot slickness of her. The slippery feel. *There,* he'd thought madly. That is where my body goes. Into that impossible heat and pleasure.

He'd heard talk, of course, but who could've imagined the utter perfection of it? Not him. Not in a million years.

But here was this perfect place again, inside Kate. He thrust harder, and watched her lips part on a moan.

Curving his body farther away from hers, he dragged his hand down her neck to her chest, lingering over her breasts to caress them until she moaned again. It was too much: watching and feeling and hearing and tasting. He would not last. He'd leave her wanting. That he couldn't bear, so Aidan gritted his teeth and dragged his hand lower, until he could just press his thumb to that pearl of nerves at the top of her sex.

Her sex tightened, and they both hissed with pleasure. He wanted to feel her climax around his cock. Wanted her to spasm and shake as he had her.

"Aidan," she whimpered, her fingers reaching for his shoulder to put her nails to his flesh. He needed to close his eyes if he was going to last, but he couldn't look away from her. The skin around her eyes tightened, she bit her lip. Aidan rolled his hips and she keened.

Now, he prayed silently. *Now. Please now, for me.*

He flicked his thumb faster, and she finally broke. Her tight face softened into wonder, she drew in an impossibly long breath, and then she sobbed. Her sex rippled around his shaft, and Aidan wanted to sob himself, but he was busy gritting his teeth and holding on. Just another moment, just one more second to watch pleasure soften her face to the innocence of that girl she'd been.

Then he finally slid his body free of her, and his own climax jerked through him with bittersweet pleasure. Bittersweet, because he wanted back inside her.

Kate slipped her arms around his ribs and squeezed him closer. He felt the slide of his seed against her skin.

"Aidan." Her voice was thick with tears. "That is all I ever wanted."

But his throat was too tight to tell her the same.

She'd risen to wash her body and Aidan's as well. Then she'd damped the fire in the stove and dimmed the lamp until the light barely skimmed their bodies. Now she was back in Aidan's arms, pressed tight against him in her small bed. It should've felt strange, tucked in so close to another person, but instead it felt lovely and right.

"I leave tomorrow," he said. "I'm sorry. I've postponed as long as I can."

"Don't apologize. I'm so happy right now."

Aidan's smile turned time back ten years; he looked so sweet and young. Kate smiled back.

"Will you come with me?" he asked.

"You know I can't."

He settled his head deeper into the pillow. "I received a letter from my brother today."

"Oh?"

"My sister is returning from her wedding trip, and my cousin's ready to announce his betrothal. There will be a grand party, of course."

"Of course," she laughed.

"After London, I'll have to return home or my mother will never forgive me."

Kate slipped her fingers into his hair, remembering again how soft it was. "There's no question you must go. Don't say it as if you must apologize."

"I want you to come to the party."

"Aidan! Don't be mad. That's impossible."

"Why?"

Kate shook her head and rolled to her back, feeling the edge of the mattress and the space that loomed beyond it. "Why even ask such a thing? My husband, my shop, my family . . ."

"Then what about London? Would you come to London? Just for a few days. I'll leave the knocker off the door. No one will even know we're there."

"I can't! Not right now. I'm still cultivating this business. I'm supporting myself."

"I know," he sighed, pulling her back to rest against him. "But I wish . . ."

She stroked his hair again, but at his next words, her hand froze.

"Perhaps . . . perhaps we could look into divorce."

"Pardon?" she rasped, her heart shuddering beneath her breast.

"Your husband could be accused of desertion. He is never coming."

She knew that better than he, but she couldn't allow Aidan to even consider the insane idea of divorce. If he even mentioned it to someone, everything would become exposed. Her name. David's death. This false life she'd built for herself. And whatever disaster Gerard had created. So she swallowed hard and dug deeper into her lie. "We no longer live as man and wife, but that hardly means he deserves to be shamed. He's still worthy of respect and honor."

"Ah." His whole body changed in that moment. His warm flesh cooled and hardened into stone. "Unlike me?"

"Aidan."

"You'd take me as your lover, but—"

"Yes, as my lover. And everything that means."

"Well, what does it mean?" he snapped.

"Aidan, I've no experience with this. But I'm given to understand that in London . . . in London . . ."

She saw his head turn slowly toward her, his eyes glinting in the faint light. "What have you heard?"

His voice had gone so hard that she lost her nerve and could only shake her head. "Never mind."

Aidan sat up and swung from the bed to pace to the other side of the room. "What have you heard about London?"

"I only heard that married women there take lovers as a matter of course. Is that not true?"

Aidan stared silently at her, his shadow a blank space in the room.

"Is it?"

"Yes."

He'd frightened her with his reaction, and now her fear turned to anger. "Why are you stomping about the room as if I've insulted you? You cast it as dishonor to be asked to my bed? Is that what you think I've done? Dishonored myself?"

"I . . . No. No, of course not."

"As if it's an insult that I want you!"

"No. I'm sorry, Kate. It's only jealousy. Of him and

his name and his hold over you. That he would come between us . . ."

Kate slumped back into the bed, all her nervous outrage stolen away. She understood, because David did still sit between them, though in ways that Aidan couldn't comprehend.

"I'm sorry," he repeated.

"I want this thing for us, Aidan. Not for the ceremony or title of it. I don't need your name. Do I?"

He moved closer and sat wearily on the mattress. "No. You're right. This is enough. It's everything. But what if there's a babe? Surely that is more than enough motive to consider divorce now, before it becomes necessary?"

"I have been married a long while, and there has never been a child." That was true enough, though David had come to her bed rarely, and never after the first few years. And every month she had said a small prayer of thanks.

His hand splayed against her belly.

"We cannot simply go back to where we ended," she said quietly. "There's no going back for us."

"I know," he said, and she could tell by the terrible weight of his words that he did.

"But we can have this, can't we? Does it have to be a disappointment?"

She waited, feeling the lovely heat of his hand against her stomach. She wanted desperately for it to be enough for him, because what if it wasn't? She couldn't give him more. She couldn't *be* more. And if Aidan left now, she'd spend her lifetime remembering what she might have had.

Aidan sighed. "Of course it is not a disappointment, Kate. Never think that. It's more than I dreamed possible."

"Then come back to bed."

He hesitated for only one heartbeat before sliding back beneath the bedclothes.

"I'll leave before dawn," he promised, but it felt so far away that Kate didn't care. This was enough for her, because it must be.

Chapter 18

He was gone the next day, and Kate's world returned to normal. She swept and filled orders and brewed samples. She interacted with her neighbors as if nothing had changed, answering the occasional question about India and her husband. No one looked at her strangely. No one commented on her transformation from wraith to woman. It was as if he'd never been there.

Yet there were the places on her body that felt different. The raw places where his roughened jaw had scraped her. The space between her legs that his cock had stretched. Her mouth felt full and sensitive. Her hands weak from clutching him to her. And her heart . . . that was altogether changed, her blood replaced by something brighter and quicker.

But no one noticed, and the secret only made it all the more delicious.

She had a lover, and it felt even sweeter than it had when she was a girl. That sweetness buoyed her courage, and she was restless to face what she'd once run from.

She hadn't meant to hurt Gerard. Not that night, nor any time before. But she'd known from the start that his feelings for her had been nothing like what a son should feel for his father's wife. She could understand that. They'd lived in the jungle, isolated from the world, and Kate and Gerard had been nearly the same age. "You should've been my wife," he'd once whispered. He'd still been young then, and Kate had only stammered and blushed until he'd left her room. But he'd grown more persistent after David's decline in health.

Still, she'd never expected his jealousy to drive him to such madness.

When midday arrived and the shop grew quiet, Kate locked the door and walked out into the bright day. The sun was high, but all its warmth was lost somewhere in the heavens. As she hurried through the busy streets toward the dockmaster's house, the air stuck to her skin like ice. By the time she knocked on Lucy's front door, she was shivering. She'd finally left the heat of Ceylon behind.

A maid let her in, but only a half second passed before she heard her name called. "Kate!" Lucy trilled, skipping down the stairs. "I was just coming to see you!"

"The dinner was lovely last night." Her last word was smothered by Lucy's hug.

"Oh, it was, wasn't it?" She stole a look around the entryway. "Come. Let's go for a walk."

"It's freezing outside, Lucy."

"Oh, I don't care! I feel like I'm going to burst."

Kate raised her eyebrows and retrieved her cloak from the maid. "Well, then. We'd best walk." Or Kate would die of curiosity.

Before they'd even reached the sidewalk, Lucy bubbled over. "He is so kind, Kate. So genteel."

"Mr. Penrose?" she asked with a grin.

"Yes! Let's walk past their office, shall we?"

"Oh, Lucy, they've already gone. Did Mr. Penrose not tell you?"

"Yes," she sighed. "He told me. But perhaps they were delayed."

Kate chuckled, but she tucked her hand around Lucy's arm and they walked toward the street where Aidan had let rooms for an office. "Are you in love, Miss Cain?"

"Come now. Surely I'm not so far gone." But her eyes sparkled with happiness. "He told me that Mr. York looked at houses yesterday afternoon. He's considering opening a permanent residence here."

Kate's heart first fell to her feet before floating high. Fear and hope tangled together and tumbled through her body. If he stayed near, she could have him whenever she liked. So many nights filled with pleasure. But if he was closer to her body, he'd be closer to her secrets too.

"Mr. York is apparently very impressed with our shipyards," Lucy said with a droll look.

Kate ignored that. "Tell me more about your Mr. Penrose."

That did just the trick, and Lucy launched into a nearly word-for-word tale of exactly what Mr. Penrose had said to her during dinner.

"His grandfather was a ship's captain, though his father did not care for the sea. But Mr. Penrose says he has spent all manner of time around ships, and he so understands my love for them."

"Ah, that must have been the passion I saw in his eyes while you two spoke at dinner."

Lucy's happy laugh echoed off the buildings of the narrow street. "He is so very kind. I cannot explain it. I've spent my life around sailors and gentlemen, and while one seemed too rough, the other was always too soft. But Mr. Penrose is very . . . Oh, I cannot find the word."

"Perhaps it's that as Mr. York's secretary, he stands in both worlds."

"Perhaps. That is what I've always felt as well. I am the daughter of a man who was once a sailor. Yet I'm not meant for a sailor, am I? But if I married a gentleman, would he think me lucky to have him? I'd rather it be the other way around."

Kate squeezed her arm. "But a gentleman's secretary? What would your father say?"

"My father would say 'Thank God' if I chose any man. And I don't think Mr. Penrose will be a secretary forever."

Kate grinned. "I think you're right."

"But it is only a flirtation," Lucy murmured, her head bent in thought as if she were weighing the truth of her own words. She slowed to a stop before Aidan's office, and they both looked up at the blank window. "Mr. Penrose says he is changed here."

"Pardon?"

"Mr. York."

Kate cleared her throat and tugged Lucy on to continue their stroll.

"He says that Mr. York is another person here. He smiles and laughs and walks with a light step. He's a different man."

"That's silly," Kate said. "Mr. York has always been the epitome of the charming gentleman. He is well known for his good humor."

"I don't think you're right."

"Of course I'm right. In fact, Mr. York said the same thing about Mr. Penrose. They are men who work together and have their gruff male conversations. That is all."

"Kate," she said softly. "I think he's in love with you."

"That's not true! I'm married. I—"

"That's what makes it so romantic!"

"No." She pulled Lucy to a stop.

"I won't tell anyone, I swear."

"Lucy, it is not romantic. Not at all." She slowly raised her head and met Lucy's gaze. The words rose from her throat without her permission. "I knew him before," she whispered, leaning closer. "I knew him long ago. That is all you see. A remembered friendship."

"Oh, Kate." Lucy's eyes filled with tears.

"Hush," Kate said, before she raised her gaze to the sky to stop her own tears. "It's only memory you're seeing on his face. Nothing more."

"And what about yours?"

That stopped her cold. Did she love him? She watched a single white cloud float across the desolate sky. Her heart was calm.

Did she love him?

Hadn't she always?

She lowered her chin and met Lucy's wet eyes. "Did you ask your father about English newspapers from Ceylon?"

Lucy's face crumpled in confusion. "Yes . . . I . . . He's found some already."

"Wonderful. Perhaps I can retrieve them after our walk."

"Oh, certainly. I'll have them wrapped up for you."

"Thank you."

Lucy nodded, and though her eyes were dark with disappointment, she changed the subject and began discussing the newest details in the saga of Gulliver Wilson's debt-ridden brother.

Kate fought the urge to race back to Lucy's house and steal away with the papers. But only just. Because she could not move forward with her life until she found out what she'd left behind. And suddenly, the future seemed so much brighter.

Chapter 19

Aidan stared intently out the window of his old bedchamber, Penrose's voice a gnat's buzz in his ear. This section of the York gardens had been his view for so many years of his childhood that he didn't notice the beauty anymore. All he could see was Kate as she'd lain sleeping the morning he'd left. She'd never been to his family home. He wondered if she would like it.

He'd been gone from her for two weeks. Two horrid, maddening weeks.

He wanted nothing more than to return to Hull, but this morning's train had brought him to the family home and all the people who loved him. Yet at the train station, he'd stared dolefully at the signs pointing in another direction.

Normally, business would be his escape from his restlessness, but now it seemed there could be nothing more mind-numbing than importing problems, and he couldn't focus enough on new proposals to make any real decisions.

Opening a drawer in Penrose's portable desk, Aidan rifled through it until he found his personal stationery, not noticing when Penrose's words slowed to a halt.

"Mr. York, is there a letter you wish me to write?"

Aidan grunted a negative as his hand closed around a pen.

"Sir—"

"You'll go to Hull tonight."

"I will?"

"Continue your search for respectable lodgings. Make sure of adequate space for my study."

"Yes. Of course. But . . . Mr. Ferris requested an answer—"

"Fine. You can send an answer just as easily from Hull. Tell him I'll meet with him in London in five days."

"Yes, sir."

"And please be sure that any house you let in Hull is furnished and available for my arrival next month. No later."

His secretary appeased, Aidan turned his attention back to the letter for Kate. Perhaps he was overstepping himself, taking a house in Hull, but if he was, so be it. It was only a house. And his pride. And his every hope. He knew from experience that those things could be lost, but Kate was worth the risk.

He spent a good five minutes deciding on a closing to the letter, finally settling on a frustratingly simple *Yours, Aidan*, then worked hurriedly through a stack of aging correspondence. Now that he knew when he would return to her, he found it easy to address business issues. Before an hour passed, he'd wrapped up the simpler problems and was walking down the stairs to finally greet his family.

He'd escaped that duty when he and Penrose had arrived two hours before. Edward and Cousin Harry had been out riding. His mother had yet to rise. And nobody knew when Marissa and her husband would arrive.

The house had been eerily quiet when Aidan had walked in, and now as he followed voices to the library, he felt a smile tug at his lips. Despite his eagerness to return to Kate, it felt good to be home. Better than it had felt in years.

"Well, Harry," he drawled as he stepped through the open doors to find his brother and cousin lounging near the fire. "I hear you've finally talked a woman into accepting your suit."

"I have." Harry rose to pull Aidan into a tight hug with a few bracing slaps to the back.

"Congratulations. Dare I ask which one? Mother has had me on tenterhooks."

"Miss Elizabeth Samuel."

"She's a lovely girl. And Marissa will be thrilled that her closest friend will become part of the family."

Harry grinned proudly. "You look well, Aidan. Your smile makes me fear for the bank accounts of the gentlemen you left behind in London. What have you gotten up to?"

Aidan looked past his cousin's shoulder and found that Edward's gaze was dangerously sharp. "I'm only excited to hear there's another wedding on the calendar."

"Good Christ," Harry barked on a laugh. "If you don't wish me to know, simply say so."

Aidan smiled. "I don't wish you to know."

"If it has you smiling, you may take your secret to the grave with my blessing."

Edward didn't look quite so enthusiastic, but his narrowed eyes couldn't pierce Aidan's mood. In fact, Aidan chuckled as he dropped into a chair and set his feet on a table.

"And," Harry continued, "if it's a business you've taken over, please consider gifting me with a share as an engagement present. I won't consider it the least unsentimental."

"Duly noted."

Harry clapped his hands together. "All right. I'd best change. I must sit for my portrait in an hour."

Aidan gave Harry an incredulous look. "Portrait?"

"Yes, a wedding portrait, to be debuted at the wedding, of course. I believe your mother whispered something about tying doves to the sheeting, to gracefully whisk it away just as we are introduced at the breakfast."

"Good God, man," Aidan croaked, picturing a flock of panicked doves tangled in linen and trampled by frightened guests. "You cannot be serious."

"Your mother is serious, and I am not man enough to defy her. Are you?"

Aidan shuddered at the thought of his mother planning his own wedding. Thank God that if it ever came to marrying Kate, it would likely be a quiet affair. Then again, his mother didn't know the definition of quiet.

"Poor Harry," Aidan said when his cousin had sauntered out. "Mother is getting her revenge for Marissa's hurried wedding, I suppose. I wonder if she has commissioned that golden carriage she spoke of?"

"She tried to sneak the bill past me," Edward said. "But I caught her out. You didn't reply to my last letter."

Aidan blinked at the sudden change of subject. "I apologize. I've been traveling."

"To Kingston-upon-Hull?"

He tried to keep a straight face. This was serious, after all. Kate was a married woman. But he couldn't help the slight quirk of his lips.

"Aidan."

"She's left her husband."

That snapped Edward up straight. "When?"

"Not for me. I mean she moved back to England without him."

"But she still has a husband," he growled.

Aidan's shoulders suddenly burned. He rolled his neck and closed his eyes before resting his head against the back of the chair. "I know that."

"Then what are you thinking?"

"I'm thinking that she is mine again and I can hardly fathom it. I'm thinking that I haven't felt this alive since I said good-bye to her ten years ago."

When his brother didn't answer, Aidan opened his eyes to find Edward frowning down at him. "You never told me what happened."

He shrugged as if it didn't matter. "I asked for her hand and her father refused me. You know that."

"But there's more. You said things sometimes, when you'd been drinking. . . ."

Aidan cleared his throat and crossed and uncrossed his feet. "We argued. There were ugly words between us. But it hardly matters now."

"Aidan . . ."

He didn't flinch. Didn't turn his gaze away at the censure in his brother's voice. Edward could call him foolish if he liked. Aidan would gladly play the fool for Kate.

In the end, Edward only shook his head. "Never mind. I'll save my breath."

"Clever fellow."

Edward laughed, his face finally relaxing as he took the seat opposite Aidan. "You'll do what you like, I suppose. You always have."

"Ha. Do you remember when I told you I meant to marry her?"

"Yes. I told you quite emphatically that you were too young."

"And I accused you of being a stiff old man who didn't know a thing about love."

"I was all of twenty-six."

Aidan smiled. "Ancient. Nearly dead, by all accounts. But the next day, you gave your blessing."

"Mother interceded on your behalf."

That was something he'd never heard. Aidan drew his chin in. "She did?"

"She said I was torturing you. That you truly loved her. That our father had only been twenty-two when he'd proposed and they'd loved each other until the day he died."

"Well." Aidan uncrossed his ankles again, then put his feet to the floor and sat straighter. "She does adore a good melodrama."

"She wanted you to be happy."

Aidan ran a hand across the nape of his neck, digging his fingers in.

"And what happened afterward . . . She didn't mean to cause more pain."

"I know. I never thought it was intentional. It was only that her desire to titillate and thrill overcame any caring she had for me."

"Aidan."

The disapproval in Edward's voice brought heat to Aidan's face. "You cannot know the effect she had."

"Can't I?"

Aidan looked away, focusing on the farthest corner of the room so he would not have to see his brother's eyes. Of course, Edward had heard all the tales. And in those first years, he'd likely seen the evidence of Aidan's debauchery with his own eyes. "I am the one who chose to take advantage of the legend she created. The young man devastated by love and grief. The heartbroken hero in need of comfort. But when I found out she was the person who'd told my secrets . . . It was a relief to have someone else to hate besides myself."

The fire snapped against the silence. Sparks shook free of the flames and slowly floated up the chimney.

"Can't you forgive her?" Edward asked softly.

"I forgave her long ago."

"I'm not sure she knows that, Aidan."

Yes, she likely wouldn't. He'd made peace with his mother's actions, but he'd never made peace with his own. Hard to distinguish one anger from another, he supposed. While he was considering that, Aidan's eye caught on the wing chair in the small alcove near the corner window. A scrap of gray fabric seemed out of place. He craned his neck, scowling.

"Is that Aunt Ophelia?"

"No, I . . . My God." They rose together and descended upon the alcove to find ancient Aunt Ophelia dozing in the weak sunlight. She opened one eye and stared balefully at them.

"Aunt Ophelia," Aidan shouted. "A pleasure to see you again. May I escort you to your room?"

She pushed to her feet before either man could help and shuffled from the room without a word.

"Do you think she heard anything?"

Edward laughed. "She hasn't heard anything in years."

"Right." Aidan frowned at the echo of a door closing farther down the hall. "Of course." He was distracted from his worry by the sound of lively voices from the entry. He prayed it was his sister and not houseguests, and soon enough he recognized her voice.

The whole household descended to greet her and touch her and ask after her journey. Aidan gave her a long hug, then solemnly shook the hand of her husband, Jude. Jude had been a good friend once. Good enough to volunteer to marry Marissa when she'd found herself compromised. But now Aidan and Jude eyed each other warily while Marissa discussed their honeymoon trip to the Ottoman.

The bronzed tint to her naturally pale skin spoke to her adventures, and her eyes sparkled like emeralds as she wove tales.

Their mother smothered Marissa with dramatic kisses. "My darling!" she exclaimed. "You're as dark as a Persian harem girl!"

"I'm sure that harem girls are kept quite fair, Mother. They are not allowed to tour the country on camelback, for instance."

"Never say you did!"

Marissa grinned. "If you'd prefer I not speak of it . . ."

"Nonsense! I can't bear it, but your brothers will want to hear it!" An utter falsehood, of course. Their mother was fairly trembling with excitement, and if Marissa wasn't careful, she'd find her next exotic trip with her husband fully encumbered by a maternal stowaway.

As entertaining as Marissa's story was, Aidan found himself drifting away, as he always did. He'd separated himself from his family long before, and now he worried that he'd permanently severed those ties. He watched his mother and brother and sister and cousin as they laughed and talked. Even Aunt Ophelia hung on Jude's arm, smiling up at some story he told. Aidan headed toward the door.

He'd take his favorite horse out for a hard run and rejoin his family for dinner. By then, he'd be ready to face them again.

"Aidan!" Marissa called just as his hand touched the door.

He froze and turned reluctantly back, but when she threw herself into his arms, Aidan hugged her hard, and planted several more kisses on her cheek. "Your new status suits you," he said honestly. "You look beautiful. And happy."

"I am happy."

Her grin turned his heart to jelly. Two months before, he hadn't even hoped she could be happy in her marriage, only content. But now she looked prettier than ever, her smile wide and wicked.

"Are you sneaking away?" she asked, her expression finally sobering.

"Just for a ride. I'll be back for dinner."

"But I've only just returned. Stay?"

He swallowed his nervousness.

"Save your rides for after the guests arrive. You'll need them then."

"Good point." Aidan let his lips form a smile and leaned in to give Marissa's cheek one more kiss. "Very well, sister." He tucked her arm into his and led her to the couch. "Tell me the most dangerous thing you did in Constantinople."

"The most dangerous?"

"Yes. I'll find it entertaining, but if your husband has put you in danger, I'll also have the perfect excuse not to apologize."

She cocked her head, puzzled.

"I did not treat him well before the wedding."

Marissa's gaze dipped to the floor. "You were quite abominable."

"I'm sorry, Marissa. Truly. I'll speak to him when we're alone."

"Thank you." She took his hand and squeezed it hard. "You'd best not wait too long. He is your only friend, after all."

"Ha. And here I thought you'd weep with feminine gratitude."

She raised an eyebrow. "Are you certain you're entirely well?"

Aidan smiled. Then he grinned. "Yes, I can honestly say I've never been better."

Chapter 20

Kate tore frantically through the new stack of papers that had been delivered to her shop that afternoon. Door locked and lamps blazing against the dusk, she spread them out over her countertop and searched every page, every word for any hint of the investigation. Gerard was alive, she knew that much. The "vicious assault" against his person had been described in detail in the papers months before.

She'd been terrified at first, and then horribly confused. She hadn't been named as the attacker. Not exactly. Instead, Gerard had happily spread a fantastical tale about a late night attack on the plantation, the night after his father's death. He'd never seen his assailant, and could not say who'd struck the brutal blow. But his young stepmother, so recently widowed, had gone missing that same night. He was "deeply concerned" about her disappearance, especially considering the timing.

He hadn't exactly damned her, but he'd skillfully painted a picture that could reveal her to be a villain or a victim . . . and it all depended upon his next words about her.

Despite her utter dismay, Kate was hardly surprised. Gerard had always been clever. Frightfully so. He'd framed this story so that he could damn her or save her. He now held the power.

The first bundle of papers that Mr. Cain had collected detailed the attack and the first days of the search for the missing Mrs. Gallow. Gerard had pleaded with the good English folk of Ceylon for help in the search. But that had been months before. He wouldn't have left it at that. So Kate scoured the papers in front of her, terrified she'd find nothing, and equally terrified for news.

Her eyes caught on a familiar name and stuttered to a halt. Her name. And Gerard's. A quick note that Mr. Gerard Gallow had sailed to India after finding evidence that Mrs. David Gallow had been seen there. The ambiguity had become less neutral and more suspicious. "Mr. Gallow refuses to address the question of whether Mrs. David Gallow was in distress during her journey or whether she fled Ceylon willingly."

So Gerard had followed her to India. And if he found where she'd been in India, then he might follow the trail here. More worrying yet, though she'd written to the solicitor in London who'd asked so many questions about Hamilton Coffees, he hadn't responded. She'd written again and received no response. It felt wrong. It felt . . . threatening.

Had Gerard hired that man to find her? And for God's sake, what would that mean?

Her hands flew over the papers as she traced the lines, checking for more news. There was none, but these papers were still months old. Kate needed more information. She needed more clues. Perhaps Gerard had given up his search. Perhaps he'd already moved on to maligning her name, accusing her of things she'd never done.

You wanted him dead. . . .

That hadn't been true, but she'd still felt terror at his words, because even though she hadn't hurt her husband, she did know something about his death that she couldn't reveal. He'd never recovered from the injuries he'd suffered in that riding accident and had been bedridden for most of those seven years after. But it hadn't been illness that had killed him.

Her hands began to shake, so Kate pressed them hard to the papers and tried to calm her heart. But her mind was racing. How could she have willingly entombed herself in such blithe ignorance since she'd landed in England? How could she have hidden beneath the bedclothes like a child? She'd thought herself so clever, moving here and changing her name. She'd been a fool.

She traced the pages for a third time, still searching for her name. Then she turned the pages over and looked again. But there was nothing.

She needed more recent news. Just as she reached for her stationery to write a note to Mr. Cain, a loud knock banged through the room.

Kate startled, jumping so violently from her seat that half the newspapers slid to the floor. "Oh, my," she breathed, looking in dismay from the scattered newsprint to the locked blue door. Knuckles rapped against the wood again, and she pressed her hand to her throat as if she could hold back her raging pulse.

Silent as a hunting cat, she moved her feet across the floor toward the front window. Once there, she edged the curtain back. Light slanted from her window, and just as she meant to jerk the curtain back into place, a man stepped into the light, his hand raised in greeting.

"Thank God," she gasped, pressing her fingers even tighter to her throat as all the air seemed to leave her lungs.

Mr. Penrose. Not Gerard or the constable or whoever else might track her down. Just Mr. Penrose.

She unlocked the door and let him in.

"Mrs. Hamilton. Good evening. I apologize for disturbing you—"

"No, of course not."

"Are you quite well?"

She dropped her hand from her throat and hid her trembling fingers in her skirts. "I'm perfectly well, thank you. Can I help you with something? Are you—?" It suddenly occurred to her what Mr. Penrose's appearance must mean. "Is Mr. York returned already?"

"No, I'm here alone, I'm afraid. But Mr. York asked me to deliver this letter personally."

Kate's first reaction was relief. Relief that Aidan wasn't here to see her exposed. But the relief lasted only a heartbeat. Then she desperately wished he was nearby. Within reach. So that she could lean on him and feel safe. As safe as she'd felt when she'd been seventeen and so sure of their place in the world.

Mr. Penrose gestured and she looked down to find his arm outstretched, offering the letter. She made herself reach for it slowly. "Thank you for coming out in the cold to deliver it."

"My pleasure." He offered a little bow before turning to leave.

"I'll let Miss Cain know of your return."

He didn't turn back, but she saw the hesitation in his next step and the edge of his jaw bloomed pink. "Please pay my respects to her. Good evening, Mrs. Hamilton."

"Good evening, Mr. Penrose."

She waited until he'd shut the door behind him before she sprang forward to throw the bolt. While she was still standing next to the door, she tore open the letter and clutched it in her hands as she devoured it.

"Next month," she breathed. He wouldn't be returning until *next month?* Now she really didn't know what to feel, though her heart was voting for aching sorrow.

She missed him, and even though she should be glad he wasn't coming, she felt only loneliness. Even with all that Aidan didn't know about her, he still knew her better than anyone in the world. But the things he didn't know . . . those were the anchors pulling her down. And Aidan was her lifeline. He always had been.

The end of his letter offered an invitation, and in that invitation, Kate found her answer. He would be in London for a few short days before he had to return to his family home for his mother's birthday.

Kate traced the words with her fingers. She could close the shop for a short time and run to London. Perhaps she could track down that solicitor. Perhaps she could even tell Aidan the truth.

But what was the truth?

Yes, her husband was dead, but did that mean she was free? Gerard's threat hung over her like a sickle, threatening to sever her from everything she'd built.

You wanted him dead. His hand had curved around the back of her neck, fingers stroking the tender flesh beneath her ears. *I saw you go in. . . .*

She hadn't known what to do. Gerard's eyes had always followed her. Always, from the moment she'd first set foot on the plantation. At first, she'd thought he might be a friend. She'd been wrong.

Though she'd pled with him that night, swearing he was wrong, he hadn't seemed to hear her. He'd pulled her closer, and then he'd pressed his mouth to her neck. "I'll help you," he'd breathed. "I won't tell them what you did."

Kate had been frozen in horror, her hands pressed to his chest, useless against his strength.

"I didn't do anything," she'd sobbed. He hadn't believed her. And he hadn't let her go.

She'd hoped Gerard would come to his senses, but she'd hoped in vain.

Would Aidan help her if she told him? Would he even believe her? Even if he didn't, he would help, but how could she do that to him? How could she let him risk his family's reputation by protecting her? And his own reputation . . . the business he'd worked so hard to build could be ruined if the world thought he'd become involved with a murderess.

She had a day or two to think. In the meantime, she needed to help herself, so she sat down to write her note to Mr. Cain, requesting more papers from Ceylon.

Chapter 21

Aidan descended purposefully late, eager to avoid spending a full six hours with the horde that had descended upon his brother's home. The air buzzed with the excitement of the impending announcement, despite that half the guests had already guessed what it must be. They milled about, reminding him of a choppy ocean as he waded in.

He'd timed his arrival perfectly. The very moment a footman handed Aidan a glass of whisky, the orchestra played a flourish and the room went silent. He was in the middle of congratulating himself on his genius when he saw who stood at his side.

"Aidan." Patience Wellingsly's voice chimed like a bell, pretty and soft and free of any intimacy despite the use of his name. "How are you?" She stared straight ahead, not granting him a glimpse of her beautiful eyes.

"Patience. I'm well. And you?"

"I'm perfectly well, thank you. I saw your sister and Mr. Bertrand. They seem well-suited."

"They are."

Patience cleared her throat and he watched her throat

work as she swallowed. Aidan turned away, looking forward again, and said a small prayer of thanks when his brother began to speak. Edward thanked his guests for coming, while Aidan tried hard to lose his awareness of the woman at his side.

It wasn't the same shame he'd felt when faced with Lady Sarah. Patience Wellingsly was a widow, after all. There was nothing particularly shameful about what they'd done.

It wasn't distaste or disgust that he felt. She was a lovely woman. Older than him by nearly ten years, but still beautiful. Still vibrant.

But his skin felt too tight as he stood inches from her body. He'd danced with her. Flirted. He'd lain in her bed and entered her body. And now it felt wrong.

He was in love with Kate, and whatever insatiable needs he'd had in the past, he wanted only her. Wanted to have only been with her. An impossibility at this late date, but he could do everything in his power to be sure that he was only hers from now on.

He turned to Patience, meaning to make a pretty farewell. "You look as lovely as always, Patience."

Her eyelids fluttered and her gaze slid briefly to him. "I spoke to Jude Bertrand before his marriage. Or rather, he spoke to me."

Despite his intention to excuse himself, Aidan cocked his head.

"I was lonely in London, and I apologize if you felt pursued."

"Of course not. I daresay I could outrun a woman in dancing slippers."

Her mouth curved briefly up. "I wanted to say that I'm not lonely anymore, and I'm only sorry we ruined our friendship."

Surprise flashed through him. Did she feel just what he did? That it was different to use someone you actually liked? "I'm sorry as well, Patience."

She smiled more genuinely then, and faced him fully. "You look happier, Aidan. Much happier. I'm glad."

"Thank you." And with that, she walked away, relieving him of the rudeness of excusing himself. Aidan felt a weight leave his chest and he drew a deep breath just as Edward announced Cousin Harry and the Honorable Miss Samuel. A brief murmur took the crowd, but they settled into silence quickly as Harry informed the mob that Miss Samuel had agreed to be his wife. "I cannot tell you how happy and proud this makes me," Harry said, looking awfully happy and proud for a man who'd spent months trying to decide between Miss Elizabeth Samuel and her cousin, Miss Nanette Samuel.

But perhaps it would end with real love. Perhaps they'd be happy forever.

Aidan kept his sneer to himself. He'd been cynical for so many years that it seemed the habit had settled in to stay. He took a sip of his drink and tried not to feel like an arrogant ass. When Cousin Harry raised a glass of champagne, Aidan raised his glass as well, determined to play the part of an enthusiast.

And when he spied Miss Nanette Samuel easing her way through the crowd toward him, Aidan was glad he'd pretended enthusiasm. He did not like her, and he was pleased that Harry had chosen the other cousin. Nanette was a young woman, but her eyes had an edge of hardness he recognized from his years of debauchery. Unlike her cousin, Nanette was an heiress and a true beauty, but he could already see the years of her life spread out before her. An advantageous marriage, the requisite two heirs, and then the boredom. The ennui. The bitter affairs.

Looking at her made him tired, but Aidan offered a polite bow. "Good evening, Miss Samuel. You must be thrilled for your cousin."

"Yes, I'm sure it's a lovely match for her." Though she smiled prettily, the message was clear. Harry might be a worthy suitor for her cousin, but Nanette had set her sights higher.

She looped her arm through his, and Aidan slanted a wary look at the hand she spread against his sleeve. "We are to be cousins now," she crooned, subtly turning him for a stroll around the ballroom. "Yet I feel I don't know enough about your family."

"What is there to know?"

"Your brother has yet to take a wife. Why is that?"

Ah. Here was her plan. "I gather he hasn't fallen in love."

"Love? You Yorks are all so very romantic." She tilted a flirtatious smile in his direction. "Sentimental, even."

Aidan waited for his muscles to turn to rock beneath his skin. She was undoubtedly referring to his ancient grief. Making a weak witticism about what he'd lost.

He waited for the tide of anger that would devour all his other feelings as it always did. But instead of fury, he found himself beset by mere irritation. Narrowing his eyes, he drew to a halt and waited. She gave him a puzzled look and tipped her head toward Edward.

"If you'll deliver me to your brother, I'd like to tell him how pleased I am that we shall all be family."

He didn't make a pleasant reply, but he did march her directly to Edward, who raised an eyebrow in question.

Nanette's smile grew stiff at the edges and her fingers

dug into Aidan's arm in clear irritation at his less than delicate approach, but she looked beautiful, all the same. She smiled coyly at Edward. "Our families get on so splendidly that I can't help but thrill at the idea of this alliance, Baron York."

Edward offered only the barest pleasantries, and Aidan fought off the urge to warn his brother against this woman's claws. Edward seemed disinclined to be trapped by them, after all. And Aidan had moved on to a more urgent concern: how to escape from this party early without offending his family. Though perhaps they couldn't be offended. They expected it of him. They called him sensitive and impatient and moody. But really, all he'd ever been was angry. Angry at himself and his mother and the ton. And truth be told, angry at Kate. For running off. For dying. For throwing his love in his face as if it meant nothing.

Now he could forgive it all, but he still wanted to leave the party. He was measuring the distance to the door when a footman stopped before him, offering a tray. Upon it sat one plain square of neatly folded paper. "Sir, you asked to see any correspondence immediately?"

"I did." And this was his ticket out of the ballroom. Aidan took the letter and held it conspicuously at his waist as he slipped toward the door. He'd congratulated Harry and Miss Samuel before the guests had arrived. His duties were done. No one would miss him.

As soon as he slipped into the corridor, Aidan turned the envelope over and studied the script. It was Kate's writing, he was almost sure of it, though it wasn't quite the same. The girlish loops were narrowed to more insistent points. The drawn-out flourishes now disappeared into impatient stops.

Aidan felt a swarm of sparks swell beneath his fingertips as he eased the seal open and unfolded the letter. He was so aware that it was his first letter from her in a decade that it took him nearly a full minute to decipher the message within the words. When it finally got through, he read over the lines again to be sure he had it right.

Kate was coming to London. To see *him*.

Allowed the space and time to think, Kate was changing her mind, it seemed, about him and about their relationship. She was open to more. She must be, to risk a trip to his home in London. His mind spun with the possibilities, and when he looked up to see Jude Bertrand stepping from the ballroom, Aidan latched on to the biggest possibility of all.

"Jude. Might we speak in the library for a moment?"

Jude's brows lowered warily. "As long as you don't plan to apologize again. That was painful enough the first time."

Aidan, embarrassed that he'd behaved badly enough to necessitate an apology, snapped at his old friend. "I'd acted terribly and I owed you an apology."

"Yes, well, I'm sure the circumstances of my betrothal to Marissa—my *last* betrothal to Marissa—absolved you of any bad behavior on your part. I was happy to escape with my bullocks intact."

"You may thank my sister. She insisted we let you keep them, though I assured her they were worthless."

"Ha."

"Now," Aidan snapped, "will you come to the library or not?"

"I see you've used up all your pleasantness for the evening. Good thing I've no use for it." Jude walked toward the library, his steps light as a stalking cat despite his intimidating size. Aidan had called him a lowborn bastard—and worse—just a few months before, but Jude had seemed to forgive him without another thought. His easy pardon only made Aidan feel more churlish. Jude had been a good friend to him, and it dishonored Aidan to admit he hadn't thought the man worthy of his sister.

"I am sorry," he said again as they stepped into the library.

"Oh, for Christ's sake, man. Leave off. You seem to think me as sensitive as a child."

Aidan felt his mouth turn up at the edges. "Perhaps I'm only afraid I'll never be allowed to visit your mother's salon again."

"Waxing sentimental over Marie?" Jude asked, referring to one of the beautiful courtesans Aidan had met there. Jude's mother was a former French courtesan, famous for her beauty and for the love of a certain duke. Jude was the product of that union, and seemed entirely comfortable with his unusual heritage. And now Aidan was counting on Jude's odd family for help.

He poured two drinks and handed one to Jude before inclining his head toward the chairs nearest the fireplace.

Jude shot him a suspicious look, but he sat down and raised his glass. "To marriage," he murmured, and Aidan winced.

"What's wrong?" Jude asked. "Finally being forced to the altar?"

"Not at all. It's something entirely different." Aidan had clearly not poured enough whisky as he found his glass empty too quickly.

"Well?" Jude prompted.

"I . . . It seems . . ." He stumbled to a halt, unable to think how to start. "Can I count on your discretion?"

"Haven't you always?" Jude scoffed.

Aidan managed a sick smile. "Yes, thankfully. But this is . . ."

"Entirely different?" Jude finished.

"Yes. It's about Katie. The girl I once meant to marry."

"The one who died?"

"Yes. Except that she isn't dead."

Jude's expression hardly budged as he shook his head. "Pardon?"

"She didn't die. Her family sent her to India and concocted the story of the shipwreck."

"What? *Why?*"

"I've no idea, and Kate refuses to contact her family, so perhaps we'll never know."

"You've been in touch?"

"Yes." He let his gaze rise to meet Jude's. "I've found her."

"Well, my God, Aidan! That's wonderful!"

Aidan let the smile spread over his face. "It is. She's alive and well and living in Kingston-upon-Hull, of all places. I happened by her on the street."

"You're kidding."

"I'm not. But please don't tell another soul. Only Edward knows."

"What about Marissa?"

"I can't tell her yet."

"Aidan . . . she's my wife."

"I know, but I can't tell her yet. It's complicated. More than complicated."

"By what?" Jude asked.

"The reason I told you . . . I don't wish to involve you. . . ."

"But?"

"But . . . I wondered if your father would be willing to help petition Parliament for a divorce."

Jude's entire body, alert and tense, relaxed slowly into the seat back as his face turned from thrilled to serious. "Ah. Complicated, indeed."

"She was sent by her father to marry him, but they're living separate lives now. He's still in India."

Jude frowned into the fire.

"I'm sorry," Aidan murmured. "I know it's hopelessly hypocritical, after I accused you of having no honor, of not being a gentleman. . . . Now I'm here telling you I'm in love with another man's wife. But I thought she was dead. And now I have her back. . . . Do you think you can understand that?"

"Jesus, of course I can. Save your apologies. If I found Marissa after ten years' separation, do you think I'd let anything keep me from her?"

Aidan swallowed hard and wished desperately that he'd brought the decanter over. He needed a drink to wash the bitter need from his mouth.

"And I know better than most how unfair society can be."

"Yes," Aidan said. They'd had a shouted version of this discussion in this very library. Jude had pointed out that despite Aidan's high birth, he'd often behaved as the basest of men. The truth had stung like fire.

"What's her basis for petitioning for divorce?" Jude asked.

"Ah, well. We're still discussing that. They've never had children. They no longer live as man and wife."

"Abandonment? Even so, Aidan . . . It's nearly an impossibility."

"But divorces are granted . . ."

"Not to women!"

"Yes," Aidan answered, his throat tight. "I know. That's why I would dare to ask for your father's help. I shouldn't wish to ruin her name, or my family's. But with the backing of a duke . . ."

"I'll ask him," Jude said easily. "If that's what you want. There is every chance he'll say no, but I happen to know he has a tender heart."

"I think perhaps he passed that on to you."

Jude smiled. "I know how long you've loved her."

Aidan rubbed his thumb over the hard, cool surface of the glass. The fire danced over the crystal as if it were trapped inside the angles. "I failed her. In many ways. I don't mean to do so again. I must find a way to fix this."

"So you are giving up your visits to my mother's salon?"

Aidan couldn't help but laugh. "I may stop in to pay my respects to your lovely mother, but no more ulterior motives."

"Marie will be disappointed."

"I'm sure she'll understand, if she notices at all."

Jude sighed and slapped one of his large hands against Aidan's knee. Aidan pretended not to wince at the blow.

"I'll speak to my father when you're ready."

"I'll call on him myself if he's willing to consider my plea."

"He'll hear you out. Don't worry, my friend. The world won't conspire to keep you apart any longer, surely."

Aidan wanted desperately to believe that himself, but it felt as though something dark and awful loomed on the horizon. As if he needed to move as quickly as possible to stay ahead of it, or Kate would be swallowed up again, disappearing from his life completely. But Aidan told himself it was only memory and worry, and he smiled at Jude and slapped the man's knee as hard as he could. Jude didn't even flinch.

Chapter 22

"You need a new dress!"

When the lilting voice exploded through the shop, Kate nearly dropped the canvas sack she'd been filling with beans. "Lucy!" she yelped as she clutched the end of the bag tightly enough that the fibers dug into her skin. "My God!"

"Sorry," Lucy said, without an ounce of regret in the word. She tossed a pile of newspapers onto the counter, and Kate's eyes widened. Kate had been so desperate for more news that she'd even considered asking the old dray driver if he'd come across any. But Mr. Fost had hired a new man, so her pitiful plan had been foiled.

She realized that Lucy had been speaking. "I'm sorry, Lucy. What did you say?"

"I said, if you're going to London, you must have a new dress. Well . . . you must have a new dress before you go, and you must have six or seven while you're there."

"Lucy . . ." Kate only barely managed to tear her eyes from the papers. "I'm only going to meet with a—"

"Oh, whoever cares why you are going? You must look pretty regardless."

Kate had too many problems to worry over pretty dresses. For example, that pile of old papers must be read. Today, tonight, at the next possible moment. But the thought of a dress intrigued her as well. The dull browns and grays of her wardrobe now depressed her. Everywhere she went these days, young, beautiful women drew her eye in their bright colors and tantalizing fabrics. She wanted to be bright and tantalizing too, but she was very afraid she'd only look foolish, like a staid widow trying to recapture her youth.

She smoothed the palms of her hands down the brown wool of her skirt and tried to look stern. "I leave in three days. There is no time for a new dress."

"Nonsense. I'd imagine the dressmaker has a ready-made piece she'd be happy to part with. I'd say you're quite an average size. There's no reason to think she couldn't take something in."

Kate didn't know whether to be happy or insulted to be considered entirely average. She decided on happy, but her gaze strayed to the papers Lucy had delivered and her happiness vanished.

"Come. Let's go now."

Kate blinked and shook her head. "I can't go now. I've too much to do before I leave. As it is, the shop will be closed for days."

"Then a half hour of time today will hardly change that. Come."

She tried to resist. She really did. But the truth was that she wanted to go. The idea of showing up on Aidan's doorstep in a brown wool dress . . . Kate had to bite back a shudder. She'd likely be sent around to the kitchen to apply as the new maid. So she let Lucy tug her from the shop and lead her four blocks over to Madame Durand's.

Bells jingled as Lucy pushed open the door of the modiste. A plump woman in a simple day dress hurried out of the back.

"Miss Cain! A new dress already?"

"Amazingly, I'm not shopping for myself this time. You should send a note of congratulations to my father. Instead I've brought along Mrs. Hamilton, who owns the coffee shop on Guys Lane. She needs a new dress. Today!"

Madame Durand introduced herself in a voice that held not a hint of a French accent, then looked Kate over assessingly, her graying blond curls a-tremble. "How do you feel about royal blue?"

"Pardon?" Kate whispered.

"I have a lovely gown of royal blue and cream stripe. With a few nips here and there, I think it will work nicely."

"Oh." Kate hesitated. "I don't know about such bright colors. . . ."

"Here," Madame Durand said with an efficient wave of her hand. "I'll retrieve it."

Kate's mind tipped between temptation and practicality. Where would she ever wear such a dress again? But then Madame Durand returned with the dress draped over her arm, and Kate was lost.

The colors were so sweet, the fine silk wool so crisp and lovely. The full skirt was gathered up at the hips, and she could imagine the sway of the bustle as she walked.

"I am a merchant," she reminded herself aloud. "A serious-minded—"

"You are a woman first," Madame Durand said. "And all women like to feel pretty." For good measure, she added a tortured "Oui?"

Oh, Kate did want to feel pretty. She wanted to *look* pretty. She wanted to descend the stairway of Aidan's London home and remind him of the girl she'd once been.

"Your figure is outstanding." The dressmaker walked slowly around her.

Lucy nodded in vigorous agreement. "The blue will be so lovely with your skin." Kate flushed.

"Yes," the modiste agreed. "Yellow would be nice, but we'll wait for spring."

"Yellow!" Kate began, alarmed at the suggestion.

"And something in green also. But later. For now, shall we fit this dress?"

Kate's doubts were trampled by the thought of Aidan seeing her dressed like a *woman*. "Yes. Let's fit it."

Lucy squealed and clapped like a child handed a new sweet, but Kate had lost her powers of speech. She stood dumbly as the modiste stripped her to her stays and pinned the dress around her. Kate was stuck simply staring at her reflection in the mirror.

When she left an hour later, head spinning, she was far poorer than she'd been, but she could hardly regret it. The dress would be delivered tomorrow evening. And two nights later she'd be in Aidan's bed. Her heart fluttered and flipped.

Lost in thought, Kate unlocked her shop absentmindedly, absorbed by picturing herself in the dress, its simple line flattering her figure. She could see Aidan's sun-darkened hand stroking the cloth over the curve of her waist.

Leaning against the door to shut it, she let her eyes fall closed, savoring the dream of his touch. She didn't want to be pretty, after all. She wanted to be beautiful. Seductive. Irresistible. A new dress wouldn't give her that, but it might come close.

She allowed herself a moment to daydream about her bright future as a seductress, but then she opened her eyes and it was just the stark lines and pale light of her everyday life. Her gaze fell on the stack of papers and she nearly groaned as she braced her hands against the door.

She had to find Gerard, or she wouldn't know what to tell Aidan when she arrived in London. The full truth? Part of it? None?

Kate set her jaw and turned her mind to the task at hand. As she flipped through the papers, it felt as if Gerard sat on her shoulder, his presence was so heavy.

His father hadn't been an easy man. He had been hard enough to endure as a husband; Kate could not imagine him as a father. Certainly, her own father hadn't been affectionate, but David . . . David had been completely removed from his family. His interest had lain a mile away at the small house his mistress Iniya had shared with her children near the entrance to the plantation. Gerard had been the heir, but David's heart had rested with Iniya and the children he'd fathered with her. Gerard had never measured up to his father's standards, never been enough, but he'd loved his father all the same.

Kate frowned. If circumstances had been different, Kate would've befriended her stepson, she thought. He'd needed a friend, and she'd sometimes tried to fill that role, but those gray eyes of his had put her off, always bright, always watching. He'd been young, a few months younger than she, but his unhappiness had lent his eyes a frightening cast.

And those first few years, Kate had been in no state to help anyone, not even herself. By the time she'd awoken from her strange state of weary suspension, Gerard had been a full-grown man, and Kate had been afraid to be alone with him, aware of the heat in his eyes whenever they touched her.

Kate shivered, feeling the ghost of that gaze on her skin. She should be thankful instead of bitter. Thankful that she'd escaped that place. It had only been ten years, after all. Ten years out of a whole life she had yet to live. Ten years taken from her in Ceylon, and the jungle could keep them. She only wanted the rest of her years for herself. But Gerard would take those too, if he could.

Spreading out the next paper on the counter, Kate searched for the answers hidden within.

"Aidan Charles York, you stop right there!"

Aidan froze, one foot on the carriage step, one on the ground. His breath steamed around the lamp before disappearing into the predawn cold. Resignation took him over as his sister's footsteps crunched through the hard frost.

"Just where do you think you're going?" she snapped as she stepped into the light.

"I'm returning to London, as I always do."

"Sneaking out in the dead of night is more like it."

"I am hardly sneaking out. I said farewell to Mother last night."

"You didn't say farewell to me!"

Aidan raised an eyebrow. "You and your husband had already retired after loudly proclaiming extraordinary weariness."

That shut her up for a moment. Even in the pale light, Aidan could see the blush bloom over her cheeks. "Right. Well. The traveling . . ."

"Please don't explain. I'm desperately hanging on to my blinders."

She raised her chin. "Well, I heard the carriage being loaded and I've come to say good-bye. And to find out what exactly is going on."

"Nothing's going on. I don't know what you mean." He noticed then that she was wearing a nightdress and robe, though her feet were protected by boots. "You should get back to bed now, Marissa."

"I'll get back to bed when you tell me the truth."

"About what?" he scoffed.

"About the letter Jude wrote to his father!"

Bullocks. Jude apparently had all the discretion of an elephant. "I don't know what you're talking about."

Marissa put her hands on her hips and glared. "Really? Then why is Jude so delicately broaching the specter of Parliament and divorce? Has my new husband already tired of me?"

"Don't be ridiculous."

She poked him in the shoulder. "You tell me what's happening, Aidan. Jude obviously knows and I guarantee I'll get it out of him. Soon. But you'll both be on my very bad side. For a long while. Not that it matters to you, I suppose."

His shoulders were nearly vibrating with tightness, but he took a deep breath and felt them slump. "Of course it matters to me."

She was trying to look stern, but a shiver worked its way through her body and exploded through her in a brief shudder. Aidan sighed. "Get in the carriage."

She narrowed her eyes.

"Get in the carriage and I'll tell you."

Marissa didn't bother hiding her triumphant smile. "Wonderful," she said as she stepped up into the carriage.

Aidan tucked a warming pan beneath her boots, then

unfolded a blanket and placed it carefully over her. He was abruptly reminded of Marissa as a small girl. The bright happiness in her eyes when he would agree to read her a bedtime story. The utter trust in her face as she'd smiled up at him. My God, she'd been so young. And so had he. Now everything was different except his love for her.

"I can't tell you everything, Marissa."

"Are you in love with a married woman?"

"I am."

She scowled. "It's not that awful Mrs. Renier, is it?"

"Excuse me?" Heat fell over him in a wave of mortification.

"Everyone knows you're lovers. She crowed about your deep affection for her all last Season."

"I . . . I . . ." His little sister knew about Mrs. Renier? What else did she know? "No," he finally breathed. "It's not Mrs. Renier."

"Thank God! Who is she, then?"

"I can't tell you. It wouldn't be appropriate."

For a moment—a long moment—it seemed she would argue. Her jaw pushed out. Her eyes narrowed. But after a few heartbeats, Marissa's face softened again. She reached out a hand and touched her fingertips to his jaw. "Whoever she is . . . are you certain you love her?"

That was a much easier question to answer. "I am," he said. "I haven't a doubt in my mind."

Marissa's eyes filled with tears.

Aidan pressed his hand over hers and felt the warmth of her fingers against his face.

"She's another man's wife. How can you be sure of her?"

"Because I know her, Marissa." He took a deep breath. "As I used to know myself."

"Oh, Aidan," she sighed. "Then you must do whatever you can, however hopeless."

"I will," he promised. "Now get back to bed."

The warmth of Marissa's hug stayed with him after she'd gone, and Aidan set off for London feeling more relaxed than he had in years.

Chapter 23

Kate had forgotten the filthy state of the Thames. The water of the Humber was smooth and clean, the Hull flowed clear and sparkling. The Thames seemed not to be water at all, but a murky brew of sewage and dead fish parts.

Covering her nose with two handkerchiefs, she tried to hold her breath as the train passed over the river. The smell didn't help the nervous rolling of her stomach, and when the train finally pulled to a stop in the station, she breathed a shaky sigh of relief.

After a quick descent with the one satchel she'd brought, Kate scanned the station. Aidan had written that a carriage would be here to meet her. There were plenty of elegantly attired coachmen milling about; no doubt one of them waited for her. She stepped quickly down the walk, not daring to glance at the people around her.

"Mrs. Hamilton?"

A young man in gray livery approached, his face friendly and trustworthy and completely unremarkable except that he had one blue eye and one brown.

"Oh. Um, yes, I'm Mrs. Hamilton."

He caught her stare and winked. "I know it's a bit

startling at first, ma'am. I'm John Dunn. Mr. York sent me to fetch you. May I take you to the carriage?"

Kate swallowed hard and clutched her bag tighter.

"No need to worry, ma'am. I'll fetch your luggage."

"Oh, no. I've nothing else." The chaos around her threw her completely off kilter. Unable to do anything but follow John Dunn, she hurried behind him, marveling at the way he forcefully parted the crowds. The mad jumble of voices thinned as they walked a small distance to the line of coaches awaiting their passengers, but her nerves still jangled.

"There we are, ma'am." She glanced with some alarm at the coach he indicated and wondered, as he opened the door, how he could know it was the right one. They were all black and very few showed any sort of arms on the door. He handed her up as she said a quick, irrational prayer that this coach was headed to Aidan's home and not to some other Mr. York.

Just as she scrambled into a seat, a hand emerged from the opposite side of the coach to squeeze her knee.

"Eee!"

Aidan's deep laugh sounded in the dark. "That's not quite the welcome I hoped for."

"My word," she gasped, pressing a hand hard to her closed throat. "You scared the devil out of me!"

"That's unfortunate. I was planning for a rather devilish woman this evening."

"Now you'll have to settle for a jumpy one." Her voice was tart, but she couldn't help melting into him when he pulled her onto his lap. Immediately forgetting her irritation, she nestled her cheek against the smooth lapel of his jacket. "I thought perhaps you were too busy to fetch me."

"Oh, I wouldn't have missed this for the world." His

hand traced a smooth path down her skirt. "But I thought it unwise to march out and collect you myself—potential for scandal and all." His last words were spoken against her mouth as they both turned to taste each other.

Kate kissed him with happy eagerness, matching each thrust of his tongue with a passion more than equal to his. She'd had the past weeks to think about him. To think about what he meant to her and what she might mean to him. He wanted her, she didn't doubt that, and she wanted him too. If only it could be that simple.

In a tender motion that brought tears to her eyes, he held her head between his hands and covered her face with sweet, small kisses. "I've missed you, Kate."

She captured his mouth again and kissed him deeply, trying to convey how very much she'd missed him too. She was afraid to say it, afraid he'd be able to hear that he'd been all she thought of.

Aidan pulled her closer until she pressed tight against him, his arousal against her hip a confirmation of his words. When his hand brushed her breast, the world shuddered and shifted.

"Oh my," she whispered, and laughter rumbled up in his chest.

"That was Dunn," he explained with a smile in his voice. "Though I'm flattered you think I'm that good."

She heard John Dunn's voice then and the carriage began to roll forward, settling into its motion. Happiness bubbled inside her as Aidan laughed, and she hid her embarrassed face against his neck.

He held her cuddled tight against him for the few minutes it took to reach his home, then escorted her quickly into the foyer. She was only able to steal a quick glance around at cream walls and gilt mirrors before finding herself before a rather dour butler.

"Madam," he intoned. "A maid will take you to your room directly."

"Thank you, Whitestone," Aidan interrupted, "but I'll give her a tour."

"Of course, sir."

The door closed behind them, the butler disappeared, and they were alone.

Kate wanted to look around, to take in the whole of his home, but when Aidan took her hand and tugged her toward the stairs, she had no urge to resist. All she could think was: *This is Aidan, holding my hand, drawing me up the staircase to a bedchamber. This is Aidan, smiling back at me with all the joy of a young boy.*

It seemed only a heartbeat passed before she was standing before a set of carved doors.

"Your chambers," Aidan said solemnly, swinging both doors open.

An enormous sitting room spread out before her, decorated in soothing colors of rose and mossy green. It was beautiful, perfect, as if it'd been decorated especially for her. A thick rug cushioned the floor nearly from wall to wall, swirling flowers of cream and pink and pale green across the room. The furniture was light and delicate, the pillows smooth silk. Evening light fell softly through the wall of windows, setting everything dreamily aglow.

The rooms were obviously meant for the lady of the house and Kate felt a thrill of frightening anticipation, picturing herself living in these rooms, receiving Aidan here every morning as she took her tea. She could just make out the foot of the bed through a doorway. A different kind of thrill shot through her body at the sight.

A footman swept past with her satchel, interrupting her fantasy, and then two maids arrived, one bearing a tea tray, the other a ewer filled with steaming water.

Once finished with their duties—and with curious glances all around—the three servants left, and she was alone with Aidan.

"Is the room to your liking?"

"It's absolutely the most beautiful room I've ever seen."

Aidan nodded, looking serious. "I'm glad. Would you like me to summon your maid?"

"My maid?"

"Yes, we found her on the best of references, and I've been assured of her discretion."

"But . . ." Kate's mind spun with the realization of what she was engaging in. "What must your household think?"

"My household? My household is happy if I am happy. And I am happy."

Kate felt such a wild warmth inside her chest that she had to swallow several times before she could speak. "Yes, I will need help dressing for dinner," she whispered, and Aidan smiled.

"Then I will ring for her and leave you alone." He started to walk out, but his steps slowed before he reached the door. When he turned back, he wore a crooked smile that turned him twenty-one again. "I feel nervous," he said, "to have you here."

She couldn't help but answer his smile. That warmth was still there, eating away at her in gentle nips. "But why?"

"It feels new, doesn't it? Being here together." He ducked his head, seeming embarrassed by his own words as he stepped out and closed the door behind him. But Kate knew what he meant. It did feel new. That same kind of newness that had urged them toward indiscretion so long ago.

He'd looked just like that when they'd walked home that day, his smile sheepish and happy, hers shy and glowing. Anything had seemed possible at that moment. Everything had been new.

Maybe that was true today as well.

Kate turned back to the luxury of the room, surprised to find laughter welling in her chest. The room was beautiful. Worthy of a princess and finer than any room in her father's home. She strolled around, taking in the little details of beauty. Whom had it been decorated for? The previous owner? A previous lover? But no, Aidan had been clear that he'd never spent a full night with another woman. Certainly none had ever lived in his home.

With a sigh, she stroked the delicate fabric of the sheer curtains.

She'd thought she'd never even consider marrying again. But now she had this feeling inside, this joy. It was a bubble in her soul, expanding every day, crowding out her pain and her anger and even all the sharp anxiety. But she was trying not to let it grow too big, because if she let it take over, if she let it grow and grow until it filled her, became her, she would be leaving herself open to terrible pain. What would happen if that bubble popped, what would she have left? What would be left of *her?*

If it were only joy or love, she could ignore it. Or be satisfied with nothing more than an occasional night with him.

But she was beginning to think that Aidan actually needed her. It would never have even occurred to her. He was handsome, witty, confident. He was rich—successful in his own right. And he'd always been a happy soul. She'd never have known his life had been changed by her disappearance. Certainly, he'd admitted to her that word of her death had devastated him, but he'd been young. He'd recovered, and quite well from what she'd seen.

But he had changed. She'd been seeing him as he once was. The lighthearted younger brother of a loving family. The kind, sought-after young bachelor. The self-possessed, funny, handsome friend of everyone he met. But there were the little things he'd said in passing. The hint of steel clouds behind the grass green of his eyes. The mouth that settled into a serious line when he was thinking.

When he was near, she'd only been aware of the changes in herself. She'd been self-conscious of the loss of her youth and good-humor. So many hours had been wasted worrying about what he saw when he looked at her that she hadn't spent enough time looking at *him*.

But now that she could see him, she didn't know what to do. How could she tell him that every day she'd spent with him was a lie? She couldn't. But she had to. Because according to the Ceylonese papers, Gerard Gallow had left for England a month ago, and she was scared to death. But here, with Aidan, she felt safe.

"I'm at a complete loss for words," Aidan said as he took in the vision of Kate. It wasn't just the pretty blue dress. It wasn't the elaborate twist of her hair. It was her spirit. She knew how wonderful she looked, how delicious.

The dress was simple—full skirt, cap sleeves, and a modest neckline. But the color lay like water against her body, bringing out the beauty of her cream skin.

She knew the effect she had on him, he could see that. The way her eyes watched, measuring his looks, laughing her encouragement. She was enjoying it, and Aidan felt his body swell with lust. He had to turn away from her to stare at the fire and gather his control.

He'd brought Kate here to spend time with her and he hadn't seen her the whole two hours since she'd arrived. The whole two hours and fourteen minutes since she'd arrived.

He'd wanted her the moment he'd seen her, but he hadn't known what to say. He could hardly ask her to disrobe the moment she crossed the threshold. She wasn't a whore come to service him.

"Aidan?"

The soft, hesitant word was a slide of silk over his spine as he turned back to her. The little coal of heat that had burned inside him all evening flared to life, sending waves of fire through his body. Then she smiled—and he melted.

"Thank you for coming," he finally said, stupidly.

"To dinner?" she teased as she took a few more steps into the drawing room.

He smiled back until he realized he'd been grinning like an idiot for nigh on a minute. "Would you like a drink before we eat?"

"That would be lovely."

He opened the bottle and filled two glasses, but one glance in her direction and he had to stop, to watch as she slowly circled the room, taking it in.

A pang of sadness struck him, a bite like the taste of medicine, bitter on his tongue. If she'd never been stolen from him, if her parents hadn't sent her away, this scene would've had a different premise entirely.

They would, perhaps, have been enjoying a drink in the drawing room before departing together for a party. Or they may have already settled in for an evening in front of the fire after an early dinner. Surely they'd have already grown into the comforting, passionate friendship of a happy marriage. There would've been children upstairs, readying for bed.

She turned then and caught him watching, so he set his melancholy thoughts carefully aside. Useless, to spend time on regrets. He only had these few nights alone with her. For now.

Tilting her head, she smiled in question. "What is it? You look so . . . mysterious."

"Mystery. An admirable addition to any romance."

"I'm sure I've had enough mystery in my life to last well into my old age."

"Yes, I'll have to agree with you."

They met in the middle of the room, but instead of giving her the wine, he set the glasses on a small table and pulled her into a gentle kiss.

"You look beautiful."

"Thank you. The maid was quite helpful with my hair."

"I'm glad she's useful, but I rather regret her attention to detail. You were locked in that room for a very long time."

Coming up to her tiptoes, Kate lightly bit his lip. "I'm here now." A pulse of heavy blood traveled to the lower parts of his body.

"You certainly are. All of you." He leered down the bodice of her gown, making her throw back her head with another of those arousingly throaty laughs.

"Perhaps we'd better have dinner."

"Appetizer," he growled, sinking to his knees before her, tugging one side of her bodice down as he went. He put his mouth to the rising mound of her breast, feeling her flesh strain against her shocked gasp. The gasp deepened, then softened to a groan when he let his hand explore the sweet curve of her calf. Dinner could wait, but he could not.

* * *

Thirty minutes later, Kate walked into the dining room on impossibly weak legs. Aidan smiled innocently when she tripped over the rug, tightening his hold on her elbow without a word.

She gratefully took the seat he offered and tried hard to hide the shaking of her hands when she touched the table. Her body was drained and limp, yet still charged with an underlying tension that likely had to do with Aidan's burning green eyes. There was a palpable heat hovering around him, and just watching his fingers as he curled them around the wineglass sent a shiver of need through her belly.

She couldn't tear her gaze away as he lifted the glass to his mouth, and when she saw his lips part, she licked her own.

"You'll have to stop looking so damned tempting, Kate, or we'll never make it through this."

"Sorry," she breathed, thinking of the way he'd touched her, the life he'd drawn from her body.

She jumped when he stood abruptly and threw his napkin to the table. "Forget the food—"

The dining room door swung open, and he froze like a wild dog interrupted during its feeding. Kate thought he might growl at the poor footman, but he only gritted his teeth and sat with a ferocious frown.

The linen of the napkin hid her smile when he turned the frown on her.

"Is something funny?"

She shook her head.

"I think I shall repay you for your distinct lack of sympathy later."

When she raised her eyebrows in mock alarm and received a remarkably wolfish grin in response, her amusement faded to a curious wonder at what he planned. She couldn't wait to see. It was obviously something worthy of anticipation.

The meal was a series of pleasant tastes in her mouth, but Aidan's hot eyes followed her every move, distracting her from the meal, just as he intended to, she supposed. He waved the footman over and gave some quiet instruction that Kate could not hear, then he turned that wolf smile back on her.

"I've asked for dessert to be served in your private sitting room. Later." He looked pleased with her "Oh" of surprise and stood, snatching a bottle of champagne from its stand. "Shall we?"

She'd enjoyed teasing him, had gloried in his tortured looks of want, but now that the time was at hand, nervousness prickled her neck. He stood, waiting behind her chair, and she fancied she could feel the tension coiled in his muscles.

"Weren't you going to give me a tour of your home?"

He choked on a laugh as he pulled her chair out. "I suppose I could, if you're really interested."

"I am!" she answered too loudly.

She jumped when she turned to find him directly in her path. He chuckled, the sound tickling her skin when he leaned in to nuzzle her throat.

"Are you sure?" His mouth paid delicious attention to the little spot just behind her ear.

"Yes." He nibbled gently. "No."

"Don't be scared, Kate. I won't bite."

A shiver set her knees trembling. She'd never even

considered he *would* bite, not until he'd mentioned it with such wicked denial, practically a promise that he would.

"I'm not scared," she protested breathlessly, wondering if it was the truth or a lie as he took her hand, looking for something in her eyes before he nodded.

Squeezing his hand with all her strength, she nodded back and followed him out of the room and up the stairs to the promise that waited above.

But she was done with waiting. It seemed she'd spent half her life waiting, so as soon as they entered her chambers, Kate shut the door and turned on her prey.

"Take off your coat," she said past a smile.

His eyebrows rose.

When he didn't move, she reached for him, sliding her hands up his chest to push the coat from his shoulders. Aidan let it slide down his arms and fall to the floor.

"Kate—"

"I never get to touch you," she said.

"That's not true." His smile went shy again, and even though her fingers trembled, that wry quirk of his lips gave her the courage to reach for the buttons of his waistcoat.

"Not the way you've touched me."

"Kate . . ." he said again, hands rising as if he'd stop her. "You don't have to—"

"Hush. I don't want to talk. I only want to touch you. Will you let me?"

"Will I *let* you?" He shrugged out of his waistcoat, then cradled her face in his hands. "You may do anything you like to me. Anything," he whispered against her mouth.

Aidan pressed a gentle bite to her bottom lip, then he sucked on that tender flesh for a moment, soothing the sting, before pressing a trail of kisses to her jaw.

Kate tugged at his cravat, loving the way the silk wound around her fingers as she pulled. The scent of his soap took her over, filling her mouth and throat and lungs. God, she wanted to taste his skin, to devour him. As she slipped the cravat off, the warmth that had soaked into it seeped into her own skin and made her shiver. He was inside her. He always had been. From that very first moment they'd touched. The scandalous twining of their bare fingers as they'd snuck through a wild thatch of forest at the edge of her family's estate. He hadn't even kissed her that day, yet somehow he'd stolen inside her and never left.

Did he feel the same?

Her fingers tripped down the placket of his shirt, freeing the buttons until she could tug the shirt from his trousers and pull it over his head. "Ah, God," she breathed as she finally pressed her face to his bare shoulder. As she rubbed her cheek against his hot skin, she knew she could never be close enough, and a few nights a year wouldn't suffice. But if it was all she could have, she'd take it.

She turned to let him undress her.

By the time he got to her stockings, Kate's breath was coming fast. The slide of delicate silk against her calf felt like a hundred trailing kisses. He rose past her shivering thighs and this time she didn't try to hide her nakedness. Instead, she reached for the buttons of his trousers, and got him just as naked as she was.

Once his body was exposed to her, he took her hand to pull her to the bed. But he didn't lay her down. Instead, he stretched out on his back like a primitive offering. His hand pressed hers flat against his stomach just above the dip of his navel, and he lay without a word, without any indication of his intentions.

Her legs were too shaky to hold her, so she sat, tentatively, on the very edge of the bed, teeth pressed to her bottom lip.

This was what she'd wanted, but now her heart churned with uncertainty. She wanted to have him the way he'd had her, but what was she supposed to do? Did he think she should know? *Should* she know? His hand fell away from hers and he closed his eyes . . . and she was alone with his body—her fingers shaking against skin, her hand a brand on his hard belly.

She was frozen, unmoving for long minutes, mortified by her indecision, but Aidan lay as if sleeping. She looked him over until her eyes rested on his straining cock.

Her nipples tightened even as her pulse trembled. Finally, Kate spread her fingers firmly, slowly, over the muscles of his belly, watching as they jumped beneath her touch. Her right hand rose to join the left, pressing lightly into his chest, stroking, feeling the warmth, the contrast of skin and hair.

Her taut shoulders relaxed by slow degrees as she touched him, gradually falling into fascination. Her hands wandered all over his torso, from his stomach to his shoulders, over the dip of his breastbone and the swell of his muscles. Crisp hairs tickled her palms, and skin smoothed under her fingers. She broadened her explorations to sweep her hands over his neck, his sweet mouth, then down, gliding over his ribs to his hips and thighs.

She stroked her fingers down the front of his legs, rough with hair, then up the inside of his thighs, marveling at how much softer and sparer the hair was.

At ease now, drunk with curiosity, she put her knees to the bed and climbed on top of him. A sigh floated from her when she nestled her backside against the tops of his knees. Her skin felt cool compared to his, but his warmth seeped into her again, leaching into her body through that small contact.

She shifted a little to set her palms against his thighs and the movement pressed her legs open, allowing the cool air of the room to caress the flesh between her thighs. The abrupt touch of air shocked her into a sharp gasp—she was wet, hot, burning.

A small sound answered her and she looked up to Aidan's face to find his gaze on her, his jaw tellingly tense. A small, fast pulse beat just under his chin.

Awareness of him flooded back to her and she smiled. He did not look half as calm as he had a few minutes ago. Fascinated, she let her hands creep up an inch or two. He swallowed hard. A different sort of heat swept through her, warming her until she had to open her mouth to get enough air. Power. She could make him pant, make him cry out. That knowledge was more arousing than all of his beauty.

Kate rocked her weight onto her knees and scooted a little farther up his thighs, settling her body and her mind to his complete seduction. She spread her fingers wide and smoothed them over the front of his hips until her thumbs crept into the dark hair around his sex. Enjoying the hard twitch of his belly, she inched her right hand closer, smoothing into his hair until she held the base of him lightly in the V of her thumb and forefinger.

Eager, her breath straining at her lungs, she turned her hand slowly up and wrapped her fingers around him until the sharp hiss of his gasp filled the room. He pulsed in her hand, large and hard and so silky she wanted to dip her head and rub her cheek against him. She did not of course; even the heady rush of power coursing through her veins could not make her so daring. Still, the feel of him in her hands drew her nipples into tight pebbles, an echo of the tightness low in her belly that throbbed with each beat of her heart.

Oh, God, she felt so restless, so strong, commanding the responses of his body. A low groan vibrated in his chest as her fingers tightened around him in her excitement.

"Mm," she grunted in pleased surprise, drawing another groan from him.

A wide, slow grin took over her face and she bit down on her lip again to keep from laughing aloud. This was heady. My God, she hoped he wanted to do this over and over again. She could spend weeks just mapping out his body like newly acquired property.

Aidan's mouth fell open on a silent sigh as his hips jerked just a tiny bit beneath her. He was growing desperate—his need obvious in the harsh line of his face.

Curious, she stroked him and he rewarded her with a hoarse curse and an impressively restrained shudder. She stroked and stroked again as beads of sweat formed on his brow and his hands clenched, white-knuckled, at the bedspread.

She bent and laid her cheek against his belly, breathing in the hot, clean smell of his skin. Her tenderness was urgent now, as if there would be consequences to not treasuring this moment, and she trailed her fingers down his cock with slow care. It jumped at her touch. He held his breath. And Kate pressed a gentle kiss to the shaft.

She did not know how this was done, or if it was done at all, but she could tell that he liked it by the way he sighed her name. So she kissed him again, letting her mouth linger this time. She set her tongue to the hot skin and tasted him. He tasted like heat and smelled like sex, and Kate smiled against him as she licked a little higher.

When she swirled her tongue around the crown, Kate glanced up, and she knew her little game was done. He reached for her, his face twisted with lust, and slid her body up so that he could capture her mouth with his.

She gasped when her slick center nestled stunningly, perfectly against his erection.

"Ah," she sighed just before he tumbled her over. His hands tangled in her hair, holding her tight as he notched his cock between her legs.

He thrust hard. The thickness of his shaft made her gasp as he forced himself deep within her. It was violent and desperate, this need. And she knew in that moment that no matter what else happened, this was good and right and what she'd always wanted.

Chapter 24

The morning light hadn't yet penetrated Kate's bedroom, but Aidan could just make out her still-sleeping form through the open doorway. The sight brought a smile to his mouth. That kind of exhaustion was enough to flatter any man. Then again, she'd done most of the work—she had a right to be tired.

He stepped carefully in, setting the tray on the table and wondering whether to wake her. The sweet rolls his chef had baked were still warm and he imagined she'd appreciate that, so he crossed to the bed and sat on the edge, meaning to kiss her awake. The beauty of her flushed cheeks and naked shoulders distracted him from his mission and he just sat for long minutes, taking her in.

He'd awakened with a stiff back, a numb arm, and skin slick with sweat where she lay pressed against him. His muscles had ached from the physical struggle to restrain himself during their lovemaking. But, more than anything, he'd felt good. So much better than his other experiences, so much more. To leave a woman's bed with a sense of completion instead of diminishment. It seemed a different act altogether.

He'd left her that morning with a gentle kiss to her sleepy mouth and returned with breakfast just to ensure she'd have no regrets. Food always seemed to smooth the way with Kate.

Unable to resist the pretty picture she presented, he trailed a finger over the graceful curve of her shoulder. Her skin was sweet and soft. He'd had little opportunity to touch her the night before and now fierce hunger rose in him. He tamped it down and settled for rubbing a thick strand of her chestnut hair between his fingers instead of pulling the sheet from her body and covering it with his own.

Lifting her hair to his mouth, he captured just a hint of her scent—flowers and spice—then he rubbed his thumb over the berry redness of her lips, tickling her until her eyelids fluttered.

Those eyes met his, soft and unfocused. A smile started to curve her mouth, then her eyes widened and he watched them clear as she glanced around.

"Good morning, love."

A pink blush stained her cheeks.

"I've brought coffee and sweet rolls."

She blinked again and her eyes slid to the dresser where the tray sat. Pulling the sheet up higher, she inadvertently drew Aidan's eyes back to her bare skin.

"Shall I bring the tray?" he murmured, admitting defeat and leaning toward one creamy white shoulder.

Kate drew in a quick breath when his lips brushed over her skin. She smelled wonderful, warm and toasty, a much tastier breakfast than the one he'd brought. A shiver vibrated through her shoulder and into his mouth as he tasted her with his tongue, sucking to draw her skin between his teeth.

"You taste lovely in the morning," he said against her

shoulder, tugging the sheets down in small increments. They were torn from his fingers when she frantically yanked back.

"What are you doing?"

"I'm kissing my way down to your breasts. Once there, I plan on licking your nipples."

"Aidan!"

Her horrified gasp made him sigh. "All right, then. I'll just bring the tray, shall I?"

She looked pained when he set it down across her lap. "I'm sorry. I'm really not very good at this."

"At what?"

"This kind of thing."

"Eating breakfast?" His words were flat with innocence.

"No! I mean . . . this . . . affair."

She looked adorable and very young all of a sudden with her tangled hair and downcast eyes. Despite her dishabille, he'd never seen her look so demure, not even as a seventeen-year-old virgin. Love, tenderness, and lust vied for domination in his heart; he wasn't sure which motivated him to pick up one of her hands and press it to his mouth.

"Do you think I expect you to behave like a courtesan? To lounge about naked, awaiting my arrival?" He smiled at her when she glanced up.

"Of course not. It's just . . . It seems a bit more awkward in the morning. It's so bright in here."

Aidan tried hard not to grin—the curtains were drawn; it was only a little brighter than it had been the night before.

"Oh, you're laughing at me!" She picked up the tray as if to move it and rise indignantly from the bed, but she had no place to set it down.

No longer bothering to hide his laughter, he took the tray from her, set it quickly on the floor, then dropped himself on top of her before she could escape from the pile of sheets and blankets.

"You—!"

Dodging her flailing fists, he straddled her and trapped her securely beneath the bedclothes, pinning her hands against the pillow.

She squirmed and struggled at his laughter until she began laughing herself, gasping out breathless giggles.

"I know you're not shy, Kate. You certainly weren't last night. So I'll assume it's only the novelty that's making you behave like a ninny."

"A ninny!" Her voice was sharp with outrage, but her eyes shone. "I suppose your other lovers aren't the least bit modest."

Aidan looked down to avoid her eyes and the sight that awaited him immediately dissolved his guilt. Clearing his throat, he glanced back to her face. "It seems you have fought your way straight into immodesty, love."

One glance down and she bleated in wordless horror.

Aidan happily followed the path of her gaze to the luscious, pink-tipped breast peeking out from beneath the bedclothes. "I think it's looking for the attention it missed last night."

Shocked into silence, Kate shook her head frantically.

He did purr then, dipping his head to suck her nipple firmly into his mouth. It hardened against his tongue and his body followed suit, thickening in eager response.

A flurry of sighs and gasps floated to his ears, spurring on his excitement. God, he'd wanted to do this so badly last night when she'd been poised above him, unselfconscious in her arousal.

He stroked her with his tongue and scraped his teeth

against the sensitive bud, loving her body's arching attempt to get closer.

When he released her hands, they flew up to grip his hair and hold him to her, while he pulled the damned sheets down and out of his way.

"You're so beautiful," he groaned, lifting his head to attend to the other breast.

Kate moaned even as she pulled his hair sharply, moving his head away from her body. "Stop. Please!"

He blinked several times to clear the haze of lust from his mind and looked up to her strained face. "What is it?"

"I'm sorry. I . . . You have to leave the room."

"What? Why would I do that?" He ducked his chin, ignoring the sharp pain in his scalp as he drew close to her nipple.

"Don't. Don't."

With a great, heaving sigh, he cast a mournful last look at the tempting pinkness before sitting up. "What's wrong?"

Kate's face turned pink, then red. "I just need some privacy," she finally blurted out.

"Oh," he replied dumbly, then, "Oh!" He felt heat seep into his own face and stood quickly. "Of course."

"Just go," she muttered miserably, her hair hiding her face.

"Sorry." Aidan hurried out of the room, slamming the door behind him, then grinned at how foolish he felt. All those lovers he'd gone through in the past years and now he was embarrassed by her need for the chamber pot. The grin widened. This sharing a bed business was interesting. How fascinating to be with someone night and day, to live with them as you lived with yourself, all the banal, commonplace trivialities exposed.

By the time the bedroom door opened he was past his fluster and feeling very cheerful. "Better?"

She cast him a look brimming with annoyance at his good humor.

"I'm sorry. I'm actually as unused to morning-after rituals as you."

She nodded and set down the tray. Aidan felt a flash of regret, knowing she'd assume something far different from the truth, but he let the moment pass.

She'd donned her shift and a dressing gown before opening the door, much to his disappointment, but he was hopeful they'd be coming off later. There was the whole day ahead, after all.

They drank the marginally hot coffee and devoured the rolls, Aidan watching her greedily the whole time. He was fascinated by her, by the knowledge that he loved her, and he didn't want to miss a thing. When he thought of her becoming a part of his family, he couldn't stop the words.

"I love you, Kate."

Her eyes went wide and he saw the clenching of her throat as she swallowed.

"You must know that."

"No," she breathed. Her head made a vague side-to-side movement. "I don't."

"There's never been another woman in my home. I've never . . . You're the only one who . . ."

She was shaking her head again. "Aidan—"

"This isn't some phantom, Kate. It's real. I won't pretend otherwise."

"I know that," she said with sudden urgency. "I know it's real. Do you think I don't feel it?"

Thank God. Aidan relaxed back into his chair, his lungs already free enough to draw more air.

"If it wasn't real, I'd never have come here. But it is so much more complicated than you know. My husband—"

"I spoke to someone," he interrupted, leaning forward again in excitement. "I raised the question of divorce."

Kate froze. The color in her cheeks seemed to dip beneath the surface, hiding itself from him.

"It might be a possibility," he assured her. "Marissa's new father-in-law is Duke—"

"A *duke?*" She surged to her feet.

He raised a hand to stop her, but she slapped it away.

"I told you to tell no one. *No one.* And you exposed me to a duke? How dare you?"

"I hardly exposed you. I only asked if he might be willing to sponsor your—"

"Aidan! You had no right. *None!* If my husband's family finds out . . . Or my husband, of course . . . I told you not to pursue this!"

Aidan stood and paced to the window, trying to calm his temper, but he couldn't understand her. "So you want to stay married?" he demanded. "You want to be Mrs. Hamilton, and I'll be . . . what? The paramour you keep in a hidden cottage?"

"No! Why must you always see things in black and white?"

"What do you mean, *always?*"

"You know what I mean! You always have. When you could not get my father's permission, you decided that was it. We could not marry, and it was over."

Frustration rolled through him as a wave of fury. "We *couldn't* marry! You were the one with no understanding. If we'd run to Gretna Green, your life would have been ruined! Both our reputations in shreds. I had no money, no house. How—"

"And," she interrupted quietly, "how could that have been worse than this?"

The softness of her voice canceled out the words in his throat. The argument. The way to make her see that he was right. Kate watched him, her eyes sad and worn.

"But . . ." He shook his head. "How could I have known?"

"You couldn't have. Just as you can't know what will happen for us now. I only want you to see that you took that decision from me then. And I am done with letting others make decisions for me. I won't have it."

He wanted to argue further. Of course he would take back that decision if he could. Knowing what he knew now, he'd have carried her to Scotland and damn the consequences. She wasn't being fair.

"I told you I wouldn't make any attempt to divorce my husband. Even if I've changed my mind, it's not up to you to force the issue."

He stood straighter. "Have you changed your mind?"

Kate ducked her head. Two bright spots of pink returned to her cheeks. "I need time to think."

The awful pain in his chest eased a little. She wasn't saying no, which was more than she'd granted last time.

"And what of your family? They will not like being dragged into this. Your brother—"

"My brother will not give a damn. And my mother always adored you."

"I only met your mother twice, and she didn't know we were . . . so close."

"She knew."

Kate's chin snapped up. "You told her? About us?"

"No, she saw me mooning about, and if anyone can recognize lovesickness it is my mother. How did you think I arranged that two-week visit to your neighbor's estate?

I told her that I was in love with you and she took over the scheming."

Kate's tense frown relaxed into a smile. "Did she?"

"Indeed."

Her temper had eased, it seemed, and she lowered herself back into the chair with a sigh. "I may not be able to have children, you know."

"Heirs are my brother's duty, not mine."

She poured herself a cup of coffee and one for him as well. "Let me think on it, Aidan."

"Yes. Of course."

"You must let me come to this decision on my own. You can't understand the damage you could do. Please, I only need time."

Time. He could give her that. He'd already given a decade, after all.

Chapter 25

Hot water lapping at her chin, Kate watched steam curl up from the lilac-scented water that filled the tub. How long had it been since she'd taken a deep, hot bath? How long since she'd set foot in a home like this?

It could be hers, she knew that. But now she was more confused than ever. Aidan wasn't a boy anymore. He was a man with all the stupid weaknesses of a man. The need to control. The need to be *more* than. She'd been ready to tell him the truth, but he'd treated her like a child who couldn't truly know what she wanted.

The irony being that he was the one in the dark.

For a moment, she felt an ugly surge of superiority. He thought he had the answers, and he didn't even know the right question.

But she immediately felt awful, and sunk an inch lower into the water. It lapped at her mouth and made her feel hidden and safe.

He wasn't truly like her father. Or her husband. First of all, he was kind, and always had been. Secondly, he loved her. Yes, he'd betrayed her with his advocacy, but she'd betrayed him in a far deeper way. And his dishonesty had been in the name of hope. Hers was based on ugly fear.

She sighed, rippling the water with her breath.

He did not care that she was older. That she dressed like a shopkeeper. He did not even care that she might not give him children.

Her heart thumped slow and steady in her body. She raised her mouth from the water. "I love him," she whispered, and her pulse stayed steady. "I love him."

Kate pictured the foundation that propped her up. The stones she'd worked so hard to replace. She imagined herself walking around a square wall, dragging her fingers along the strong edges. Yes, there were still parts of it that had been damaged beyond repair. She could shore those up but never replace them. But the foundation, which had been riddled with holes, looked untouched in places now. Certainly strong enough to see her through a life.

Her heart lightened, and she knew she would tell Aidan the truth. Not out of fear of Gerard Gallow, but out of love for Aidan. Today she was a woman with a life ahead of her. Now she only had to get rid of the past.

Kate did not like the contrast of her drab brown dress against the flower blue runner that carpeted the stairs. She lifted her skirt higher in an attempt to lessen the comparison, but then she felt vulgar and lowered the fabric again. She could not wear the blue dress every day. And she had greater problems than her sad fashions, but she still wished to look beautiful for Aidan.

When she glanced up and saw him waiting at the bottom of the stairway, Kate's awareness of her dress grew heavier for a brief moment. And then he smiled and it disappeared altogether.

"Good afternoon," he said with a solemnity that clashed with his boyish grin.

"Good afternoon, Mr. York."

He stole a quick kiss when she joined him.

Though she blushed, she couldn't bear to pull away. "Your servants . . ." she murmured.

"I'll pay them extra to recover from the scandal of it all. They'll be begging me to have you back again."

She let her fingers trail against his as she stepped away.

"Now," he said, strolling with her toward the morning room. "We have luncheon in a few moments, but perhaps you'd like to see some of London afterward. Much as I'd like to keep you locked in the bedchamber for days."

"Surely we can't be seen together."

"We'll take a closed carriage. No one will know."

It sounded wicked and dangerous, but she couldn't enjoy it until she'd set her deception aside. "Aidan, I need to tell you something."

His teasing smile faded to a frown.

"Could we sit for a moment, before luncheon?" Her heart thundered in her chest as if danger were approaching at a fast run.

"Kate, what is it?"

She was just opening her mouth when danger became all too real, though it appeared in an unexpected form. The front door opened, and there stood someone she hadn't thought to worry over. Young Mr. Penrose.

Kate could not see her own face, but she imagined it mirrored Mr. Penrose's expression perfectly: utter, sudden shock.

"Mrs. Hamilton," he gasped.

Aidan cursed, and Penrose's eyes shifted to his employer for a moment. When he looked back to Kate, realization hit his gaze, and his mouth dropped open.

Kate's face burned with mortification. They stood frozen in an awkward triangle until Aidan finally spoke. "What the hell are you doing here, man? I sent you to Hull!"

"But I . . ." Penrose stammered. "I found a house. And I thought . . . I sent a letter last night, sir. I thought . . . Um . . ." He swallowed so hard that the sound echoed through the room.

"I received no letter," Aidan snapped, but Kate felt sorry for poor Mr. Penrose. If a letter had arrived, surely Aidan had been too occupied to notice.

"I'm sorry, sir. I . . ." His voice faded into a small leak of air from his throat. He swallowed hard again, his natural color disappearing behind a wave of red. "I'm so sorry."

"Oh, for God's sake," Aidan said, throwing up his hands in exasperation. "Wait for me in my study."

"Yes, of course!" Penrose offered a quick bow in her direction. "Excuse me, Mrs. Hamilton." Then he raced so quickly toward the far corridor that he slipped on the marble floor and nearly fell. "Pardon me," he gasped before lurching away.

Kate and Aidan both stared at the archway to the corridor until they heard the sharp clap of a door closing.

"I'm so sorry," Aidan said, turning to take her hands. "I'll explain to him that you've come for a tour of my home while you're visiting London."

"I'm not sure he'll believe that," she whispered.

"It doesn't matter. He'll be happy to accept the explanation, whether he believes it or not."

"Don't be cruel to him. It's not his fault."

"Well, for God's sake, I'm not a tyrant."

"He's afraid of you."

"That's ridiculous," Aidan snapped.

She almost smiled at his disgruntled scowl. Everyone liked Aidan. He was probably put off by the idea anyone could be afraid of him. She gave his hands a reassuring squeeze. "Don't worry over me. Mr. Penrose wouldn't tell a soul."

"He'd better not. Excuse me for a few moments." He gave her a distracted kiss on the cheek before turning on his heel.

Kate took a deep breath as his footsteps echoed down the corridor. Her lungs hurt a tiny bit at the strain, but otherwise she felt strangely undamaged. She did not want Mr. Penrose to think her a loose woman, but then again . . . wasn't that exactly what she was?

She smothered a smile at the thought as she headed for the morning room to wait. What a journey she'd taken, from colorless wife to gentleman's mistress. What a sweet, swift descent into unrespectability. A natural journey, though. She hadn't exactly started life as an obedient daughter.

A maid came to serve her tea before disappearing into the kitchens to complete preparing luncheon. "Just tug the bell if you need me, missus." Kate agreed, then wandered over to the window to look out at the street beyond. She stayed close to the curtains to hide herself from prying eyes, but Kate devoured the scene before her. Aidan's home was on a large corner lot in an intimidatingly wealthy part of the city. She wasn't familiar with the neighborhood, but hopefully Aidan would give her a tour when they took their carriage ride. The street was quiet this early in the day, and likely half-deserted during the winter, regardless, but Kate enjoyed the short bursts of traffic that traveled by.

As she watched, an unmarked coach slowed to a stop just in front of the window. The driver descended and approached Aidan's entry stairs. He was too close to the house for Kate to see, but she heard the three sharp raps against the thick door.

A few moments later, the butler passed the doorway of the morning room. Though she heard the murmur of the two men's voices, she couldn't make out the words. The driver came back into view outside, but instead of resuming his seat, he approached the door of the carriage.

As he spoke, the curtains of the carriage window slid open an inch, but Kate could see nothing inside.

The driver shook his head and raised his hands. A few more words were exchanged, and then he opened the door and a woman emerged. Though her face was hidden by a large hat and a pale gray veil, her dress was startling in its beauty. The dusty red fabric draped over an underskirt of dove gray silk that perfectly matched the gray ribbon at her neck. Kate was so entranced by the gorgeous colors that it took her a moment to realize the woman was ascending Aidan's front steps.

"My word," Kate gasped, pressing a hand to her throat. Who could it be? Marissa, perhaps?

Another knock this time, much softer than the last. This time when the butler passed the morning room, Kate snuck closer to the hall to eavesdrop.

"I know he is here," the woman snapped. "I was informed yesterday that he'd returned."

"Madam, I assure you that—"

Kate snuck a peek just in time to see the feminine

vision brush past the butler and stop in the middle of the entry. "I will see him," she snarled.

"Madam, he is not at home!"

Ignoring the butler, the woman turned in a slow circle. Kate's reflexes were dull, weighted down by the boulder of anxiety that had formed in her stomach. This was not Aidan's sister. Even past the large hat, Kate could see a coil of black hair.

Before Kate realized that she should retreat, the woman faced her and stopped cold. A glove of pearl gray kid rose up to adjust her veil and lay it back against the hat, and Kate was faced with one of the most beautiful women she'd ever seen. The boulder in her stomach turned, grinding her belly into sand.

"Well," the woman said. When she stepped forward, Kate stepped back, and the woman followed her into the morning room. "Who are you?" she asked archly.

Kate just shook her head, her hand still pressed to her throat.

"Mrs. Renier," the butler said, his face a portrait of pained discomfort.

Mrs. Renier ignored him. "You're not a maid." She swept her eyes down Kate's dress. "Quite."

Kate bristled. "I'm a guest of Mr. York. My family . . ." The lie turned to ash on her tongue and she couldn't think what to say.

"A guest?" the beautiful woman hissed. "Aidan York doesn't have *guests*. Or friends. Or pleasant visitors from the country. You're his new lover, aren't you?"

"I . . ." Now she truly couldn't speak. *New* lover. Which meant that this beautiful creature had once been—

"You're hardly his type," Mrs. Renier sneered, sweeping

another damning look down Kate's body. "But perhaps he's run through all of us by now."

The backs of Kate's knees hit the settee, but she refused to collapse onto it. She registered the movement of the butler rushing away, but her gaze stayed locked on the woman in front of her. Aidan's lover.

Mrs. Renier smirked. "You look distraught. I hope you weren't so foolish as to think yourself special, though I understand the temptation. We all know the tales about him, don't we? The countless women, the whispered tales of his . . . *prowess*. But once you're alone with him, it seems you must be different."

Kate tried to gather some strength, but it seemed only enough to shake her head. "No."

Pain twitched briefly over Mrs. Renier's face, turning her sneer into a grimace, but she laughed to cover it. "Of course you must be different, because he's *insatiable*. Four or five times a night. It's never enough for him. *You're* never enough for him. Until you are."

"Mrs. Renier," she managed to plead past her collapsing throat. Something seemed to have come loose in her head. She knew that this was terrible, knew this information was going to hurt, and badly, but it was far away, softened by the distance of shock, by a haze of denial.

The woman's smile gentled, and her voice lowered to an intimate murmur. "He is so skilled. So handsome. We want him to *belong* to us. But we are just like a hundred other women, you and I. And he has had us *all*."

The pain finally caught up with Kate, sinking in its teeth with the viciousness of a small, rabid beast. Now her throat wasn't the only thing collapsing. It seemed the whole room was falling in on her. Bile rose to sting her throat. She sucked in air and swallowed the sickness back.

Disgust and shame rippled through her stomach, and the bile surged up, gagging her. She choked it back but must have made some noise, some sound, because Mrs. Renier stepped back in alarm.

"There's no need to be melodramatic, you fool. Have a little pride at least. It's the only thing he admires."

Kate pushed past Mrs. Renier and stumbled from the room, her eyes locked on the curve of the stairway.

"Kate," she heard Aidan's voice say. She didn't look toward him as she finally reached the first step and started her escape. "Kate, what's wr—"

"Pardon me." Kate was amazed that she could speak so clearly. In some distant, still-functioning part of her mind she felt proud of her quiet voice, proud of the way her legs carried her up as if she weren't dying inside.

Her legs carried her all the way to the second floor and down the hall to her room. But once she was inside, with the door safely shut behind her, Kate fell to her hands and knees, and put her forehead to the floor, weak with something she couldn't understand and didn't dare examine. How could she have imagined that Aidan York was lonely? His whole being defied the idea.

He was young and handsome and charming. He was rich, strong, and vibrant. Women loved him. *She* had loved him.

"Oh, God," she said. She'd thought he needed her. An image filled her mind—of Aidan bent over Mrs. Renier, his exquisite body flexing, entering, filling her up while the woman cried out. Just as Kate had.

"No," she moaned, closing her eyes, struggling to blind herself. Again the scene played itself out, a different woman this time. An icy blonde, screaming her pleasure.

Oh, all those beautiful, primal things they'd done, she

and Aidan, all of them part of some traveling show he trotted out for anyone who asked. Hundreds of them. She dug her nails deep into the wool of the carpet.

Insatiable.

Laying her cheek very carefully against the wool, she cursed the softness, wishing it the cold of hard stone.

Insatiable. Kate had likely been just like the other women to him, except perhaps in that respect. He'd never been insatiable with her. He'd gotten more than enough of her, easily, quickly, had often found nothing better to do with her than fall asleep. *I've never slept with another woman.* My God, she'd been unsophisticated enough to take that as a compliment.

This newfound understanding of him was painful in so many ways, but humiliation struck her hardest.

Opening her eyes, she stared across the blurred colors of the rug, stared at the pale fall of drapes over the window. What had he even wanted with her?

It was true she was not his type—she could see that easily enough with that glimpse of only one of his women. Cool, effortlessly elegant, completely at ease among his peers. Mrs. Renier was beautiful, if a little older than Kate would have suspected. Older. More experienced. Less naïve.

The thought of her own inexpert responses to him brought tears to her eyes. Eagerness did not make up for lack of skill.

What was the appeal? The only explanation she could conjure was simple: sheer nostalgia. She was a reminder of his youth. It was possible he'd even meant to marry her. People married for less compelling reasons than nostalgia, certainly.

But she'd actually thought she was saving him, rescuing him from a bleak existence. My Lord, she'd been about to save a man from a harem. They would have married, she'd have left everything behind to be his wife, then watched, helplessly, as he began to drift away, back to those women.

This revelation of his true nature was a blessing, she told herself with desperate practicality. A gift to keep her from shackling herself to another endless, fathomless misery. This excruciating pain was better than the dull, eternal ache of yet another life spent with a man who didn't love her and spent his nights elsewhere.

This was a rescue. She still had what she'd owned a few months ago. She'd come so close to throwing everything away for him, but she hadn't stepped over that cliff. Nothing had changed.

Something wild scrambled inside her, screaming that she lied. She smothered it mercilessly and pushed herself to her feet. It was time to leave this place.

He knew who was waiting in the drawing room. The butler had whispered the name "Mrs. Renier," in his ear with a tone that managed both alarm and censure.

So he expected to see Beatrice Renier when he stepped into the drawing room, but the sight of her still sunk knives of fear into his chest. "What the hell are you doing in my home?" he ground out, as if there were some mystery as to why Kate had floated up the stairs like a ghost.

"How dare you?" she spat, her lovely features twisting into ugly fury.

"How dare I what?" He glanced over his shoulder, his mind already straying to Kate.

Beatrice grabbed his chin and pulled his face back toward her.

He shrugged and jerked free of her grasp. "What did you tell her?" he demanded.

She crossed her arms and smirked. "I waited for you, idiot that I am. I dressed with such care, imagining what you might like. I had Chef prepare your favorite dishes. And then I waited for hours, like some doxy who'd lost your favor!"

"What the hell are you talking about?" he snarled.

Her sneer wavered. "You don't remember."

"Remember what?"

Beatrice's shoulders slumped and she became smaller. "You sent a note that you'd come to me, and you don't even remember it."

Damnation. He remembered now. Just before he'd left to retrieve Kate's watch, he'd promised Mrs. Renier he'd come for dinner. And more. "I'm sorry," he muttered. "But you've overreacted. What did you say?"

"Overreacted?" She laughed, tossing her head back. "I reacted exactly as you treated me. Like a whore beneath your consideration. Exactly the same thing that other woman is to you, I assume, as you treat none of us any better than the next."

"Get out of my home," Aidan snarled. "Go back to your husband."

"Ha!" she barked, brushing past him as she tugged the veil over her face. "I love how you say that as if you're better than I. You were no better than I when we were rutting on the good china under his roof. The only difference is that I have someone to go home to, and you don't." She stopped at the threshold of the door and turned back. "Not even her, Aidan."

His blood went cold. "What did you tell her?" he asked again.

"I told her the truth."

* * *

He stood before her door for an endless moment. Fifty heartbeats. A hundred.

He was waiting for this to get easier, to convince himself that it wasn't that bad. Beatrice was only one woman, after all. Kate must know he hadn't lived like a monk. But the look on her face when she'd passed him . . .

No. It wasn't that bad. Couldn't be. He knocked on the door and waited. When she didn't answer, he knocked again, then pushed it open, his heart skipping as the door stirred the scent of her soap in the room.

"Kate?" When she didn't answer, he pushed the door open farther. "Kate?"

"Yes. I'm here." She rose up from where she'd been kneeling next to the bed.

"I'm sorry about . . . that."

She stared at him oddly, saying nothing, looking as beautiful as ever, but very pale, very stiff. He stepped into the room, and when he drew nearer, he could see why she'd been kneeling. Next to the bed lay her satchel. It gaped open, and he could see the blue dress inside.

"What are you doing?" he asked past a tight throat.

She clasped her hands together and did not look at him. "I'd like to go home early. Today, in fact. As soon as possible."

That tightness choked him, closing off his throat in a painful grip. The tension grew, sinking impossibly deep in his chest. Fighting against it, fighting the terror, he opened his mouth, drew in a breath. "No."

Her eyes locked on his in a shock of dark fury before sliding deliberately away from him. "It seems the best thing."

"I'm sorry that she came here. But I haven't seen her in months. I swear to you." His voice sounded distant, shushed by the loud rush of blood in his ears.

"That's not it."

"What did she tell you?" he snapped. There was only one thing Kate could have heard about him, but perhaps it wasn't that, he told himself ridiculously. Perhaps she'd heard something else, something entirely untrue.

She didn't want to speak, he could see it in her twisting hands, the muscles working in her throat. He wanted her silence as well, wanted her to shake her head and smile and tell him it was nothing, nothing, just a misunderstanding. When her lips finally parted, when she finally spoke, she stared hard at his shoes, as if she couldn't bear to see his face.

"She told me that you are well known for your impressive displays of indiscriminate sex. That you've been with seemingly vast numbers of women. That you may, in fact, have already run through the whole of the ton." She deigned to glance at him then, a terrible blank look that bore straight through his heart. "I did not receive any estimates as to the number of the lesser classes you've offered your services to. I'd rather not know."

Services. She'd captured it exactly, though she could not know that. Rage rose up—unreasonable, illogical—as if to make an effort at shielding him from his shame. "It's not what you think."

"I'll be very pleased if that's true."

"You make it sound like I've been with legions of women. I haven't. Not that many." Jesus, he couldn't stop himself babbling. "Only ever widows, or married women who made it well known that they . . ." He snapped his jaw shut, refusing to explain further. It was the past, surely he could make her see that.

"Married women? Like me?"

"No! They never meant anything to me, Kate. Not one of them."

She drew back from him as if he'd reached for her, though he wouldn't have dared. "How can you say that? How could you s-s-s—" He winced at the sharp edge of hysteria in her voice and watched her stiffen and stamp it down in response. "—Sleep with all those women if they meant nothing to you?"

"I never slept with any of them," he spat, wanting to make her see.

A gasping, coughing sound jumped from her throat, startling him and her as well, it seemed. She slapped a hand hard over her mouth with a clap that made him cringe.

"I know," she gasped, giggling behind her palm. "You already told me."

"What?" Frightened by her laughter, he lurched forward to clasp her elbows, to shake her. "Stop it." Her eyes caught him with their flat, unnatural gaze. "Don't look at me that way. Please."

She only closed her eyes against him.

Mad fury swept through him—fury at Kate, fury at Beatrice, but mostly, truly, fury at himself for the depths he'd sunk to in the past few years. "Goddamn you," he ground out between clenched teeth. "If I'd known you were alive, I would never have done any of it."

He expected anger, outrage in response. The calm that came over her body frightened him.

Pale as the white silk wallpaper that glowed behind her, she nodded and dropped the hand from her mouth. "That is something between us then. If I had known I was still alive, I'd have done things differently too."

The veil fell away from her eyes, just for a moment.

Aidan dropped his hands from her in shock. That brief clarity in her eyes had allowed him a glimpse into her heart, and he'd seen nothing but bleakness. She had no hope for him. And what could that mean for his soul?

"I'm sorry. I'd take it all back if I could. All of it. But you had a life these past years too, Kate. You lived your life with another man, you loved him once. You shared your bed with him and I'm sure you enjoyed it. But I didn't even—"

"Is that what you think?" She knocked his hand roughly from her arm, and he felt it fall away, weightless as mist.

He watched her watching him. She looked wary and disgusted and ready to attack or flee or both. "What?" he asked, confused.

"You think that I loved him?"

"You said you were happy," he murmured stupidly, wanting it to be true for the first time. "I may not like it, but I understand."

"My God. You don't understand. I don't *want* you to understand." She backed away from him, her feet drawing her too close to the fire.

"Stop."

Her foot shifted. She meant to step back again, to retreat even if it meant letting her skirts brush the flames. Cursing, Aidan grabbed roughly for her arm, meaning only to pull her away before she set herself afire.

She tried to twist away, but he held tight to her arm and yanked her clear of the danger, shifting her past him so he blocked the path to the fireplace. His heart thumped wildly with alarm; it took him a moment to realize she was struggling in his grasp.

"Stop it," he growled.

"No!" Her voice was shrill as she wrenched her arm free and stumbled a few steps away. "Don't touch me."

An icy flush crept over his skin, crawled beneath his flesh, tunneled into his bones. "You said you were happy. You loved him."

"That's what you think?" She spat the words out as if they burned her mouth. "You think I was just a stupid, fickle girl who was denied one man and decided the next was just as good? Well, you're right on one count. I was stupid. I was *stupid,* do you hear me?" One trembling hand rose to press against her throat.

She began to cry then. Aidan wanted to cover her mouth to stop the welling sound, to halt the words, but he couldn't move.

"You think I just decided to make the best of it?"

"Kate—"

"I was not a horse to be broken to another rider."

The meaning of her words was a searing pain in his chest. He'd thought it torturous to imagine her enjoying another man's touch, but it was unbearable to think the alternative. "Oh, Kate."

Her fury spilled out of her, deaf to his words. "How could you think I loved him? I loved you. I was *your* wife, not his. Despite that we'd never made it to the church, I was yours. I kept telling myself that, even when it seemed hopeless. Even when he held me down on his bed and took me. Even when I waited and waited and you never came. Even when I thought myself too used for you to love. I knew I was yours. *I was yours.*"

Horror and grief stretched his soul thin until it was as tight as the skin of a drum. Every word set off a vibration of pain in his chest. "Oh, Katie. You didn't tell me." The disgust in her eyes when she looked at him made him cringe.

"I didn't want that pity I see on your face. I still don't. And how could you possibly understand? You gave yourself to every woman with a friendly glance and a warm bed! How could you understand what I felt?"

Thoughts and fears wrestled, fighting inside his head. He wanted to scream, to rage, to injure. But he tamped that need down and tried to reach for her. She slid from his grasp and stumbled back to her bag as tears streamed down her face.

"Kate, what happened?" he rasped.

She stuffed things into the bag, giving up any semblance of order. "I was sent to the other side of the world. I was given to a man I'd never met. I was as dead as my parents named me. And you did not mourn me at all."

"That's not true!"

Kate paused, both hands clutching the edge of the bag. "I'm sorry," she whispered. "It wasn't that I thought you hadn't had lovers. I understood that I wasn't the only woman you'd—"

"No," he barked. "No. You are not just one of them. I love you. I love you, Kate. I want to marry you. I want you to be my wife."

She shook her head. "We can't marry, Aidan. We have very separate lives. You have an important business here in London, a life—" Waving a hand, she gestured to indicate his family, his friends, his tawdry affairs. "I have the shop in Hull. And a husband."

"No. I've already planned. I will move to Hull, work from there until a divorce can be arranged. Most of my business is correspondence anyway. I could travel to London every few weeks. . . ."

His frantic words faded into silence as she paced away from him to stare out the window.

"I don't want to marry you," she said softly to the glass. "I do not wish to become less than, again."

"Less than what? I want to give you everything. Everything I have—"

"I can't marry you." The abrupt loudness of her words hung between them. She couldn't hide her disgust, her utter hatred of him at that moment. It glowed from her skin.

"Kate, please," he pleaded. "Please let me explain. Will you?"

She turned back to the window, but then she met his eyes in the reflection of the glass and nodded once, very slowly.

Aidan held her gaze for a long moment before he turned away to sit on the bed. He hung his head, staring at his shoes.

"You died. And I was lost. I didn't know what to do with myself except drink, so that's what I did. One night, a month or so later, an innkeeper's daughter took pity on me and coaxed me upstairs. Afterward, I thought I would die of the guilt. . . ."

He glanced up, but her reflection only watched him in cool silence.

"The guilt was enough to keep me living like a priest for a few weeks—a drunken priest. But at some point . . . at some point, the liquor stopped doing its job. It ceased to banish your ghost, ceased to make life tolerable. I would dream of you, and that was the worst thing—waking up in the morning thinking you'd returned, then realizing it was a dream.

"I wanted another way to lose myself, and I found I was the object of a flood of feminine interest. I didn't know why."

"You're handsome," she said bitterly. "Charming."

"That wasn't it. It was you, actually. My mother spread the tale of our young love and its tragic end. She titillated the ladies of the ton. Apparently there is something unbearably attractive about male pain." His laugh was a bitter shell of humor that grated from his throat.

"The interest took its natural course and I found, to my extreme relief, that I could set your memory aside, could forget the sad state of my life, if only for a few minutes, a few hours, at a time."

He looked up at her and saw that she'd finally turned toward him.

"I was entertainment for them," he said. "And they were a distraction for me. I offered nothing except the use of my body for a short time. I never seduced, never promised. But, of course, my reputation precedes me." His mouth twisted around the words. "I am a purebred stud. Unbroken. Spirited. Highly recommended for my gait if not my temperament."

Kate sucked in a hiss of breath at his words. Her fingers curled in, forming fists.

"I made myself into this." He let her see all the unflinching shame in his eyes. "I debased myself for a peace that I never even found."

A dozen heartbeats passed. She said nothing. Why would she say nothing?

"I would change it if I could." Looking away from her again, he stared down at his clasped hands. "I'd take it all back if I could, but I can't. I can't. I thought you'd never find out. I didn't want you to find out."

"I can understand that, at least," she said. "I didn't want you to know either, but the difference . . . The difference is that I was ashamed of something done to me. Your shame . . . it's something you embraced."

"I never wanted it. And I never want it again."

Minutes ticked by. She stared at him, measured him, and apparently found him wanting. "I can't do this, Aidan. I can't."

"Fine," he made his mouth say. "But stay. I'll leave you be. Only stay."

She shook her head, and in that moment he hated her. He snarled, "You act so self-righteous, as if you've done nothing wrong. But you let them do this to you. They did not bind your hands and legs and ship you in a crate, did they?" Her face blanched to a sick white, and Aidan was horrified by his own words, but could not stop them. "You let yourself be put on a boat and shipped East like some prized mare."

"You did not want me anymore!" she shouted. "And they were my parents. Who could gainsay them?"

"Christ, did you really think I wouldn't help? Or were you still holding on to your stubborn anger? Either way you were a fool, Kate. If you'd run, if you'd come to me, I'd never have let them take you away."

Her jaw trembled and her eyes filled with tears.

"We've both been fools for different reasons. But we both deserve this chance. We do. Please."

The trembling in her jaw stopped and turned to steel. "No. We both wanted to go back, but neither of us is the same. Don't find me again. We are not worth it." She looped her fingers in the handle of the satchel and picked it up, and then she walked past him. Out the bedroom door. Down the stairs. Through the entry, and then she was gone.

Aidan stood staring at the open door, his heart dead cold in his chest.

"Mr. York?" Penrose's voice asked weakly from the corridor. "Is something wrong?"

"Follow her," Aidan said dully. "All the way to Hull. Just make sure she stays safe until she gets home."

"Yes, sir." To his credit, Penrose asked no more questions. He didn't even protest that he'd only just arrived in town and needed a bath or new change of clothes. Penrose only shot Aidan a wide-eyed question with his eyes, and then he hurried out the door and disappeared in the same direction Kate had.

He'd have duties in Hull regardless. Aidan would no longer need a home there or an office. In fact, he'd never set foot there again.

Chapter 26

Kate sat very still in the train station, her ankles crossed and tucked beneath the bench. The next train to Hull didn't leave for four hours and darkness was already falling. Still, she didn't feel frightened. She felt cocooned. Sheltered by a gray pall that hung over her person. It would keep her invisible—she knew that from experience. People could walk past her without seeing her. They could look straight at her and feel nothing.

It was safe, and yet she didn't want it. Not again. She didn't want to spend years living with no feelings and hardly any thoughts. It had been a relief in Ceylon, but it was no relief here. She wasn't a seventeen-year-old girl without options. And if someone tried to put her on a ship to Ceylon, she'd fight tooth and nail to stay.

Aidan had been right about that. She'd let herself be sent away out of weakness and resentment. She'd done what they'd told her to, and then they'd named her dead. Her father had gotten his secret dowry. Her husband had gotten a new governor of Ceylon. And Aidan had received the generous sympathy of a hundred stroking hands.

All she'd gotten was a false grave and the knowledge of how stupid she'd been.

That was what she could not bear now. That she'd been a fool again, thinking Aidan broken and lonely without her. He hadn't curled up into a ball and wished himself dead. He'd built a fortune and filled his life with beautiful women.

He'd touched them, filled them, kissed them, just as he had with Kate.

She touched one gloved finger to her lips, remembering their last kiss. She could hardly fathom that she'd tasted his mouth only hours before. That mouth—beautiful, sensual. How many women had it kissed, licked, sucked, worshipped? How many women had craved that mouth, dreamt of it endlessly, awake or asleep, just as she had?

And Aidan had craved them right back, far more powerfully than he'd ever wanted her. *Insatiable,* that beautiful woman had called him. Relentless. But not with Kate. With Kate, a few simple moments had been enough, as if he were touching a comforting memory before falling asleep. But Kate wanted to be more than a memory to him. She wanted him to need the woman she'd become. She'd already spent half a lifetime married to a man who didn't want her. She wouldn't be that again.

A train hissed and chugged from somewhere out of sight. Metal screamed against metal as it drew nearer. It wasn't the train to Hull, but Kate watched intently as it slid toward the platform in a crazed cloud of steam. It would pull away again in thirty minutes and chug toward someplace very different from Hull. A place so far removed that Kate could hardly imagine it, and yet it had once been her whole world. This train would stop in Derby, at a station only two bare miles from her family's home.

It was a coincidence, surely, but Kate couldn't stop staring at the black beast flaunting itself in front of her. It would take her to the place where it had all begun. To the family that had sent her to Ceylon. To the people who'd rather she be dead than bothersome.

Kate was filled with the overwhelming urge to tell them that she'd survived.

What could they do to her, anyway? If they exposed her, they'd have to explain to the world how she'd managed to return from her watery grave. And it no longer mattered, regardless. Gerard had found her.

As soon as she'd left Aidan's home, she'd hailed a hack and driven straight for that solicitor's office. He'd refused to see her. What kind of planter's agent would refuse to see a coffee seller? She'd waited for hours, standing on the street outside, willing the solicitor to come out. He had never emerged, but someone else had, and all her suspicions had been confirmed. The white-haired dray driver who'd worked for Mr. Fost. He hadn't seen her as he'd shut the door behind him and descended the stairs. He'd looked like a man without a care in the world. As if spying on her had meant nothing. As if ruining her life was just another coin in his pocket.

And so it was. He'd taken a job with Mr. Fost, solely for the purpose of reporting back to this solicitor, and Kate had no doubt now, none at all. This life she'd built was about to end. Gerard had found her. She had to leave. So what did it matter if she made one small detour? Another day, a few hours. It could make no difference when the whole world was running through her fingers like sand.

Kate rose, purchased a ticket, and she boarded the train for home.

Everything was so familiar. Even the coming and going of the light as she walked down the drive. The even spacing of the chestnut trees broke the road into sun and shade, sun and shade. She must have walked up this drive a thousand times. Five thousand times. On Sunday mornings, after church. On Tuesday evenings after their weekly dinner with her widowed aunt. On every bright, sunny afternoon after visiting friends or exploring the woods. And always the light was sorted by these trees.

For a moment, Kate forgot the past and felt so free she nearly floated. She was home, at last. And it felt so right that she almost didn't care what they'd done to her.

Kate had missed her mother. She was a soft woman, and that quality had made her both comforting and weak. The weakness hadn't mattered to Kate until those last months. Before that, her mother had been a warm and pleasant presence in Kate's life.

Her brother had been less accessible. He'd always been away at school or off in London. Then he'd developed a passion for Italy. As a matter of fact, he was likely there now. He'd loved to spend his winters in Italy, and their father had only admonished him not to bring home one of those "dark-blooded women" as a wife.

The thought that she might find her mother alone sped Kate's footsteps until she reached the expanse of green lawn that stretched to the front steps. She flew across the lawn, racing all the way up the stairs. But then her eagerness deserted her.

Something about standing at the front door cut through

her fantasy of a happy return. After all, when had she ever stood here, begging entry? She'd tripped in and out the side doors or been ushered up these stairs by footmen, but she'd never stood on the lonely stone as if she were a stranger.

Kate turned the handle of the door and slipped inside.

The entry hall was dark and quiet. The curtains were open, but the windows caught no sun at this time of day. Somewhere deep within the house, Kate could hear the murmur of servants talking, lending a comfortable hint of life to the otherwise silent building.

Kate turned in a circle, but it was a restless spin. She was done with introspection now. Instead of looking over her old home and marking the changes, Kate moved quietly to the staircase and headed for her mother's upstairs parlor. Even before she reached the door, she could picture her mother, small and plump and curled up on her chaise with her needlepoint or tatting.

And there she was. Smaller now, and older. So much older than Kate had expected. Her hair had been the same dark brown as Kate's, but now it was liberally streaked with dull gray, and she squinted down at her needlework through tiny glasses.

Emotion swelled in Kate's chest, expanding until she couldn't breathe. Her mother stitched on, unaware.

Kate watched until she couldn't bear it anymore. "Mother," she croaked.

Her mother's frown intensified, then her gaze rose. For a moment, she didn't recognize her own daughter, and Kate could only hope her eyesight was to blame. Finally, shock overcame her, and the creases in her face relaxed as her eyes widened. "Katie?" she breathed, her work falling to her lap.

"Yes."

"Katie?" she repeated. "Is it really you?"

Kate nodded. "It's me." Her throat tightened, cutting off a chance to say more. When her mother smiled and opened her arms, Kate rushed forward to hug her.

She smelled the same. Of roses and starch, and it seemed so impossible that so much could be the same after ten long years.

"Oh, I've missed you, my sweet Katie. I thought I'd never see you again!" Her mother pulled back and frowned. "But whatever are you doing here in England?"

Kate ignored the question. "I can't stay long, Mother. I'm only passing through."

"But to where?"

"I . . ." She shook her head. "I wanted to see you and tell you I was well. Are you well?"

"Of course! Very well."

Kate nodded and made herself continue. "And I wanted to find out . . ."

Her mother watched her with clear, guiltless eyes.

"After I was sent away, Father told everyone I had died." Her mother's only response was a slow blink. "Is that true?"

"Well, yes, I'm afraid it is. I can't pretend I liked it. It was all so incredibly awkward. But . . . your father thought it best." Ah, yes. This was always her mother's response. How many times had Kate heard that as her things had been packed for Ceylon? As she'd begged her mother to intervene? Kate tried to bite back that old rage.

"I just want to know *why*. Why would he say I'd died? And why would you let him?"

"He did what he thought best—"

"You always say that!" she fumed. "Always!"

"He was the head of this family, Katie. He knew what was best."

"Do you honestly believe that? That it was best to send me to the ends of the earth to live with a *stranger?*"

"Well, he did not know, did he? He thought Mr. Gallow was a gentleman. He came with the highest recommendations. By the time your father heard about his troubles—"

"Troubles?"

"He was quite distressed that Mr. Gallow had presented himself as a respected member of the English community of Ceylon when in reality, he was . . . less than . . ."

"He'd gone native, Mother. That's what they call it when a white man takes up with a native woman. He did not want me. He only wanted the illusion of a white wife because the governor had threatened him with arrest!"

Her mother's cheeks turned bright red. "If your father had known—"

"Oh, certainly! There is nothing at all wrong with sending your only daughter across the sea to marry a stranger! Nothing at all! So long as he is a *respectable* stranger."

"Katie, please don't speak of your father in such a—"

"He told everyone I was dead!"

Her mother shook her head so hard that her cheeks quivered. "He thought it was best, Katie."

"Best?" Kate screamed. "Are you mad? Can you even hear yourself?"

"Once your father realized that the circumstances were . . . less than respectable . . . Well, it was too late to stop the marriage. You'd sailed two weeks earlier, and he was only afraid that it would appear mercenary. . . ."

Kate was so overwhelmed with confusion that she collapsed weakly into a chair. "Mercenary?"

"To have it known that he'd betrothed you to a man of such low moral fiber. The title, the family name . . . He was quite upset with Mr. Gallow for his dishonesty. He wrote and told him that he wasn't to use your name. He wasn't to advertise the family connection. It appeared . . . sordid."

"It *was* sordid, Mother."

"Yes," she finally conceded, her gaze falling to the floor. "I'm sure it was, my sweet girl."

Sweet, Kate thought with a sneer, feeling anything but sweet. "So he dusted off his hands as if he'd taken me out to the rubbish pile. He had his money—"

"Katie!" her mother gasped, still horrified by the mention of something so base.

"He had his money! Thirty-thousand pounds and another five for every year of the marriage, wasn't that it? A suspiciously high price for a bit of used goods like me."

Another gasp. Shock for the sake of propriety, but none for Kate herself, it seemed.

"And when Father realized just how mercenary it would appear, to have sold his daughter to a man so far outside polite society that even his friends had shunned him . . . when he realized how that would appear, he demanded it be kept quiet. But he did not ask for me back."

"What could he do?" her mother whispered. "It was done already."

"Yes," Kate said softly. "It was done. But I would still have liked to come home."

"I'm sorry, Katie," she said. The words were sincere, but still helpless, as if she could not fathom why Kate couldn't understand the issue. "But Mr. Gallow would never have sent you back."

Kate nodded, a ghost of an agreement. Even with the

new governor in place, David had needed her as a shield. An excuse for people to pretend they saw nothing. "I should go," she breathed.

"But you've only returned! And you haven't told me what happened!"

"What do you mean?"

Her mother looked sideways, as nervous as if they were in a roomful of people who might overhear. Then she leaned forward, eyes wide and secret. "We received a letter from your husband's son. And a visit from his solicitor."

Kate's skin turned to brittle ice. It was nothing more than what she'd suspected, but it still stunned her. "Whatever he's told you is a lie."

Her mother's voice dropped to a childish whisper, her eyes like saucers. "He implied that you . . . encouraged . . . your husband's death."

"And you believed him," Kate said flatly.

"No! I never did! And your brother didn't either. He said you weren't capable of it."

Well, more fool he. She'd smashed Gerard over the head and left him to bleed. She was capable of killing, but she hadn't been capable of killing David. They'd reached a truce, she and David. After the accident, when his legs had ceased to work properly, Iniya had moved into the big house to help care for him. And Kate had begun to see him as a human being instead of a monster.

David had been almost as trapped as she, because he'd truly loved Iniya. He would've married Iniya if he'd been able. He'd done everything but marry her, and that had been his mistake. He'd been shunned, mocked, reprimanded. And when he'd become an embarrassment to the English community of Ceylon, he'd been threatened with imprisonment. The governor had taken David's household as a personal affront. He'd made it his mission to see it changed. So David had made it his mission to replace the governor, and Kate's family had been his means to do that. That was all. It hadn't been personal in the least, even when he'd occasionally taken her to his bed.

The same accident that had scarred her cheek had broken David's spine. And though his health had improved over the years, he'd never truly recovered, and Iniya had stayed in the house. Kate hadn't found it in herself to resent the obvious love between them, but it hadn't helped her loneliness. Nor had it helped Gerard's resentment.

"I must go, Mother."

"But where have you been? Where are you living?"

"It doesn't matter. I won't be there long. But perhaps I'll visit again someday. You look well, and I'm happy for that."

"Oh. I see. Be careful, dear." Her hands fluttered as if she were helpless to say more.

Kate rose and kissed her mother's cheek before leaving. The scent of faded roses enveloped her, but she turned and walked out, ignoring the awful tug at her heart. She should stay the night, but she couldn't bear it. She needed to return to Hull and leave that place before she missed her chance.

David Gallow *had* been poisoned, and Kate couldn't prove she hadn't done it. She had no choice but to flee, and there was nothing to hold her back anymore.

Chapter 27

She woke on the train, disoriented and weary. The rocking kept her submerged in a half-sleep, and the dim light of dawn urged her to close her eyes again. There was so much to do when she got back to her shop. She couldn't simply walk away or she'd lose every cent of her investment. Better to sell everything outright. Even if she took a loss, she'd leave with something.

As she floated along through the countryside, she tried not to think of Aidan. She was almost glad for her current predicament, because she had no time to feel all the hurt and guilt and doubt.

But the next time she opened her eyes, he was there with such a sweet, sharp intensity that Kate gasped. Not him, but a man who looked almost exactly like Mr. Penrose staring at her over one of the seats. Kate jerked around to check behind her, certain that Aidan must be close by. Why would Mr. Penrose be on this train with her alone?

But Aidan was nowhere to be seen, and when Kate looked again to the man dropping hurriedly back into his seat, she wasn't entirely sure it *was* Mr. Penrose. This man, after all, was missing his hat, his hair looked as if it had been mussed and then matted down, and his normally pale skin was beet red . . . or at least the shell of his ear was. He hunched deeper into his coat.

Frowning, Kate checked behind her one last time before concentrating all her attention on the man ahead. A whole minute passed, maybe two. Then finally, his head poked slowly up, and he arched a look over his shoulder. When he saw her watching, his eyes widened, and she knew it was him.

Kate narrowed her eyes and surged to her feet. Mr. Penrose slipped low again as if she might give up at this sign of furtiveness. She marched forward and planted herself at his side. "What do you think you're doing?" she hissed, trying not to wake the sleeping passengers around her.

Penrose kept his eyes clenched shut.

"Mr. Penrose, I know it's you."

In the end, he could not suppress his compulsion toward good manners, and he rose to his feet, putting his hand to his forehead as if he'd remove a hat he did not have. Still, he didn't meet her eyes or say a word.

"Mr. Penrose," she said sharply, and his gaze finally rose to her. "Are you spying on me?"

"No, Mrs. Hamilton. Of course not."

"Where is Mr. York?" she demanded.

"In London, ma'am."

"He sent you after me? To follow me?" As she recognized that it must be the truth, her voice rose, and the people around them stirred.

Mr. Penrose slid over and gestured her to take his seat. "No," he whispered as she sat stiffly next to him. "He only asked me to see that you made it safely home. Nothing more. He didn't expect . . . I wasn't prepared . . ." He touched a hand to his forehead again. "I apologize for my appearance, ma'am. I've lost my hat. And I have no luggage."

Her anger softened. Poor Mr. Penrose. "You swear he didn't send you to watch me?"

"I swear on my honor. I was only to look out for your safety. I didn't expect you'd go anywhere but home. Mr. York would never mean for me to spy on you."

He had a point. Kate was getting her difficulties confused. Aidan wasn't the one who would follow her across the globe. "Well, I don't appreciate knowing I've been followed, sir. Though I suppose I must thank you for your care. As always, you are an amazingly dedicated employee."

Penrose flushed. "Mr. York deserves dedication. He is an exacting employer, but I'm learning more about the world of business than I could ever have hoped."

"I wonder who taught him," she murmured. "He is not very analytical."

Mr. Penrose frowned, looking uncomfortable. "I apologize for disturbing your rest, Mrs. Hamilton. Please pretend I'm not here."

She nodded, but didn't budge. She didn't want to go back to her seat now. Being near Penrose was a reminder of being near Aidan. Despite that she felt like a lovesick, broken fool, Kate missed him. Whether she'd meant anything to him, he'd meant something important to her, and that was gone now.

So Kate ignored the hint that she should return to her seat, and simply settled into this new one. From the corner of her eye, she saw Penrose staring at her. "What is it, Mr. Penrose?"

He shook his head and turned to stare straight ahead.

"I'm sorry that my trip to London has put you out. And I'm sorry that . . . you must have been upset to see me there."

"No, of course not. It's not that."

"What is it, then?"

He turned slowly back to her, and she met his troubled gaze. "He *is* very analytical. Mr. York, I mean."

That was what had upset him? Kate offered an appeasing smile. "I'm sure he's quite good at what he does."

"He is. He's efficient and cold and ruthless. He lives and breathes nothing but investments and income."

She held back a bitter laugh. "It may seem that way to you when you're working, but I assure you that he's always known how to enjoy his life, Mr. Penrose."

"That's not true."

She stiffened at his tone. "I believe I know him better than you."

"You don't, Mrs. Hamilton. I mean no disrespect, but I'm not sure you know him at all."

Kate gasped and drew back, letting him see every ounce of her outrage.

"I'm sorry. I know I'm being unbearably rude, but it seems likely I'll never see you again after this, and . . ."

"And that gives you leave to say outrageous things?"

His gaze fell for just a moment, and Kate was sure he would retreat. And so he should. How dare he pretend he knew *anything*.

But Penrose didn't retreat. When he looked at Kate again, his gaze was sharp and sorrowed. "I'd never seen him smile. Not truly. Do you know that?"

"That's ridiculous."

"I'm not saying he never smiled, Mrs. Hamilton. Just that I never saw it. Until he went to Hull."

Kate shook her head again, but she was the one who retreated, rising to scramble back to her seat and gather her cloak around her as if she could hide in it. Her stomach churned, and she held her breath, terrified that he would follow and say more ridiculous things. More stupid, hopeful nonsense things.

Despite that she'd donned her cloak, the cold from the window at her shoulder seeped into her as she sat, first chilling her hands, then her arms, then up to her chest and face. She shoved her hands into the deep pockets of her cloak, but her right hand touched something smooth and cold.

Her fingers instinctively clasped it tight, and she drew her hand free. When she uncurled her grasp, there was her grandfather's watch. It had comforted her on the train ride to London, but she saw it with much different eyes now.

It was the only jewelry he'd given her during this affair, and now it seemed symbolic. Simple, sentimental, used . . . pretty in a worn way. If he'd given gifts to his other mistresses, they'd been nothing like this. He would've given those women glittering jewels. Expensive baubles. Things to enhance their beauty.

She squeezed the watch hard in her fist, as hard as she could, wishing she could crush it, break it with her bare hand, destroy what he'd given her. The hinge dug into her palm, gifting her with bright spots of pain to distract her mind.

When she let it go, her palm throbbed and her mind flared back to clarity.

Aidan had let her believe he'd been empty, lonely, and now his man was trying to convince her of that too. That his life had been joyless before she'd reappeared. *Joyless*. As if it had been misery he'd been visiting between those women's legs.

He'd said himself that it had been the only way he could forget her. He'd buried her inside those women, and she couldn't forgive that.

But if her heart was so hard, why was she so terrified that Penrose would follow her and tell her more? Why did she feel sick at the thought?

In the end, it didn't matter. She wasn't forced to confront her fears, because Penrose let her be. She stared out the window, avoiding even a twitch in his direction as she watched the sky lighten into a gloomy day. And once they arrived in Hull in a flurry of sparks and steam, Kate pretended not to see him hover at the edge of the platform until she'd safely descended and turned toward home.

But this was not Ceylon, and she was not as weak as she'd once been. There was no gray pall to smother her feelings about Aidan. She tried to walk faster and leave them behind, but they gripped her, clutched at her, no matter how quickly she moved. They stayed with her past the docks and into the lanes and followed her down the dim alley toward her shop.

She unlocked her door, then shut it hard behind her. But a terrible foreboding followed her in. Her heart whispered frantically that she'd done something very wrong.

She answered it with stubborn silence.

Plodding up the stairs, Kate stopped at the top and looked listlessly around—saw her tiny, neat parlor, her undersized bed. She had to leave it all, but surprisingly, she felt no grief at that. After all her hard work, it seemed to mean nothing to her at all.

Chapter 28

The power of the horse beneath him was a relief. Each strike of hoof against ground felt as if it channeled some of Aidan's rage out of his body and into the depths of hell. But in the end, it channeled nothing, because as soon as he wheeled his mount to a stop and jumped down, his rage was back. He normally felt better after a ride, but today he was buried in his own emotions, and the idea of walking back into his brother's home made his skin crawl.

Still, he hadn't been able to stay another moment in London, in his big house full of nothing and no one. The house seemed nothing more than the building that had once held Kate. At least she had never been here.

His instructions to the groom were interrupted by the breathless voice of a footman. "Mr. York!" He rushed across the horse yard. "A letter, sir."

Aidan snatched the paper from the footman's outstretched hand and tore it open. Finally . . . news that she'd arrived in Hull. And that was it, he supposed. If she could not forgive him his past, what could he do? He hadn't died ten years before any more than she had. He'd had a life. He'd made mistakes.

But his outrage was as hollow as the rest of him. Mistakes, after all, were accidental. He'd made his willingly, and so they weren't mistakes at all. Just awful, awful choices. And he hated her for knowing them.

He'd come to his family home without thought. His mother's birthday was in two days, and she'd never forgive him for missing it, but that hadn't been his primary motivation. No, he'd returned home like any injured animal would. For comfort. Understanding. Or simply to howl in rage.

But it didn't matter where he was; he still thought of her. Why had she visited a solicitor's office in London? Surely she couldn't pursue divorce on her own? The cost would destroy her.

Her next stop had been even more mysterious. Derby. Her family's home. Had she visited them? Or just stopped to walk through her old world? Penrose hadn't offered details. And Aidan was too proud to ask, though he suspected he might change his mind sometime in the future.

Stealing in through a side door, Aidan rushed toward his room, intent on ordering a bath and dinner. Then he'd drink his way to sleep, God willing.

But as he passed the library, he knew he'd made a mistake in coming home. He wasn't alone here. Marissa called his name, and he came to a reluctant halt as she rose from a chair by the window, her face tight with worry.

"Pardon me," he growled. "I need a bath."

She frowned as if he were speaking a foreign language. "Come in, Aidan. Please? I need to speak with you."

He tried to temper his voice. "I'm sorry. I'm not in the mood for idle conversation right now."

"It's her," she said softly.

"I don't have the patience for riddles or—"

"It's Katie. Katie Tremont. You found her." The hope in her face made him scowl.

Aidan gave in with less grace than a mad dog, stepping into the library and slamming the door behind him. "Your husband has been telling tales."

"I was worried. You were—"

"It hardly matters now," he snapped. "I found her, yes. Congratulations on ferreting out the story, Marissa. It must be quite exciting for you."

"Stop it!" she ordered, her spine snapping straight. "You've no call to be cruel to me. Nor anyone else in this house. What are you even doing here?"

That stopped his raging heart. Did even his family not want him now? "What?"

"If you've found Katie, if you love her, what are you doing here, moping about?"

"She's married."

"And? You've already looked into dispensing with that obstacle."

"And?" he snapped. "And she knows about me."

"Knows what?"

This was not a conversation a man had with his sister. Aidan crossed his arms and glared at her, but Marissa simply stared back, eyebrows posed in a question. He cleared his throat and tried not to squirm.

"Well?" she pressed. "What is it?"

His outrage floated away, escaping him. "I'm not . . . That is . . . I have not been the man she expected me to be. I have not made myself proud, much less anyone else."

Aidan half-expected his sister to shush him and tell him how wonderful he was. But she only pressed her lips tight together.

He tried to feel irritated instead of embarrassed. "I see that you agree."

"You have spread yourself thin, by all accounts."

"Jesus," he bit out. When she shrugged, Aidan spun toward the door. "Well, then. You have your explanation."

"Don't. This is important. It's important to all of us, Aidan. Don't just leave."

"I don't want to talk about it."

"Well, you never want to talk about it. You want to hunch over it like a hermit with his treasure, raging at anyone who comes near. Is your pain so precious to you?"

"Don't be ridiculous."

"Do you think you're the only person who's ever lost anyone?"

"That's not it at all!" he shouted. "I'm ashamed of myself, and all I wanted was for her not to know. I just wanted to go back and be that other man. The man I was meant to be. But there's no going back, and no hiding the truth, and she will not have me now."

"Did she say that?" Marissa asked calmly.

"Of course she said that. What else could she say?"

"Perhaps she will change her mind."

"But she will know, and I can never take that away. Everywhere we go, every woman we meet, she will have to wonder, won't she? Every sly word or cunning smile . . . She will suspect, and sometimes she will be right. Could you live with that? Would Jude ask you to?"

"I don't know, but I suppose I have asked him to. Perhaps he is the one to advise you."

That brought him up short and pulled him from his selfish world. "That's not how it was with you, Marissa."

She shrugged again and dropped into her chair. "Not quite, no, but I was hardly pure, and every man wants a pure wife, doesn't he? But I am the woman he fell in love with, and so he accepts it."

"But it's different for Jude. He had his own life. He wasn't forced to live in misery while you 'spread yourself thin' as you said."

Marissa's face finally softened into sympathy. She took Aidan's hand, and pulled him to sit beside her. "Is that what happened to her, Aidan?"

"I don't know," he answered honestly. "I thought she was happily married. She implied that she'd been content. But then . . . she said things. I don't know what happened to her, and that hurts worse than I could imagine."

His sister squeezed his hand and laid her head on his shoulder. "Give her time. Go see her in a month or two. If she loves you, she'll forgive you."

He shook his head. "She deserves better."

Marissa sighed and wrapped both her hands around his. "You loved her so completely, Aidan. There is nothing better than that."

They sat in silence for a long while before Marissa kissed his cheek and rose. "I'll leave you to your brooding, then. For now."

"Pest."

She blew him another kiss and hurried out. He did not like this writhing hope she'd left with him. It was an awful thing and he wanted it gone. It reminded him too much of what Kate had said. That she'd waited for him. That she'd thought he would come for her.

What had been done to her?

Thoughts and fears wrestled inside his head. He wanted to scream, to rage, to injure. His imagination raced to provide him with fuel for his turmoil, filling his mind with things he could never wish to see. My God, she'd been so young and sweet and everything good in his life. What had been done to her?

Perhaps she did not need a divorce. Perhaps Aidan could rid the world of her husband. Hunt him down and kill him.

I was not a horse to be broken to another rider. A chill spread beneath his skin. He'd thought that he resented her love for another man, but he would take that back in an instant now. He'd give her the perfect husband to have loved for those ten years. Anything not to know that she had been broken.

"Ah, God," he groaned, pressing the heels of his hands to his eyes.

"Well, don't weep like a mewling child," a voice rasped from across the room.

Aidan sprang to his feet, twisting toward the sound. "What the devil?"

No, not the devil, only that sneaky old Aunt Ophelia pushing up from her chair hidden in the arch of the window. Again.

"Blast it," he muttered, stepping toward her automatically to help her rise. "I knew you were eavesdropping before, weren't you?"

"What?" she cried. "Speak up!"

Aidan closed his eyes and took a deep breath. She'd heard nothing. Thank God.

"Nothing, Aunt Ophelia!" he shouted.

"When's dinner?"

"Eight o'clock!" he yelled, then muttered, "Same as every night," under his breath. Her cane knocked his shin, ringing it like a bell.

She shuffled past him, her kerchiefed head reaching only half the height of his body. "You're a fool."

Aidan frowned and leaned closer, clasping her elbow to steady her frail body. "Pardon?" But she ignored him and shuffled all the way to the door, pulling her elbow from his grasp halfway across the room. "I've been walking for eighty years."

"Yes, ma'am."

She narrowed her half-blind eyes in irritation. "Puling babe."

Aidan tucked his chin in. "I'm sorry . . . What did you say?"

"Some men never get over teat-sucking for comfort."

He stumbled back in horror. "Aunt Ophelia! What did . . . ? You . . ."

She spun back toward him with surprising speed and pointed a crooked finger in his face. "I said grow up or I'll dress you in short pants like you deserve!"

Aunt Ophelia escaped before he could stop her, likely because he was paralyzed with confusion. He now had no idea if she had been eavesdropping or was simply mad as a fiend. He could certainly hear her muttering to herself as she moved slowly down the corridor. Aidan could only shake his head and hope that everything would make more sense tomorrow.

Chapter 29

Kate woke exhausted, and the irony was not lost on her. All day yesterday, she'd kept the shop locked and shuttered, too weary to even greet her neighbors. But despite her daytime exhaustion, she'd lain awake in a sea storm of twisting sheets for most of the night. Now that it was morning, she was finally tired again.

It wasn't fair, and she wanted to lay abed and weep, but there was no time for that.

She took her boots from the wardrobe, avoiding the sight of her blue dress and the memories of him. In the near dark of the room, she washed with water that she was too tired to heat, sending trails of goose bumps marching over her skin. Lamplight flickered, softening the angles of her body, sparkling off the small drops of icy water. She smoothed the cloth between her breasts, watching, remembering. Her nipples tightened almost painfully at the cold touch, but her eyes saw them peak and harden for Aidan, saw his hands stroke over her instead of her own.

Lust swept over her, startling and unexpected. Its

intensity nearly buckled her knees. The very core of her tightened and heated, and the urge to close her eyes and stroke again, to think of Aidan and his jaded skills . . . it took her breath away.

Oh God, her body was not her own anymore. Of course, that had been true in her marriage also, and she'd learned to live with that. But this was a different sort of ownership altogether, binding her with her own needs, her own memories. This was so much more insidious, so much easier to embrace.

Angered by her desire, she finished washing quickly, scrubbing with a harsh hand at her body. Without even taking the time to dry, she pulled on her clothes. The worn linen shift, the woolen stockings, the loose corset and shapeless brown dress. Nothing that any of Aidan's other women had worn, she was sure of it.

She could not imagine living like this every day. A tight, uncomfortable ache weighted down her stomach, a feeling that she'd forgotten something important, something crucial. A sense of foreboding had overtaken her last night, and she'd been on guard before she'd even opened her eyes.

"It's Gerard worrying me," she whispered to herself as she pulled on her worn, ugly boots. "That's all."

But that wasn't one of the thoughts that had tortured her through the night. Instead, she'd thought of Aidan. She couldn't seem to steel her heart against him.

If she still loved him, it didn't matter. The fantasy that she could take him, take his body, his heart, everything he offered, now seemed impossible. How could it work? Even in the short-term, how could she please a man who'd likely had every woman he'd ever asked for?

The answer was that she couldn't. *Insatiable,* the woman had called him. *Insatiable.*

It still stung like fire, seared her lungs, her throat. How many women had said the same about him?

Every moment with him, every touch, every kiss they'd shared had seemed special, almost sacred. She felt betrayed and foolish now. Beyond foolish—stupid. She'd trusted him. She'd trusted him to overlook her hesitance and fear when they made love, to not even notice her lack of skill. Now, with the truth between them, she realized how hopeless that must have been. He'd likely been bored.

Perhaps that was the greatest source of her anger, that he had offered her such joy—such fierce joy—under a false pretense. The pretense that he found her arousing in some specific way. The truth was that his arousal was an easy thing. He'd admitted it himself. Those women had meant nothing to him, and still he'd had them.

Muttering a curse, she pushed to her feet to stomp downstairs. The stove didn't dare to defy her this morning, and her coffee and salt pork were both hot within minutes. Perhaps this would be her last small meal here. If she could sell the shop today . . . But no, that was a ridiculous fantasy. She'd never sell it so quickly, but there still might be a way to steal away today.

She couldn't in all good conscience call on the Cains this early, so Kate spent time going through her ledgers and copying everything she wished to take with her. It was only then that the sadness hit her. She hadn't been born with this dream, but she'd made it hers out of necessity. Now what would she do?

Undoubtedly, it could be nothing to do with coffee this time, not if she wanted to leave Gerard behind. Perhaps she would simply sail to America and decide what to do with herself once she'd landed. Plenty of others did exactly the same, and surely Gerard would never find her in a place so immense. She could disappear as she had before. It would be as if she'd never returned to England. Just as well. She never should have.

When she looked up from her ledgers, thin bars of light slanted past the edges of the curtains over the front window. It was later than she'd thought.

She snuck out the back, pulling the hood of her cloak low against the vulnerable feeling she'd worn since returning to Hull. The Cains lived blocks away, but Kate kept her head down and avoided meeting anyone she knew along the way. By the time the housekeeper let her into the Cain home, Kate had held her breath so long that she was dizzy. She gulped air and paced in the entry hall until Lucy rushed out of a room halfway down the wide corridor of the house.

"Lucy!" Kate called, hurrying toward her as if she were a lifeline. "I'm so glad you're here. I need another favor, I'm afraid."

Lucy glanced over her shoulder, raising her hands.

"I'm sorry to impose. And it is an imposition, but—"

"Kate!" she whispered, her hands wrapping around Kate's wrists. She looked behind her again, and kept walking so that Kate had to move backward.

"Lucy, what . . . ?"

"Your husband!"

"What?"

And then he was there. Not her husband, of course. Not his ghost. It was Gerard stepping out of the same room Lucy had come from. He was here. Right here. His mouth stretching into a smile, his arms opening in welcome.

Kate gasped out a choked cry and scrambled two steps back.

"Darling," he said. "It's me." Though he smiled even wider, his eyes were like coals burned to ash.

"Poor thing," Mr. Cain said, patting Gerard on the back. "She looks shocked to her very core. You should have warned her you were coming, sir."

"Well, I thought to surprise her, but I see it's too much. She always was a delicate thing. Come, Mrs. Hamilton, and greet your long-lost husband."

Though she was standing still, she felt as though she were speeding down a tunnel. Choices flashed past her and she couldn't grab any of them. What should she do? What should she do?

If she exposed him, then he would expose her. He could accuse her of assault and calumny and murder, and who would defend her? They'd only know her as a liar. A woman who'd used a falsehood to settle into their midst. How could she claim innocence when she'd lied about so many things already? Her name, her husband, even the place she'd come from.

In the end, she made no decision at all. She simply let herself be swept into his embrace, wincing as he hugged her. Oh, God. Oh, God. What was she going to do?

Mr. Cain made a joke, seeming unaware of Kate's horror. But just before Gerard released her, Kate met Lucy's gaze. Her friend's eyes were filled with confused fear. Kate wondered what her own looked like.

"I am so thankful for your hospitality, Mr. Cain," Gerard said, turning to shake the man's hand. "I was quite at a loss when I arrived in port and could not locate my own wife!"

Male laughter filled the hall. It sounded like the horrid barking of wild dogs.

"Come," Mr. Cain said, "we've just poured tea."

"I should really . . . I should get back to the shop. . . ."

Another round of loud laughter.

"She's in shock," Gerard said with a pleased smile. "But much as the sight of my lovely wife renews me, I'm still parched. And Mr. Cain was just telling me that you'd gone to London, darling. Whatever were you doing there?"

Kate watched Lucy flinch and tried to school her own features to calm. "A coffee roaster," she made herself say with only a slight tremor to her voice. All she could think was *Gerard is here. Gerard is here.*

And everything was over.

"A roaster?" he asked.

"Yes. I was hoping to strike a deal with him directly."

Her mouth was working, and her feet too, as they were moving past open doorways now. Once they reached the morning room, Gerard led her to sit next to him on the settee and Lucy filled another cup for her.

Luckily, Mr. Cain asked a question about the ship that had brought Gerard to Hull, and Kate was free to indulge in panicked thinking.

She was trapped. Trapped by her own lies. She'd flown so far from her past, and yet it was here again, and there was nothing she could do to change that.

"—didn't you, Katherine?"

Her head jerked up at her name, and she realized she'd been concentrating on her tightly clasped hands. "Pardon?"

"I think perhaps I'd better take her home, after all," Gerard said. "And after all your kind words about the shop, Mr. Cain, I find I can't wait to finally see it."

"Yes, yes," Mr. Cain said, helpfully waving them toward the door. "Go and enjoy each other's company. But I insist you return for dinner tonight."

"We couldn't," Kate said quickly, shaking her head as she stood and backed toward the corridor.

"Nonsense," Gerard offered with a hard smile. "I'm eager to acquaint myself with your new friends. All of them."

Even Lucy paled at those ominous words, though her father still smiled indulgently.

"Kate," Lucy said too loudly, and Kate jumped at the sound. "I have the gloves my maid mended for you."

"Gloves?" Kate whispered.

She nodded. "Yes, let me fetch them." She grabbed Kate's hand and pulled her from the room. Kate saw that Gerard wanted to follow, but he was stuck with Mr. Cain, who was speaking about the timber trade.

"What is he doing here, Kate?" Lucy whispered.

"I don't know."

"Does Mr. York know he's here?"

Kate shot a nervous glance toward the door of the morning room. "Shh. Of course not."

"Then I shall write and—"

"No! No, you can't."

Lucy took Kate's hand between both her own. "Please, Kate. You look so scared. He can't be a good man."

"Katherine," Gerard's voice called. "Are you ready?"

Kate eased her hand away from Lucy's. "It will be fine. Don't worry. And thank you for being a friend to me, Lucy."

"But if you—"

His shadow darkened the doorway, and Kate pushed Lucy toward the front hall. "The gloves!"

There were no gloves, of course, but surely Lucy must have a pair she was willing to part with. And indeed, by the time Gerard looped her arm through his and steered her toward the door, Lucy was rushing back with gloves clutched in her hand.

"Thank you," Kate said. "Thank you so much."

Lucy gave her a tight hug, but Gerard retrieved Kate's arm as soon as her friend let her go. Kate allowed him to hold on to her until they'd stepped into the street and the Cains' door closed behind them. Then she jerked away and stumbled a few steps back.

"Katherine," he said in warning.

"Why did you pretend to be my husband?" she demanded.

"I needed to find you. What else would you have had me say? Surely not the truth."

She shook her head and started walking, rushing as if she could escape him. Heads turned in her direction, but she didn't care. Gerard's footsteps stayed close behind her, though he didn't try to touch her again.

There was no point in rushing to her shop as if it would offer sanctuary, but she simply could not maintain this ruse for more than a few moments. Gerard made her skin crawl and her belly draw up. She could not stroll down the lane as if he were a beloved husband.

When she reached the shop door, she hit her knuckles far too hard against the bright and cheerful wood. The pain rang up to her elbow and slithered to her shoulder. The keys dropped to the ground.

"Here, darling. Let me."

"Mr. Hamilton!" a voice called. Kate glanced back to see Gulliver Wilson standing in the doorway of his tobacco store. His eyes were bright with hostile pleasure. "I see you found your wife!"

"I did. Thank you for your assistance, sir."

Kate heard the keys clink and then the gasp of the door opening. She closed her eyes against Gulliver Wilson's grin and let herself be led inside.

Chapter 30

"How could you have done that to me?" he growled, slamming the door behind him, plunging them into the dark.

Kate backed up, arms stretched out behind her, trying to find the archway that led to the back rooms. But his hand snaked out and grabbed her shoulder. His other hand curved around the nape of her neck, fingers tightening like a vise.

"After what you did to my father!"

"Stop it! I didn't do anything."

"Don't lie to me. I was trying to help you—"

She tried to shake her head, but his grasp was too tight. She latched her hands around his wrist. "You're hurting me."

"As you have hurt me!" But he let her go, pushing her aside with a curse.

Her eyes had adjusted, and she could see now, but so could Gerard. When she edged toward the back, his gaze slid to the alley door.

"Let me make this clear, Katherine. If you run off, I'll

tell everyone who'll listen that you killed my father. I'm done chasing you."

"I didn't kill him!"

"Don't treat me like a fool! Am I to think he died naturally, with blue lips and white fingers? With the smell of poison on his mouth? I saw you go into that room, damn it. And I saw his body afterward."

Kate pressed her hand to her mouth and shook her head. She knew exactly what David had looked like. It had haunted her dreams for weeks afterward.

"I'm trying to help you."

"By tormenting me?" she shot back.

"Would you rather go to prison?"

"I didn't do it! I would never have hurt him. Never!"

"Good Christ, Katherine, you were the one who hurt him in the first place!"

"Oh," she breathed, shocked at having it said aloud. Yes, she'd wanted to blame herself for David's accident at first, but David had brushed aside her apologies. It had been her first hint that he was a human being and not the monster she'd considered him. "It was an accident," she said.

"I can understand your feelings, Katherine," Gerard said, as he paced across the room to idly open one of the bins. "You were forced to marry a man you didn't want, then even made to live in the same house as his mistress. He refused you his affections, gave you no children. How could you not hate him?"

"I didn't hate him."

"You told me you did."

"That was *before,*" she argued.

"Before you tried to kill him the first time?"

"Stop it!" she yelled. "I never tried to hurt him, and

you're the only person who's ever said such an awful thing."

"Ha! You don't really think that, do you? The whole island has been transfixed by my father's story for years. Add in a mysterious young wife, a tragic accident, a sordid living arrangement, and a suspicious death. . . . Good God, they suspected you of murder even before you tried to kill me."

"You attacked me."

"I wanted to *help* you. No one else believes anything you say. Look at the liar you've made of yourself, Katherine."

Terror opened up inside her. He was right about that, if nothing else. She slid one foot back, taking herself closer to the door. "Why did you come here? What do you want?"

"That's up to you." He offered a flat smile. His black hair slipped over his forehead, and he looked startling young when he pushed it back. When she slid her foot back again, he glanced toward the door and shook his head. "You've already proven yourself guilty by running once. The authorities wanted to charge you with murder, but I talked them into waiting."

That stopped her in her tracks. Ice formed inside her chest. "What?"

"I can't hold them off forever."

"What did you tell them?" she demanded.

"I haven't told them anything. You're not listening to me. I'm trying to help you. I was trying to help you the night you left—"

"If that's what you call help—"

He lunged for her, wrapping his hands around her upper arms to shake her. "Listen to me, damn it. I hardly think one kiss is too much to ask for saving your life.

And to think you repaid me by nearly breaking my skull open."

"I'm sorry. I didn't mean—"

"You will have to answer to the authorities one way or another. Did you think you could flee Ceylon after my father's death, and people would shrug and say fare-thee-well?"

"I don't know. I . . ."

His eyes burned like dark ice in the dimness of the shop. His lips pressed tight to his teeth when he spoke. "You need me, Katherine. Come home with me and I'll tell them you were out riding the day he died. I'll swear you couldn't have hurt him. Or stay here and I'll tell them the truth."

"I didn't hurt him!"

"Damn it, I don't care if you hurt him, don't you see that?"

His hands were squeezing bruises into her arms. The sound of his panting filled her ears.

"He was supposed to bring you to Ceylon for me," Gerard said. "And he ruined everything. Even when that bastard died, he ruined everything."

She saw true sorrow in his eyes then. Torment instead of madness. "Gerard . . ."

"I want to take care of you. You were the only good thing in my life. Ever. I just want you to come home."

"I'm sorry," she whispered. "I can't go back. I don't belong there."

His hands slowly loosened. The sorrow in his eyes faded to disappointment. "You're tired," he said.

"I'm tired of being afraid."

He shook his head. "There's no need to be afraid of me. I'd never hurt you."

"Just go home. Please. I'm begging you."

Gerard opened his hands and stepped back as if to show that he meant no harm. "You've had a shock. Lie down and rest before dinner tonight."

"Just go," she begged, but she could see he didn't mean to respond. He kept his mouth flat and gestured toward the stairs.

Kate couldn't escape today, not truly. So she walked up the stairs and tried not to remember the way she'd walked onto that ship to Ceylon. She felt that helplessness again. That same weakness.

And yet . . . And yet this was a moment. A choice, just like the choice she'd faced when she'd let her father lead her onto that ship. She could give in to whatever Gerard planned. She could be terrified and foolish and certain of her powerlessness . . . or she could make the right choice this time. The choice she hadn't made before. She could be strong.

Yes, this time would be different. And if Gerard wanted the truth, she'd have to give it to him, no matter what she'd promised David.

Gasping back a choked cry, Kate opened her eyes to blackness. Her neck tingled as the tiny hairs at her nape rose, warning her of the danger.

Though her eyes rolled wildly, she could see nothing, nothing. For one long, terrible moment, she was back in Ceylon, where night fell like black wool, where this feeling came often. She was suddenly sure that Ceylon had reclaimed her, that England had been a dream, Aidan a fantasy. In that moment, brief and heart-wrenching, she thought she would dare anything to have him back again. Anything.

Lying there, stiff with shock, too frightened to even

shake, she sensed the minutes tick past. Her heart finally receded, dropping back into her chest where it usually lived, and reality eased its way closer.

This was not Ceylon. This was England. She gulped at cold air, fighting to ease the sharp burning of her lungs, to calm her driving pulse. Her panic was fading, but the sense of wrongness remained.

"Gerard," she whispered, holding herself still.

He'd shut the curtains and the bedroom door, but he was waiting in the parlor.

She could scarcely believe that she'd slept, but her sleepless nights had caught up with her. He'd be coming in to wake her soon. Dinner couldn't be far off, and he was determined to go. Determined to play at being her husband, just as he'd always wanted.

Her heart jumped at every sound, every creak of the old building. Her eyes continuously slid to the parlor door, imagining footsteps. Eventually, though, her pulse began to slow to a more reasonable pace.

She was left in the company of a different sort of anxiety, not based on fear, but on hope. Aidan. When she'd awakened, certain that her time with him had been a dream, she'd thought she'd dare anything, risk everything, to be with him. The thought had been straightforward, uncomplicated: Nothing mattered except the chance to love him.

But only the chance. When he found out that she had no husband, he'd hate her for that. He must.

Still, there was a chance, and this time she'd take it.

She rose and lit the lamp, then washed in the basin and opened the wardrobe.

"Wear the blue," Gerard said from the doorway.

Her muscles tightened painfully as her heart forced

a wave of blood through her veins. She hesitated, staring at the blue stripes aglow against dark wood.

"The blue," he repeated, and she heard the scrape of his boots turning to retreat back to the parlor. Kate dressed as quickly as she could, afraid he'd reappear again without warning.

Though he swept her with an approving look when she emerged, he didn't say a word during their walk to the Cains'. He was like his father that way. Quiet and serious. At least he didn't try to force her to laugh and flirt with him. They simply moved through the cold night like strangers, both staring straight ahead.

After dinner tonight, she'd tell him the truth, and then perhaps he'd go. If she could get him to leave on his own, to return to Ceylon without her, everything would turn out well. Better than well, because her masquerade would be stronger than ever after her mysterious husband had made an appearance.

She would not be ruined. She would not have to leave.

She shot him a look from the corner of her eye. "I can never be your wife, you know."

"I know. Not legally. But I hate that place without you."

"But, Gerard . . . I am happy *here*. Can't you see that?"

He shook his head, but as they walked, he frowned down at the ground as if he were puzzling through a problem. Was it possible he was actually listening to her?

"I have my shop here. A simple life. It's all I want."

"We're late for dinner," he muttered.

Kate let it be. They obviously weren't sailing for Ceylon tonight. She had time. And better than that, she had a plan. He wasn't mad. He'd only been grief-crazed that night he'd pushed her onto the bed and kissed her.

He lusted after her, yes, but he did not hate her. She could fix this. And if she couldn't, this time she wouldn't be a fool. Aidan had promised his help before, and if it came to it, she'd run to him. She could pretend that she didn't trust him, but that was only hurt and jealousy. She trusted him with her life. She always had. It was why she'd given herself to him in the first place.

By the time they reached the Cain home, she was almost relaxed, but when the door opened, she found it was more than just Lucy and her father awaiting them.

Gulliver Wilson was there as well, and his wife, a sharp-nosed woman with icy eyes. They both stared at Kate with gleaming interest as everyone was ushered toward the dining room. Mr. Cain made a joke about their lateness, observing that it must have been a happy reunion.

Kate avoided speaking to any of them, even Lucy, until they were all seated.

"Well, Mr. Hamilton," Gulliver Wilson drawled, "I can assure you that we've all been looking after your lovely wife."

"Thank you, Mr. Wilson," Gerard said without a hint of deceit in his expression. "I can't pretend I haven't worried."

"I am surprised you would send her ahead on her own. . . ."

Gerard made a dismissive noise and brought the soup spoon to his mouth without responding. Mr. Wilson looked irritated.

"The shop is quite popular!" Lucy said into the silence. "What did you think of it?"

But Gulliver Wilson was determined to make trouble. "Your friend Mr. York was especially attentive to Mrs. Hamilton," he said. Kate felt her face flush. Even Mr.

Cain could not miss the implication and frowned in Wilson's direction.

"York?" Gerard said.

"Yes," Wilson said with a smile. "Mr. Aidan York of London. He visited several times. Said he was an associate of yours."

Gerard's gaze slid to her. "Yes, of course. I hadn't thought he'd made it back to England yet."

"You'll be happy to know he's been here for months," Wilson said, his sly grin widening.

Lucy glared at him. "How is your brother, Mr. Wilson?" she asked loudly.

Wilson coughed and blustered, but Gerard's eyes were still on Kate. She tried to keep her expression flat, but she couldn't keep the color from her cheeks. She wanted to leap over the table and stab Mr. Wilson with her fork. She wanted to jump up and scream at them all that Gerard was not her husband and she was free to do as she pleased. But she only sat there, eating slowly so that her knotted stomach wouldn't betray her.

Lucy's eyes were wide and liquid with worry, but Kate avoided her gaze. She did not like lying to her friend, but she had no choice.

The tension remained all through dinner, with Gulliver Wilson continuously hinting that she'd been a less-than-perfect wife during her stay in Hull. No one suggested they linger over port. Indeed, Mr. Cain seemed eager to see everyone out the door. Gerard took her arm too roughly, and soon enough she was whisked away.

"You are happy here?" he hissed into her ear. "Because of the shop? Because you enjoy slaving away like a merchant's wife? By God, you are a damned liar, is what you are."

"I am not."

"Who is he?"

"Gulliver Wilson despises me. He is goading you, hoping I'll get a beating."

"You didn't answer my question."

Kate hesitated, but finally his fingers dug so deep into her arm that she couldn't stay quiet. "Mr. York is an importer, nothing more."

"Yet you told people he was a friend of your husband."

She swallowed hard, focusing on the stones of the street. "What does that matter? I was trying to shut that awful Mr. Wilson up. I don't even have a husband."

He didn't say another word, and she thought he'd left the matter behind, but when they reached the shop, he locked the door behind him and threw the key across the room so hard that it cracked against a bin. "I actually thought you were telling the truth. That you wanted to be here, alone, at peace."

She hurried toward the stairs. He tried to grab at her arm, but she scooted around him and stormed up the steps. "I've done nothing wrong, just as I did nothing wrong in Ceylon."

"It doesn't matter. You're returning with me. Whoever this man is, he can rot for all I care."

She paced across her small parlor, back and forth, while Gerard watched her. "I am free, and you will not take that from me!"

"We shall see about that," he growled.

"Listen to yourself! What happened to you? You were a boy with hopes and dreams when I met you. You wanted things from life that had nothing to do with Ceylon. But you can have any life you want now, don't you see that? You are free too. As free as I am."

"I am not free," he snapped.

She reached out to grab at his sleeve. "Sell the plantation. You can go anywhere. Be anyone."

His hand closed over her arm with brutal speed. "He paid a fortune for you."

She tried to pull away and failed. "What?"

"He paid *my* fortune for you. All that money he sent your father just to shut up that blasted governor . . . he mortgaged the plantation to the hilt. But he didn't give a damn because he had his beloved Iniya. So don't tell me I'm free. I'll be buried in that cursed place as surely as my father was."

She'd had no idea. David had never said a word. "I'm sorry, Gerard. I truly am. I would never have wanted that for you."

Gerard cursed and his hand fell away. He ducked his head, fists on his hips, and glared hard at his boots.

"I need to tell you something," she finally said, hating the words that were about to come out of her mouth.

"What?" he asked, sounding exhausted already.

"About your father."

His head rose. "What?"

"Your father. He . . . he did die from poisoning."

"I knew it." For a moment his face twisted with rage.

Kate raised her hands. "But I did not give it to him."

That caught him back from his anger. He pulled his chin in. "What do you mean?" Then his eyes widened. "Good God, it was Iniya, wasn't it? I can't believe that never occurred to me."

"No, it wasn't. . . . That is . . . she didn't kill him, Gerard."

"Well, somebody damn sure did, and you seem to know a lot about it."

She said a silent prayer. An apology to David for revealing the truth. "Gerard . . . he did it himself."

Gerard frowned at her, clearly not understanding what she'd said. She felt a sharp stab of grief for him. Despite all their differences, Gerard had loved his father.

"What the hell are you saying?"

"For a long while, he thought he was getting better, regaining strength. But for those last few years, he left the bed less and less often. He could no longer ride. He asked me to bring him poison, and I refused. For weeks. But someone must have brought him some."

"Iniya."

"I don't know. It could've been one of the servants. Any of them. He took it, and called me up to him. He'd already said good-bye to Iniya. He wanted to say good-bye to me."

"But not to *me?*" Gerard roared.

"You were his heir. He felt he'd done what he could for you. But he had money for me. Enough so that I could leave. And Iniya, of course. He wanted to see her settled. And . . ." She swallowed hard. "And he didn't want you to know that he'd taken his own life. I'm sorry."

"I don't believe you," he said simply.

"He didn't want his son to think he was weak—"

"I don't believe that he committed suicide!"

"Oh, Gerard. He was tired. I tried to talk him out of it, I swear. So did Iniya."

"You should've told me!"

Kate's shoulders dropped. She'd hoped it had been idle talk on David's part. She hadn't thought he'd really do it. "You're right, of course. Perhaps you could've stopped him. I could not. But he made us promise we would never tell you. In the end, there was nothing I could do but hold his hand. . . ." Her throat closed with the memory. Iniya had stroked his face and whispered comfort into his ear. At least he'd had her there at the end.

Gerard dropped into a chair and slumped over the table, head in his hands. Though he didn't make a sound, she knew by the way he shook that he was weeping. Whatever was between them now, she'd known him for so many years. Kate put her hand to his shoulder. "If it's a comfort to you . . . he didn't have any doubt that you could run the plantation. None at all. He was proud of you."

His silent sobs eventually faded. Kate poured a glass of wine and brought it to him. He drank it all in one long draw.

"Are you all right?"

"Go to bed," he growled.

"Gerard . . ." She reached to touch him again, and that was a horrible mistake. Gerard spun and caught her to him, crushing her with his strength. He pressed his forehead to her bosom and wrapped his arms around her waist.

For a moment, she let him hold her, thinking he needed comfort. She kept her hands high and tried to breathe past the vise of his arms.

But then he shifted, dragging his face higher until his mouth touched the bare skin of her chest. "My God, I love you."

"Don't . . ."

"Please," he whispered, opening his mouth against the rise of her breast. "I need you. I need you."

"Stop. Stop!" She dug her fingers into his head and pushed as hard as she could.

He finally shoved her violently away. "Go!" he shouted. "Get out of my sight."

She stumbled toward her bedchamber, relieved he'd let her go, afraid that he'd follow. But his next words turned that fear into despair.

"We'll book passage to Ceylon tomorrow."

Kate grasped the doorjamb and whirled back to him. "What?"

He poured himself another glass and downed that one as well.

She shook her head. "No. I told you what happened. I'll write a letter, explaining it."

His face had twisted with rage. "You can tell them yourself. And see if they believe you."

Worried that she was making everything worse, Kate closed the door and sank down to sit on the edge of the bed.

If Gerard hadn't come to his senses by morning, she would have to send for Aidan after all. It was her only choice. Hopefully, he'd find a way to forgive her. Whatever happened, she would not set foot on that ship. No one could make her go this time.

Chapter 31

"Penrose!" Aidan shouted, slamming open the door of their rented quarters. "Penrose! Damn it, man, what the hell did you mean, sending that ridiculous message?"

He sped up the stairway, his boots echoing like explosions against the plain wooden stairs. "Penrose!"

His secretary didn't greet him when he reached the rooms. Aidan threw back the covers of Penrose's rumpled bed in case he'd somehow flattened himself into the mattress.

Christ, he was losing his mind.

Miss Cain has requested your urgent assistance. Please return to Hull as soon as you're able. Discretion prevents me from saying more.

What the hell could that mean? He couldn't wait to find out. If Penrose couldn't tell him, then Lucy would.

Growling in frustration, Aidan wheeled around and pounded back down the stairs.

It had to be Kate. Perhaps she was with child. What other kind of emergency could possibly call for such discretion? If she was . . . Despite all the impossibilities of such a thing, his heart beat with hard joy. He'd marry her. He'd kill her husband himself if he had to, but he'd marry Kate if she carried his child.

If she was still determined to resist, he'd convince her. He'd move to Hull and sit on her doorstep every day and show her that he deserved her love.

Aidan burst from the door, nearly knocking down a boy running past. "Sorry," he muttered to the startled child as both of them blinked at each other in shock. Finally, the boy ran on, and Aidan snapped the door shut behind him. But he'd only taken two steps when someone called his name.

"Mr. York!" Penrose rushed toward him, one hand raised in alarm.

"Penrose, where the hell have you been?"

"I thought you'd be on the eight o'clock train. I meant to meet you. . . ."

"I came through Leeds. The first train I could get."

Penrose leaned over, fighting to catch his breath, but Aidan wasn't sympathetic. He grabbed the man's collar and hauled him up. "What the hell is going on? Is it Kate? What's happened?"

"Mr. York," Penrose gasped. "Mrs. Hamilton has . . ." He gestured vaguely toward the coffee shop.

Aidan gave him a shake, then forced himself to let Penrose go when passersby began to stare. "Spit it out."

He didn't realize just how hopeful he'd been until Penrose spoke four awful words. "Her husband is here."

The shock forced Aidan back a step. "What?"

"Mr. Hamilton. He arrived on a ship three days ago."

One more step back and Aidan's heel hit the wide stairway of a bank. He sat down hard.

"Mr. York!" Penrose reached out, but Aidan waved him off with a slow sweep of his hand.

"What did Kate say?"

"I didn't speak with her, sir. Miss Cain asked me to send for you. She seemed . . . overwrought."

Fear took over his gut. "Why?"

Penrose's gaze darted up and down the walk as if he were afraid of being overheard. He leaned closer. "She said that his return was unexpected and that Mrs. Hamilton seemed quite alarmed, but otherwise nothing was amiss."

"What did Kate say?"

Penrose cleared his throat. "I don't know that she said anything at all, but I thought you should like to know."

"Yes," he murmured. "Of course. Thank you, Penrose."

His secretary cast another nervous look around. "Sir, perhaps we should discuss this in your rooms. If—"

"I'll go see her now. Wait here for word."

"Mr. York, are you sure that's—"

But Aidan waved him off and surged to his feet. Her husband was here. Aidan tried to find some way this could be a good thing, but it couldn't be, no matter how quickly he turned it in his mind. Neither could he find a way to convince himself that rushing to see her was a good idea, but here he was, nearly running down the lane. What would he say? How could he look this man in the face?

Aidan had no answers. All he could think was that he must get to her now, now, before she was lost for good.

The front of the shop was still locked up tight, so he circled to the back, his heart beating so hard he could hear nothing but his own fear. He tried the alley door as if he had the right to simply walk into her home, but that door was locked tight too.

Aidan banged his fist against the wood, then waited, glaring a hole into the tops of his boots. When there was no answer, he banged again, harder this time, until the door bruised his hand. Still nothing. “Answer, damn you.”

Where was she? Where had she gone?

He let his head fall back in frustration, staring up at the narrow slice of blue sky above the alley. The view felt right, as if he were sinking beneath the ground and clawing uselessly at the earth.

A few deep breaths later and he only felt more determined. A quick look ensured that not one other soul graced the alley. Aidan tried the lock one last time, dared another glance around, and then he slammed his foot into the door as hard as he could. It shook and creaked, but the lock held. Offering a quick, unspoken promise to pay for the repair, Aidan put all his strength into one hard thrust with his foot, and the wood cracked and gave. He tugged it open and half the lock fell to the brick ground.

Dark silence greeted him. No outraged cries, no pounding feet. Just silence. He hesitated for a moment, foot poised on the threshold, worried what he might find inside. But stillness had never been his gift, so he moved forward, checking the shop first, and finding nothing out of order.

He made himself take the stairs at an even pace, though he kept his footsteps light. At first, Kate’s rooms looked perfectly normal too, but as his eyes adjusted, he realized something was . . . off. Her neat parlor was still neat, but things were out of place. He pushed the curtain back from the small window to let in more light. The first thing he saw was a crate packed with books and plates and silver . . . and the folded chess set he’d given Kate. Next he saw a bare table where there had once been a clock and a flower vase. A small chest sat next to the table, and Aidan crouched before it and slowly raised the lid.

It was clothing, packed carefully as if for travel. Men's clothing.

All his muscles seized up and he jumped to his feet, letting the top fall shut. He turned to the bedroom, but there was no relief there. Kate's bed, small as it was, took up most of the space, and he did not want to look at it. Not now. But there was nowhere else to look. The small dresser had once held her brush and comb and mirror. They were gone, along with the pots of cream and powder and the pins that held her hair. And at the foot of her bed, another chest, this one standing open and filled with Kate's clothes.

Her husband was here, and she was leaving. Going away from Aidan without a word. Again.

The strength he'd always felt in her, the passion and certainty . . . What had that been? Nothing solid. Nothing real.

She'd rather go back to India with a man she didn't want than stay here and fight for their love. She was angry at him, hurt, and so she'd leave again.

Barely able to feel his own movements, Aidan turned away from the bedroom. He turned away from her. She was someone else's wife now. That was what she'd chosen. He would've fought the world for Kate, but he couldn't fight her.

Aidan was tempted to find a tavern and drink until the serving wench seemed a fine idea. Or he could get himself invited to a dinner party and make friendly eyes at the women until one of them took him home.

But no. He wasn't going back to that, not even for the sake of loving Kate. It was killing him, slowly turning his insides to dust.

He closed the alley door as best he could and walked away, blind to the people around him. He could do this.

He could. It wasn't so bad as being told that she'd died. And he was older now and sick of grief. This would be easier to bear. He was done with her.

But as he walked through the morning, through the streets that had become as familiar as his own, he looked up and she was there. Distracted, frowning, her hand rested on a man's arm though her head was tilted away from him.

Aidan didn't want to see him, but his eyes had a will of their own. They slid up the man's arm, up to his shoulder, and his neck, and then his face. Younger than Aidan had expected. Much younger.

Kate's chin kicked up, and his gaze was drawn to her. Her eyes widened, her lips parted in horror, and she stared at Aidan as if she could will him gone with just a look. But he didn't disappear. In fact, his feet became rooted to the ground and he stood in their path like a tree.

She did not touch her husband easily. Her hand lay stiff on his sleeve and she kept distance between them. Sadly, Aidan found this satisfying. Small comfort when she was married to the man. But then he remembered her words about being broken like a mare, and Aidan felt ashamed. She might not be brave or strong, but that did not mean she should be miserable. Sudden, fierce hatred for this man rose up in Aidan's chest like a serpent unfurling. The need to strike tightened all his muscles and his hands rose.

Kate's face paled. She tried to shake her head, but her husband caught the movement and followed her gaze. Aidan's eyes locked with his, and he saw the man's knowledge as if it were a fire sparking to life in his dark gaze. In that one moment, her husband saw everything, and Aidan realized his horrible mistake.

The knowledge in those dark eyes had already blazed

to fury and hate. Aidan welcomed it, but it would be turned on Kate soon enough, and Aidan couldn't let her pay for their transgressions.

So instead of tipping his hat and allowing them to pass, Aidan held his ground and let his anger show.

"Mrs. Hamilton," he said, though her name emerged as a low growl.

She didn't respond. Aidan raised an eyebrow.

"Katherine," her husband said, his gaze not leaving Aidan, "why don't you introduce me to your friend."

Katherine. Aidan wanted to slap the sound of her name from this man's mouth. The fact that he had more of a right to say it than Aidan did . . . that only turned his anger to rage.

"This is Mr. York," she whispered. "Mr. York, this is . . . Mr. Hamilton."

The man's mouth smirked.

"Are you going with him?" Aidan asked her simply. *Please say no. Please say no so I can take you away from this*.

Her eyelashes fluttered.

"She's coming home," her husband said, and Aidan's rage curled around his heart and squeezed.

"Kate?" he breathed. This wasn't the place for this. He knew that. He could feel the stares of people as they edged past, but this was it for him. He couldn't leave without hearing it from her lips.

"No," she finally said.

Aidan frowned.

"No, I'm not going with him."

"Katherine," the man said, his hand curling around her wrist.

Aidan stepped forward. "What are you saying?"

"I'm not getting on the ship, Aidan."

It would've taken him some time to believe. He needed to breathe and ask her if she meant it, but he saw the way she tugged at her arm and failed to free herself.

"Let her go," he growled.

Her husband's hand held her still. "Don't do this, Katherine. I can't be responsible for what will happen."

"I don't care," she hissed, yanking her hand free just as Aidan rushed forward to help her.

"Keep your hands off her," he said, leaning in close so that the passersby couldn't overhear.

"You're as much a fool as I," her husband said, offering a hard smile. Aidan didn't care what was said. His mind was overwhelmed with hope. But he'd misjudged the blow this man could deliver.

His black hair fell over his brow when he leaned close to Aidan. "I'm not her husband, you know," he said casually.

For a moment, Aidan thought he was telling a ridiculous lie, but Kate's face had paled at his words. "What?" Aidan asked.

She shook her head and started walking, and Aidan had no choice but to catch up to her. She rushed toward the shop, but the man followed close behind them.

"It's true," he said loudly. "I'm not Mr. Hamilton. In fact, there is no Mr. Hamilton."

"Kate?" Aidan asked, but she kept her head down until she reached Guys Lane.

She scrambled to open the front door, then nearly fell to the floor when she finally slid inside. Aidan put his hand under her elbow and followed her in before he turned to block the doorway.

"Get the hell out of here," he ordered, but the bastard only smiled again.

"You really don't know, do you?"

"Know what?" he barked.

"There is no husband, you fool."

He was a madman. There was no other explanation. Aidan just wanted him gone.

"My father died months ago."

"Your father?" Aidan scoffed. He put a hand up to stop him from stepping past the threshold.

"She was my father's wife."

"Kate, what the hell is he talking about?" When she didn't answer, he looked over his shoulder. "Kate?"

"I'm sorry." Her face twisted into a sob before she pressed her fingers to her mouth to stop it.

"My name is Gerard Gallow," the man said, stepping through and shutting the door behind him. "And I don't know what she's told you or who you think she is, but there is no Mrs. Hamilton and there never has been. She's a fraud, and the authorities in Ceylon want to question her about my father's death."

Aidan didn't know what to do, so he went with his overriding impulse and grabbed Gallow by the lapels of his coat to push him against the wall. "She's not going anywhere."

"Didn't you hear what I said? You don't even know who she is!"

"You're the fool," Aidan said softly. "I've known her since she was a girl." Despite his confusion, Aidan was supremely satisfied to see the man's face pale at that. "You don't get to tell me who Kate is. I know who she is."

But his words were far more certain than his heart. His heart was holding on to Kate's expression of horrified regret. "If you're not her husband, then you have no right to be here. None. So get the hell out and never return."

"She's coming back with me."

Aidan pulled the man closer, only to give himself the

satisfaction of slamming him back into the wall. "She'll never go back!"

"She has no choice. She may have killed my father, and she has to answer for that."

Kate gasped. "I've told you what happened! Aidan, I had nothing to do with it."

But Aidan didn't need to hear that. He actually smiled at the audacity of the man's lie. "You're ridiculous. Whatever she's done, it wasn't that." He cocked his head and stared into Gallow's stone gray eyes. "Even you don't believe that." Something dark and liquid moved behind those eyes. "You don't believe that," Aidan repeated.

Gallow held his gaze and didn't say a word.

"Kate, did he hurt you?"

"No," she whispered.

Aidan slowly loosened his hold and stepped back. He dusted his hands off while Gallow tugged his coat into place. "Then go get his things. All of them."

"Aidan." Her hand touched his arm, then fluttered away. "He'll tell everyone. The truth. And the lies. You should go. Your reputation and your family . . . You don't need to be involved."

"Go get his things. He won't tell anyone anything."

Gallow laughed, but Aidan watched Kate calmly until she'd turned up the stairway and he heard her steps ascend. Then he swung back to Gallow. "How did your father die?"

"He was poisoned."

"By whom?"

"The authorities suspect Katherine. They meant to arrest her. I am the one who stopped them."

"And what does she say?"

His eyes shifted to the side. His cheeks reddened. "She says he took the poison himself."

"Did he?"

Gallow shrugged, his jaw so tight that Aidan could see the muscles straining beneath. "The authorities will have questions about it. That's why she must return."

The stairs creaked behind him. Kate set a small trunk on the floor and pushed it forward with her foot.

"Is that everything?"

She nodded.

Aidan picked up the trunk, strode to the door, and tossed the trunk outside. "Which ship has he booked passage on?"

"The *Talisman,*" she whispered. "It sails tomorrow night."

"Wait here," he said to Kate before gesturing for Gerard Gallow to step outside.

"Aidan . . ." She reached out as if she'd touch him, but Aidan pulled away. "What are you going to—"

"I said *wait here.*"

He was left with the image of her stricken expression as he stepped into the street. Gerard Gallow rounded on him, fists clenched and face purple with rage. "I won't stand for this. She will be ruined and arrested. I'll see to it."

Aidan gathered up all his hurt and fear and rage. He thought of the lies she'd told him and the danger she was in. And then he let it all gather in his fist and drove it into Gerard Gallow's face.

The man went down like a sail with its rope cut. The crowd that had gathered around them gasped and drew back. Several of the ladies shrieked.

"Drunkard," Aidan explained as he heaved the trunk up to his shoulder. He was crouching down to grab the back of Gallow's collar so that he could drag the man to the dockyard, but Penrose raced up to take the trunk from Aidan's shoulder.

"I'll take that, sir. Is there someone you need me to get? A constable, perhaps?"

"No, thank you, Penrose. I'll take it from here."

Aidan bent down, lifted the unconscious man by the shoulders and slung him over his back, staggering a little at the weight. "Find out where the *Talisman* is docked."

"Yes, sir."

Penrose raced off, running right past Lucy Cain without seeing her. Aidan made a point of nodding in greeting as he passed her, and smiled a little to try to erase some of the fear from her eyes. But her startled blink told him that his smile was more of a snarl, so he ducked his head and walked toward the docks.

Once there, it was a simple transaction. He paid the captain of the *Talisman* to keep Gallow locked in a cabin until he set sail. "He's to have no visitors. I'll return tomorrow to ensure he's still here. There'll be another hundred pounds in it for you if he's still aboard when you shove off. And I'll have a letter to be delivered to the governor of Ceylon. Agreed?"

"Absolutely. An honor to do business with you, Mr. York."

Two sailors disappeared below with Gallow slung between them. A third toted his trunk. God willing, Aidan would never see the man again.

Still . . . he'd rather fight Gerard Gallow like a dog in the street than return to Kate and find out why she'd lied to him. About everything.

He had no choice, but he eyed the train station as he passed it, wishing he could simply board a train and go somewhere else. Anywhere else. But he walked on until he reached the door of her shop. The small groups of people still loitering on the walk studied him as he approached. Lucy tried to stop him, but he shook his head and did not pause once. He could not stop or he might not be able to start again.

When he opened the door, he found Kate standing in the center of the room, her arms wrapped around her middle. "Aidan. Are you all right? What happened?"

He could not speak yet, so he only gestured toward the stairway. Kate trudged up the stairs and Aidan followed. He tried to sit down, but his muscles twitched beneath his skin, so he rose again. And every second, Kate watched him with eyes so wide he thought he'd fall into them. "Tell me," he finally rasped. "Tell me the *truth*."

He heard the rush of air in her throat as she inhaled. "I'm sorry."

"Just say it!"

"My husband died ten months ago," she whispered, and Aidan felt his stomach drop so far that he felt hollow.

"I didn't know how to tell you. Or when."

"What does that mean, you didn't know *how?* You simply do it! And when? When I asked about him. When we made love. When I begged you to divorce him! Jesus Christ, Kate!"

"I couldn't tell anyone. I couldn't. You heard Gerard. He'd accused me of killing my husband!"

"Did you?"

"No!"

Aidan scrubbed his hands through his hair. "I feel like I'm going mad. Was any of it true? Any of what you told me? Were you even sent away at all?"

When she didn't answer, he looked up to find her so pale that she looked gray. She nodded. Her hands gestured as if she'd say more, but when Aidan saw the way they shook, he cursed and moved to hold her. Her skin felt cold when she leaned into him. "You need to sit down, Kate."

He settled her close to the stove and fed the fire. Then he poured her a glass of Madeira and pressed it into her hand. "You have to tell me everything. Everything or I'll leave right now. This is cruel, what you've done to me."

"I know," she murmured.

Aidan paced to the window and stared out. He waited and she finally spoke.

"I was sent to Ceylon, not India. And you were right, you know. I didn't want to go. I fought them at every turn. But when I stepped onto that ship, part of me thought, 'Well, this will show him. He'll feel sorry when he hears I'm gone.'"

Aidan winced, hating her in that moment.

"But," Kate said quietly, "I got over that soon enough, long before I arrived in Ceylon. . . ."

Determined not to offer comfort, he clenched his jaw to bar any soft words from escaping.

"I thought I'd be able to talk my way out of it somehow. But when the ship docked, a cart was waiting to take me into the jungle. Two servants and me and a pastor . . . He did not even introduce himself, my husband. I didn't have time to change out of my dusty clothes or wash up. I was led into the house and the pastor married us. And then, I think . . . I disappeared."

Aidan turned to her to find her staring down at her hands as if she'd never seen them before. "What do you mean?"

"I still thought it wasn't too late. I was shown to a bedroom, and when he came in . . ."

Aidan tensed and held up a hand, thinking he would stop her, but it was too late.

"I told him it was all a mistake. That I'd been promised to you. That I'd already made love with you. I thought he would send me back, but he didn't."

"Kate—"

"He only said, 'This will be easier then,' and he laid me on the bed and h-h-he—"

"Kate, please—"

"—he *had* me. Just like that. As if it meant nothing to him."

Pain spiraled through Aidan as if a knife was twisting straight through him. He'd said those words to her. That those women had meant nothing to him. But he couldn't imagine . . . He didn't want to imagine what those words had meant to Kate.

"So yes, I was telling the truth about that, but I was married in Ceylon, and his name was David Gallow."

She went quiet then, but Aidan could hear his own breathing, too loud and fast. "And he's dead," he growled.

"Yes."

"So I will not have to kill him?"

She looked up, surprise in her eyes. "He didn't deserve to be killed."

"He did!" Aidan shouted. When she shook her head, he pounded his fist onto the table as hard as he could. "He did, Kate. How can you say that? He *raped* you." He thought of her, young and bright, laughing over her shoulder as he'd teased her. Looking up at him as he'd eased inside her body while his heart shook like a bird in his chest. Smiling across the table the first time they met.

He didn't know how she'd lived with what had happened to her. Aidan wasn't sure that he could.

"I thought he was a monster," she said quietly, "but he was just a man. He was in love with a woman named Iniya. He'd bought her from her father when she was sixteen and made her his mistress, and that was why he needed me. The good Englishmen of Ceylon all had women they kept, but he was too open about it. He took his children into town to buy them treats. He lived in her cabin instead of the big house. He scandalized the other wives with his indiscretion. None of them wanted the truth flaunted in their faces. He needed me as a shield against scandal, and that was all. David was as miserable as I."

Aidan eased down to sit next to her. "How can you say that? No one forced him to anything. No one put their hands on him."

Kate shrugged one shoulder and stared down into her glass.

"How did you live like that?"

She flashed a quick smile with no humor in it. "I didn't. I ate and breathed and slept. I existed. Nothing more. Sometimes I took laudanum to help me sleep longer because there were so many endless hours in the day. Have you ever noticed that? How many hours there are?"

He shook his head.

"One night I woke up and I simply walked out. It was the middle of the night. I had nowhere to go, but I just couldn't stay another moment in that house. I walked for miles. Miles. Into the jungle. Into the rain. I just kept walking. After the sun rose, I heard hoofbeats behind me; it was David. He didn't say a word, he just put his hand out to pull me up. I tried to run up a hill, and he followed. The hillside wasn't stable, and the horse slipped. . . . The whole world seemed to fall away." She touched her cheek and the scar that lay there. "In the end, his spine was broken. He was never the same, but I came to know him as a person after that. I helped care for him. Iniya moved into the house. I wasn't happy, exactly, but I was alive."

"Did he kill himself?" Aidan asked.

"Yes. He never fully recovered. When he didn't want to live that way anymore, he took poison. Gerard thought I'd done it. He accused me and so I ran. And I came here. I changed my name to hide from him. And I thought that would be the end of it, I swear. I had no idea that others suspected the same thing."

"You could've told me," he said roughly.

She nodded. "I could have. But I didn't."

The color had returned to her cheeks, but Aidan wondered if she'd stolen it from him. He felt shaky and ill. He did not know if he should be furious or if he should go to his knees before her.

"Gerard will tell everyone. He'll see me ruined."

"No, he won't. He's locked in a cabin on the *Talisman*. He won't get off until it reaches Ceylon."

"Oh," she said, her eyes wide with surprise. "That was very smart."

"And very expensive," he joked, amazed that he was able to smile. "But worth every shilling."

"I'm not sure about that." She waved her hand toward the front of the building. "I'm not sure my reputation is salvageable after all this."

"It will be fine. I'll send a letter to the governor, explaining what I've witnessed. I'll have my brother send one as well."

"I don't know. If that doesn't work . . . I do not even care for my reputation, but yours . . ."

"Kate . . ." he started, but what could he say? He hated her and loved her. He wanted her still, but she didn't want him. And when she turned to him, he was sure he imagined the yearning in her eyes.

He cleared his throat. "Speaking of . . ." He tossed a glance toward the window. "I should go before there's even more talk."

"Oh. Yes." Even as she nodded, tears welled in her eyes and spilled over her lashes. "Of course you must go."

Every muscle in his body ached with the need to hold her, but he had no right to touch her. She'd made that clear in London in no uncertain terms. So he stood, and his eye caught on the doorway to her bedroom and the open chest inside.

"Were you going to go with him?"

"No."

"You were already packed, Kate."

"I wasn't . . . I thought I would have to flee, but I wasn't going with him."

"But you were leaving."

"I . . ." She shook her head and didn't bother saying more.

Aidan gave a small bow. "Well, you can unpack now at least. I'll be back. I need to compose that letter, but I'll need more details first."

"That's very . . . I can't thank you enough."

"Yes, well . . . If Lucy is waiting below, I'll send her up."

His foot was above the top step when Kate said his name. He stuttered, turning back to her.

"Don't go," she breathed.

Kate stood, her hands twisting so hard together that her fingertips tingled and flashed. "I know you might never forgive me."

His brow fell and he started to shake his head.

"Please," she said, holding up one shaking hand. "It's all right. I just wanted you to know that . . . This morning

I was lying in my bed, waiting for the sun to come up, and all I could think of was you. I knew I'd never let Gerard take me to Ceylon, because I needed to tell you I was sorry."

"Kate, I understand. It's—"

"No, not about the lies, but for what I said in London. And what I thought . . ." Tears stung her throat at her own bitter resentment. He'd apologized, he'd revealed to her his shame, his regret, and she'd turned from him just as she'd turned from him ten years ago.

But did she have the courage to turn back now? Could she offer him mercy, accept that it was natural for a grieving man to turn to visceral pleasure for comfort? And how could she please a man who'd had so many women?

That morning, in the cold hours before dawn, Kate had thought of the glorious implosion of her first climax with Aidan, right there in her bed. Each one after had been just as intense, just as surreally pleasurable. And in the aftermath her body and mind had been unresponsive, so lax, so drained that she'd always fallen immediately asleep. As had Aidan. She could imagine that blankness as comfort. She could imagine how he'd crave that.

"That woman," she whispered. "She said you were insatiable. That you never stopped. But you weren't insatiable with me, were you?"

Red burned into his cheeks, not of embarrassment it seemed, but helplessness. His hands rose from his sides as if he were searching for some diplomatic way to phrase his words.

"It's all right, Aidan. You don't have to lie."

"I don't know how to explain it, Kate. It can't make sense to you. . . ."

She nodded. "I've been humiliated, thinking that I

could never satisfy a man who'd known so many women—"

"For God's sake, never think that. There's nothing true about it."

But Kate realized that she didn't need him to say the words to her. She understood. She did. "Insatiable," she said again, and Aidan flinched from the word. "That doesn't mean satisfied, does it?"

"Pardon?" he murmured.

"It means unsatisfied. Starving. Desperate. And you weren't that with me . . . were you?"

His brow wrinkled for a moment, a spasm of confusion passing over his face, but then his eyes cleared and he looked at her. He truly looked at her for the first time that day, though pain shone clearly in that gaze. "No," he said. "I wasn't. Not with you."

He hadn't been lying to her. He had been alone . . . lonely, *lost*. He hadn't found comfort with those women. Not at all.

At that moment, even knowing he might not forgive her, Kate felt brave. Felt she could throw her soul into the void and trust that she would be fine. She nodded.

"I hope that you will forgive me some day. For the things I said to you. And the things I never said. And for letting them take me away from you before. I won't go away again." She managed a smile past her tears. "Perhaps not even if you want me to."

He moved toward her, and he looked so large, suddenly. So strong and safe. He'd always just been Aidan before, but now she saw him with new eyes. He was the Aidan she'd always known, but he was more than that too. Strong and steady and a man she'd love even if she'd never known him before.

"Katie," he murmured, reaching to touch her cheek.

She could not tell what was in his eyes. If he was saying good-bye or something much better. But she would say the same thing to him regardless. "I love you so much," Kate whispered. "More than you can ever know. You are such a *good* man."

"Don't say that. Please."

"You are good. But not perfect. If you were perfect, I'd never have even met you. You would've kept your hands to yourself, just as you should have."

He pulled her into his arms, his laugh sounding suspiciously rough. Kate just closed her eyes and breathed him in, thankful for every second that she could touch him. It might have to last her for years.

He drew a deep breath, the sound of it a comforting rumble in her head. "I haven't been good for a long time. I couldn't imagine life without you, Katie. I never could. That's why I was so lost. I just . . . I couldn't make myself want anything more than you."

That was when she began to cry, because she knew he would forgive her, and he'd love her, and they would have this chance. Finally. A real chance to love each other on their own terms. She was on solid ground again. Every stone back in place.

"I love you," he breathed against the top of her head. "I'm not perfect, but I'm yours, if you'll have me. I've never been anyone else's."

Chapter 32

"He is very tall, don't you think? Elegant even?"

Kate smiled down at Lucy as she fastened a simple pendant around her neck. "Mr. Penrose? Yes, he is quite elegant."

Lucy sighed and swung her feet against the legs of her stool. "He may be too cautious for me. He hasn't even tried to steal a kiss!"

"He respects you. Perhaps he has something more permanent in mind."

"Bite your tongue!" Lucy gasped, tapping a playful slap on Kate's arm. "Whatever would I do with a respectable man like that?"

"Liven up his life, I'd say."

"Well, he does need a bit of livening. All he ever does is work."

"He's very dedicated. That's important in a man."

"Mmm." Lucy sighed and resumed her pose of a forlorn maid. "Well, you have Aidan in your bed and my beau is nowhere near mine."

"He's a beau then, is he?" Lucy's blush wasn't the least

bit innocent. "I don't want to disappoint you, Lucy, but he doesn't seem the type to fall happily into an affair." Lucy groaned in exaggerated misery, but Kate threw her a cheeky grin that held not a trace of sympathy. "But I, for one, think Lucy Penrose is a lovely name."

"Ha! Can you imagine that? Me, a nice married woman?"

"Yes, and so can you. I can tell by the frighteningly devoted way you watch him."

"Never say so!" Lucy laughed, jumping up from the stool. "Are you ready then?"

Kate drew a deep breath. "As ready as I'll ever be, I suppose."

"You look so beautiful."

Kate ran a shaky hand down the skirt of her new dress. The silk was a deep ruby red shot through with hints of black. She loved it so much and could not wait for Aidan to see it. But the thought of being surrounded by his family set off butterflies in her stomach. What would they think of her? Did they blame her for his unhappiness?

She was so glad she'd brought Lucy along as her guest. Since the moment they'd set foot in the York family home that afternoon, she'd done her best to distract Kate from her nervousness. But though Lucy kept up her chatter, Kate was still trembling as they descended the stairs. There were so many people to meet, and she felt like a lone warrior entering battle.

As soon as her feet touched the floor, Kate looked up and saw Aidan's mother headed straight for her. Kate squeaked, but her squeak was smothered in Baroness York's arms as the woman pulled her into a tight embrace.

Hoping she was being hugged and not strangled, Kate tentatively patted her back.

"You!" the baroness sobbed.

Kate stared wide-eyed at Aidan as he approached with a smile. "Lady York, I'm sorry if I've—"

"My darling girl, you are the best birthday gift I could ever receive!"

"Oh, I . . . Are you quite sure?" Kate made helpless eyes at Aidan, but he only crossed his arms and watched with a wide grin. *Help me,* she mouthed when his mother squeezed even tighter. Aidan shook his head.

"My dear, dear girl," his mother sighed before finally leaning back to hold Kate at arm's length. "Returned from the dead! Imagine that! I tell you, I fainted when I heard the news. I did!"

"Mother," Aidan warned quietly.

"Oh, hush. I won't tell a soul. Not a soul!"

Her voice carried clearly through the crowd, and Kate laughed at the way Aidan winced. They'd agreed it would be best if no one knew who Kate Gallow truly was. She was being introduced as a distant cousin from Hull, but his poor mother was fairly vibrating with the need to tell everyone the real story.

"And thank you," the dowager baroness whispered loudly, "for bringing my son back. He has been ever so grumpy for years."

Aidan sighed loudly, newly irritated again, it seemed.

"Oh, it's true!" the baroness whispered, though her whisper carried as far as her normal voice. Aidan claimed she had practiced that for years. "He has been a trial, I tell you."

Kate pressed a hand to her mouth to try to stifle her laugh. She thought she heard Aidan growl, but the tension was defused by a tiny elderly woman who shuffled over to the baroness's side. She eyed Kate from behind wrinkles so deep that Kate wondered if she could see past them.

"Aunt Ophelia," Aidan said with a small bow. "May I present Mrs. Gallow of Hull? Kate, this is my great-aunt, Mrs. Ophelia White."

"It's a pleasure," Kate said, dipping into a low curtsy. The tiny woman looked so ancient that Kate had to fight the urge to reach out and support her.

"Hmph." Aunt Ophelia looked her up and down, then turned her gaze on Aidan, her nose wrinkling. "Well, I see you've finally located your bullocks, young man."

Kate blinked in shock, while Aidan seemed frozen, his lips parted.

Aunt Ophelia turned her eyes back to Kate. "Good news for you, I suppose. Would've been a disappointment otherwise."

"Um . . ."

Lady York merely smiled and patted the woman's hand. "Oh, Aunt Ophelia. You do go on so. Come, let's get you a glass of lemonade."

"I can get my own lemonade," the woman muttered, shuffling off the same way she'd come. Apparently she'd completed her mission.

"Aidan," Kate whispered.

"Don't bother asking me," he answered back. "I suspect she may be a spy."

"Whatever do you mean?"

"I have no idea."

Lady York grabbed both her hands. "Katherine, you must tell me all about the East. What was it like to live in the jungle? How did you—?"

"Mother," Aidan said loudly, glancing around to be sure no one had heard. "Come. I believe I hear the music starting. Would you honor me with the first dance on your special day?"

"Oh, do you see?" the baroness crowed to Kate. "Do you see how sweet he is now?"

"Yes," Kate laughed. "I think he's nearly tame."

"Exactly."

Aidan aimed a look at Kate that promised retribution, but he asked, "Will you be all right?" under his breath.

Kate took another deep breath. "I think I shall."

It was a small party, by Aidan's account, but it seemed overwhelming for Kate. Lucy had already been led off to dance by an old man in a dashing red cravat, so Kate wandered through the party, trying to take it all in. Laughter swirled through the air, tripping, dancing along the currents, spinning around her. Women trilled and giggled and tittered. Men chuckled and huffed and guffawed. Some of it was bitter, hardened by sarcasm, but most sounded good-natured. Kate let it all wash over her.

"Mrs. Gallow!" a friendly voice called. Kate turned to see a beautiful woman with strawberry blond hair. "Marissa?" she asked in shock. "I mean, I apologize. . . . It's Mrs. Bertrand now, isn't it?"

"Oh, nonsense." Kate was enveloped in another hug, though this one was not quite so melodramatic. "Call me Marissa. I'm determined that we shall be sisters, after all. Has Aidan asked yet?"

"I . . . It's . . ."

Marissa waved a dismissive hand. "All in good time. Believe me, I was in no rush to marry myself. Men are such moody creatures, are they not? Funny that we are considered the delicate sex when they are so obviously inferior in strength of mind. Oh, hullo, darling."

Her husband, a great hulk of a man, offered an ironic smile through the introductions, but he graciously excused himself a moment later. “I wanted to meet Mrs. Gallow, but I now fear I’ve already overheard more than I meant to.”

“Oh, I wasn’t speaking of you,” Marissa said.

“We’ll discuss that later, dearest wife,” he said with such a warm warning in his tone that Kate blushed to hear it. “And endeavor to decide who is the weaker sex.”

“I shall win that argument.”

“Or you shall enjoy losing,” he said.

Marissa wore a wicked smile as she watched him leave, but she was serious again when she turned back to Kate. “You look well.”

“As do you,” Kate offered with complete honesty. “You’ve grown into such a beautiful woman.”

“Thank you, but . . .” She waved a hand. “I really mean that you look well. I’m sure you were . . . I can’t imagine. . . .”

Kate smiled. “I am very happy to be home,” she said, feeling a startling jolt of pleasure as she said it. When she and Aidan married, this would be her home at least part of the time, and what a grand place to feel welcomed.

“Aidan mentioned that you wished to pierce your ears.”

Kate blinked at the strange change of subject. “He said that?”

“He did, along with a hundred other things. He was quite eager for you to arrive today. He talked incessantly. I almost wished him silent again, though I never truly would. So would you like to?”

Kate stared blankly. “What?”

“Pierce your ears! Come to my room tomorrow. I’ll

have Cook send some ice. It is just the sort of thing that sisters do."

"Oh." She smiled tentatively and touched her bare ear. "All right. Perhaps I shall."

"Wonderful! Now you must excuse me. A waltz is starting, and I promised my husband. . . ."

"Of course."

Kate couldn't help but grin, but she moved closer to the French doors in the quietest part of the room. Aidan's family was a bit overwhelming all at once. Her father had considered them quite vulgar, which is why she'd never been able to attend one of their famous hunting parties.

But now she could do whatever she liked. She watched the party unfold around her and began to relax.

But then an icy wall of air touched her back. A strong grip circled her arm. The hand tugged her carefully through the French door and out onto the terrace where her body was instantly warmed by the press of him against her back.

"You promised to dance with me," Aidan said. His deep voice rumbled through her body and tickled the skin of her neck.

Arching into him, Kate purred. "I certainly did not. I said I'd think about it and that was only after you badgered me for fifteen minutes."

"We've never danced together."

"I know. I just . . ." She shook her head, then softened and smiled when his arm curled around her to offer a glass of champagne. Taking a sip, she shrugged. "I've never had much practice, Aidan. You know that."

"I do." He wrapped his arms around her waist and rested his jaw against her temple, and they stood, quietly, comfortably, and watched the guests in their bright finery, talking and laughing and flirting, unaware of the couple nestled outside in the shadows.

Champagne bubbles tickled her tongue and Aidan's fingers stroked the line of her ribs, setting off twin vibrations of pleasure. The icy air was a balm to her heated skin, the soft notes of music from inside soothed her fraying nerves, and the body of the man she loved set her heart tripping happily.

She didn't realize her glass was already empty until Aidan plucked it from her fingers and turned her in his arms.

Staring up at him, his hair highlighted blue with moonlight, his hard jaw softened by a smile, she felt a painful swell of love build in her chest. The stroke of his fingers over her lips set off a shock of heat low in her belly, and she wondered that she'd thought she could live without this, without him.

"Dance with me," he whispered. "Here. Beneath the stars."

"Here?" Her voice was high with surprise and arousal.

"Here." His hand slipped down her arm, leaving nerves dancing, and slid into her hand to grasp her fingers. "Listen."

She took a deep breath, closed her eyes and heard the strains of the waltz.

They began to turn, to step and revolve, and she felt the magic of the cold night air seep into her. He was a strong lead and his ability let her imagine she was graceful and light, young and confident.

The world around her spun, and she felt pleasantly dizzy—with love, with champagne, with pleasure. Opening her eyes, she found Aidan watching her with a smile. The dance was over.

"Marry me," he breathed.

Kate's heart thundered. She'd known he would ask, but for some reason it still shocked her. Or perhaps her heart was simply flooded with joy.

"We can marry here," he said. "This week. My family is all here. And Lucy."

"Here? So soon?"

"Yes." His voice was strong as steel. "So soon. As soon as possible. We can live in Hull if you like. Or London. Or here. Wherever you want, as long as you're my wife."

Her impulse was to ask for time, but time for what? Time was the one thing she didn't need. "Yes," she whispered. "Yes, I'll marry you."

"Thank God," he breathed against her lips as his mouth sought hers out. "You're shaking," he said just as she realized her teeth had started to chatter. "Are you cold?"

"Yes. Or excited. I'm not sure."

"I'll pretend it's excitement even as I whisk you inside and into the warmth."

"Thank you."

He paused and turned back to kiss her one last time. "Thank *you*. You've made me the happiest man in the world. And you'll have the happiest mother-in-law too. Another wedding to plan . . ."

"Perhaps we should wait a while longer. To give her time for preparations—"

"No! I mean . . ." He cleared his throat. "You may do what you like, of course. You're the bride. But I urge you not to give her time. Believe me . . . less is more in this case."

"If you insist," she said with a doubtful look.

"I'm only trying to protect you. And she has Cousin Harry's wedding in a few months. Best to space them out, right?"

She stopped with her hand to the door. Her breath fogged against the glass. "This week, Aidan? Are you sure?"

"Are you?"

She watched the people move through the bright lights of the house. She and Aidan were separate here. In their own world. And she'd rather be out here in the cold and dark with Aidan than anywhere else. "Yes. I'm sure."

"Good. Because we've waited long enough."

He pushed the door open, and she slipped back into the heat.

"Look," Kate murmured. "There may be yet another wedding in our future."

Mr. Penrose and Lucy strolled past, her arm twined snug around his. Penrose looked down at her with a slightly dazed smile.

"Do I detect a hint of redness to her lips?" Kate asked. "As if she's just been kissed?"

"By *Penrose?*"

"Yes, by Penrose. Are you blind?"

"I'd like to be!"

"Aidan," she laughed, but her laughter died on a sigh when he whispered a hand down the back of her neck.

"Shall we tell my mother the good news? Or would you like to hold it secret for a time?"

Kate smiled, arching her neck into his hand. Even if someone looked straight at them, they'd never notice the sensual dance of his fingers down her spine. "Let's hold it secret. Just for tonight."

"Like old times," he said, his voice low and deep in her ear.

"Yes." And it was. That secret love and joy. The happiness of being together. And the knowledge that they'd never be apart.

She'd hold it close for one more day. And then she'd tell the world.